A LADY'S KISS

"I don't care a fig about the gossips. What I *do* care about are my friends. Whether you approve of Marigold or not, she is my friend, Garth, as you are, and I will do whatever I may to get her out of this muddle."

She had said more than she meant to. Did Garth realize? Georgie stood so very close to him that she could feel the heat of his skin. Or maybe it was the heat of her own skin. Georgie knew her cheeks were flushed. Did Lord Warwick look as if he wished to kiss her? He did not. Instead Garth looked very much as if he were about to scold her again. Georgie was very tired of being scolded. She stood on her tiptoes, grasped Lord Warwick's lapels, and pressed her lips to his.

It was not a skillful kiss, perhaps, but what Georgie lacked in experience she more than made up for in enthusiasm, and Lord Warwick possessed enough experience for them both. His arms moved to enfold her and draw her close. Georgie melted against him. It was a most romantic moment.

BOOK YOUR PLACE ON OUR WEBSITE AND MAKE THE READING CONNECTION!

We've created a customized website just for our very special readers, where you can get the inside scoop on everything that's going on with Zebra, Pinnacle and Kensington books.

When you come online, you'll have the exciting opportunity to:

- View covers of upcoming books
- Read sample chapters
- Learn about our future publishing schedule (listed by publication month *and author*)
- Find out when your favorite authors will be visiting a city near you
- Search for and order backlist books from our online catalog
- Check out author bios and background information
- Send e-mail to your favorite authors
- Meet the Kensington staff online
- Join us in weekly chats with authors, readers and other guests
- Get writing guidelines
- AND MUCH MORE!

Visit our website at
http://www.kensingtonbooks.com

CUPID'S DART

Maggie MacKeever

ZEBRA BOOKS
Kensington Publishing Corp.
http://www.kensingtonbooks.com

ZEBRA BOOKS are published by

Kensington Publishing Corp.
850 Third Avenue
New York, NY 10022

All Kensington titles, imprints and distributed lines are available at special quantity discounts for bulk purchases for sales
promotion, premiums, fund-raising, educational or institu-
tional use.

Special book excerpts or customized printings can also be created to fit specific needs. For details, write or phone the office
of the Kensington Special Sales Manager: Kensington Publishing Corp., 850 Third Avenue, New York, NY 10022. Attn.
Special Sales Department. Phone 1-800-221-2647.

Zebra and the Z logo Reg. U.S. Pat & TM Off.

First Printing: September 2003
10 9 8 7 6 5 4 3 2 1

Printed in the United States of America

One

The beach at Brighton was deserted, shortly after dawn. Waves murmured softly in the distance. Seagulls fed on the debris left in the wake of the receding tide. The scene had an eerie, otherworldly quality. Sunlight had not yet dispelled the last tendrils of fog. Later in the day the sands would be busy with bathing machines and fishing boats, but at this hour the seaside belonged to the screeching gulls, lending it an aspect of Eden after the fall.

Into this secluded paradise galumphed a great beast, a canine of some exotic lineage with fat, flat paws that sent the damp sand flying in all directions, and long, multicolored fur that wafted about him in the exhilarating sea air. Indeed, so varied were his hues that the creature appeared to have bounded unrestrained through a number of paint pots. And so abundant was his coat that one end could be distinguished from the other only by the glimpse of a pink and damply lolling tongue or an energetically wagging tail. Over the beach, the great beast gamboled, mightily disarranging the sand and destroying various specimens of marine life, startling the feeding seagulls into annoyed squawks—and dragging an irate young lady in his wake.

"Lump!" she cried, grasping at her straw bonnet with one hand while with the other she clutched the dog's stout leash. "I vow you shall have no stew bones for a fortnight if you do not slow down, you wretched beast!"

Thus scolded, the dog did slow his pace, due less to his mistress's dire threat than to his discovery of an especially intriguing morsel of seaweed. As he snuffled and drooled upon this latest object of his interest, his mistress readjusted her straw bonnet, which had slipped forward to rest on her nose, thereby revealing herself as a lady not so young as she had first appeared, a slender female of medium height with attractive features, dreamy gray eyes, and blond hair that escaped her bonnet in riotous wisps. At six-and-twenty, she was beyond her first youth—indeed, Miss Georgiana Halliday knew herself to be a confirmed spinster, firmly set upon the shelf. Her gown also was beyond its first bloom, as was the shawl she had wrapped around her shoulders as protection against the chill air.

The fog was lifting. Soon the fishing vessels would return laden with fish for the London markets. Miss Halliday drew her shawl more tightly around her as she gazed out at the horizon. Once a simple fishing village, Brighton had been turned into a popular resort by the Prince Regent. It was not the thing, perhaps, to stroll along the seashore escorted only by a dog, but the fashionable world did not rise to greet the sunrise, would not venture forth until much later in the day to engage in morning rides and afternoon calls, to inspect the expensive shops on North Street and promenade along the Steine, and later still to disport themselves at card parties and soirees. Considering herself quite free from observation, Miss Halliday returned her attention to the letter which she was trying to peruse, an effort made difficult not only by Lump's perambulations, but also by lines that were crossed and crossed again. As best she could determine from these pothooks and hangers, Miss Halliday's oldest friend had landed herself in a pickle, not as unusual a circumstance as Georgie might have wished. "'Things could not be in a worse case. I am in a dreadful pucker!'" she read aloud and commented, "Yes, and when were you not? Oh, Marigold!"

Grown bored with the seaweed, which he had reduced to a mere shadow of its former splendor, Lump raised his shaggy head and peered about. Unlike his mistress, he was disappointed to find the beach so deserted; he would have been very excited to chase a fishing boat or a bathing machine. Alas, there was nothing to pique his interest but seagulls flocking to a distant point. Yes, and why were they so doing? Lump thought he must find out. With a happy woof, the dog bounded forward. Caught off-guard and off-balance, Miss Halliday sat down smack on the damp sand. "Oh, Lump!" she wailed, as she struggled to her feet. Oblivious to censure, the dog galloped down the beach, barking and panting and dragging his leash behind. Eventually he would return to her, of course, but Miss Halliday dared not wait for that felicitous event. Appalling, the amount of damage that could be wrought by Galumphus unrestrained. Muttering unladylike sentiments, Miss Halliday lifted up her skirts and set out in pursuit. At least at this early hour there was no one to see her disgrace herself.

In that, she was mistaken. Miss Halliday was not the

only member of the polite world not snugly still abed.
A tall, dark-haired gentleman walked along the es-
planade that bordered the beach. He wore a drab
greatcoat against the chill air, and beneath it an exquisitely cut black coat and kerseymere waistcoat,
pantaloons, and Hessian boots. No early riser, he; the
Earl of Warwick had not yet been to sleep, having
marked his arrival in Brighton with several rounds of
cards, and several more bottles than were prudent of
various potent beverages. Not that his lordship was so
inexperienced in the ways of the world as to allow
himself to be either fleeced or foxed, but he admittedly had the devil of a head. Brighton's bracing sea
breezes were famed for their salubrious effect on sluggish livers and general debilitation. Lord Warwick
had hoped they might also be of some benefit in
blowing away residual brandy fumes. Thus far, unfortunately, this foray had only increased his discomfort.
In addition to having an aching head, he was now also
cold and damp and surrounded by a clutch of
screeching seagulls demanding more than the meager biscuit he'd brought with him from the gambling
hell. "Away with you!" he said, and irritably swatted
at the birds with his curly-brimmed beaver hat. The
gulls squawked and settled down a short distance away
to watch and wait, putting his lordship strongly in
mind of a bevy of gabble-grinders prepared to dish up
the scandal broth. Once Lord Warwick had been as
amused as anyone by the latest scandalous story fab-
ricated in the bay window at White's. He was less easily
diverted since his own name had been bandied about
the clubrooms of St. James's Street and Pall Mall.
Now, even on the seashore, he was the cynosure of
bright, malicious eyes. "The devil fly away with all of

you!" said Lord Warwick, and flung a seashell at his tormentors.

The gulls shrieked, flapped their wings, rose into the air, but Lord Warwick's seashell failed to frighten them away. Instead they flew straight at him, causing his lordship to wonder if he was to be pecked to death on Brighton Beach by seagulls in search of biscuit crumbs, an ignominious prospect which inspired him to perform windmill-like maneuvers with his beaver hat. Miraculously, the birds flew past. Nipping along smartly on their tails came a large and multicolored canine. Lord Warwick glimpsed a pink and damply lolling tongue and what seemed an inordinate number of gleaming, sharp teeth as the beast scampered by. Stumbling through the sand in pursuit of the creature was a young woman with her skirts snatched up and her straw bonnet tilted precariously low on her forehead. Lord Warwick had barely time to note the neat turn of the damsel's ankle before she fetched up hard against his chest.

Of course, he clutched her to him. Lord Warwick might be despondent, and devilish out of humor, and embittered by the harsh hand dealt him by unkind fate, but he was not adverse to an armful of frail femininity. Indeed, she felt damnably good to him, even soiled doves being less prone than once to cast out their lures in his direction. That he clutched a lightskirt, Lord Warwick never doubted. An unusual sort of lightskirt, he conceded, with a novel manner of presenting herself to a gentleman, but Lord Warwick had been accosted by ambitious Cyprians often enough not to be surprised. "Well met, fair charmer," he murmured. Doubtless this enterprising daughter of pleasure knew not who he was. Lord Warwick thought he would not enlighten her. Then he scowled. Or perhaps the vixen had some ulterior motive in seeking him out.

Miss Halliday, meanwhile, was subject to conflicting emotions. She had no notion of why this strange gentleman had accosted her, was holding her so hard against his chest. Unaccustomed to being treated in this cavalier manner, she was forced to admit that the sensation was not altogether unpleasant. Improper, certainly; she must make a push to free herself. "Oh!" gasped Miss Halliday. "Do let me go! I am not a, er, what you seem to think, but a respectable female!" Her protests might have been more effective, certainly would have been more intelligible, had they not been muffled against the stranger's thick coat. So tightly was he clutching her that he must surely bruise her flesh. "I insist," cried Georgie, "that you release me this instant!"

Whether or not Lord Warwick would have released Georgie remains a moot point; his lordship had a certain perversity of nature that made him frequently reluctant to oblige. However, Lump had by this time wearied of terrifying seagulls into heart attacks. Upon hearing his mistress's voice raised in anger, the dog loped back along the beach. No doubt she was all of a muck of sweat about his disappearance. He would present himself to her unscathed, so she would see that all was well. But what was this? She was not alone. Lump contemplated the spectacle of his mistress struggling with a strange gentleman, and decided that she was embarked on some new game. Incapable of refraining from involving himself in any frolic that took place in his vicinity, Lump leapt forward with a happy bark.

That bark, unhappily for Lump, ended the fun straightaway. Confronted by a large and enthusiastic canine, Lord Warwick released his captive, whose straw bonnet had slid forward to rest once again on the bridge of her nose. Miss Halliday drew in a deep breath. "I have not the most distant guess why you should treat me in this odious fashion, sir! But I will do you the courtesy of assuming that it was due to some awkward misapprehension—oh, get down, you clunch!" This last remark was addressed not to his lordship, but to Lump, who sought to assure his mistress of his continued well-being and joy in their reunion by saluting her cheek, thereby knocking her bonnet to the sand. Miss Halliday shoved her troublesome pet aside and snatched up her hat.

As she straightened, she saw her accoster clearly for the first time. He was scowling at her with the expression of a man who finds himself abruptly thunderstruck. Miss Halliday could perfectly share in his feelings. She felt suddenly dizzy and flushed, and wished she might sit down. "Garth!" she gasped. At forty, Lord Warwick retained the muscular figure of a noted sportsman, although there were now faint strands of silver in his windblown, raven hair. His finely chiseled features were sterner than she remembered, his dark eyes more remote. Scant wonder, thought Miss Halliday. Her heart gave a queer little lurch.

The silence stretched out unbearably between them. "Will you not speak to me?" she said at length. "Must I apologize for giving you a rake-down? It was your own fault, Garth! If you assume that every female you meet is a fair unfortunate, you are bound to find yourself in disgrace." Reminded of his far-from-blameless reputation, Lord Warwick's expression grew even more shuttered, and Miss Halliday could cheerfully have bitten off her tongue. "You know I did not mean *that!*" she said.

Lord Warwick did not answer, but instead reached for her hand. As he drew her closer to him, Miss Halliday wondered faintly if he could feel the hammering of her pulse. Hot with embarrassment, she fixed her eyes on his exquisitely tied cravat. Lord Warwick's other hand moved to her chin. "Look at me, Georgie," he said.

Slowly, she raised her eyes. Lord Warwick's expression was unreadable as his fingers moved across her cheek to tangle themselves in her hair. With a sudden oath he pulled her abruptly against him. His mouth descended upon hers. His lips were soft, and then demanding. So startled was Miss Halliday by this onslaught that she made no demur, even slid her arms around his strong shoulders so that, she told herself, he would not sweep her altogether off her feet.

As abruptly as he had embraced Miss Halliday, Lord Warwick let her go. "I wondered if I would still wish to do that," he said.

Georgie stumbled, caught herself. "Oh?" she murmured, with considerably more nonchalance than she felt, and no little interest in his reply.

Lord Warwick's expression was shuttered, his voice bleak. "I find that I still do." Without another word, he stepped back from her and turned and walked away.

"Garth!" cried Georgie, but he did not look back. Her emotions in turmoil, she stood and watched him disappear into the distance. Then she stooped and picked up Marigold's letter from the sand. Why was

Garth so angry? If anyone had cause to be in a pucker, it was Georgie herself. Yes, and she very well might be, once she caught her breath. Georgie had not had a great deal of experience with kissing, or with the after-tingles and tremors that left her both light-headed and weak-kneed. Why the devil *had* Garth kissed her? Could his lordship have been foxed? If only she had been other than windblown and disheveled and covered with sand! With the still-unread letter, she absently fanned herself, thereby attracting the attention of a seagull, which swooped and snatched the missive from her hand.

Lump had settled back on his haunches to observe these queer proceedings, which had exhausted the limits of his short attention span. Now that his mistress gave signs of returning to herself, he leapt to his feet. First she would give him a rare trimming for jauntering about, and then she would forgive him, and then all would be as it had been—which seemed to Lump a great fuss over nothing. But if his mistress was made happy kicking up a dust over trifles, it was all the same to him. His mistress was very quiet. Lump did not care to see her sunk in a fit of the blue devils. He butted her hip with his great, shaggy head and uttered a sympathetic woof.

Thus distracted from her musings, which did *not* concern the possible contents of Marigold's lost letter, Miss Halliday firmly grasped Lump's leash and set out toward home. "You are an incorrigible jingle-brain," she said sternly, although it was uncertain whether she addressed this comment to the dog or to herself.

TWO

Along the Brighton road rattled an elegant travelling carriage, drawn by a beautifully matched team of grays. The horses were proper high-bred 'uns, beautiful steppers; the carriage was richly fitted out with copper springs and iron shafts and silver-plated fastenings, dark paneling, and huge wheels. "God's blood!" cursed the coachman, as one of the wheelers, for reasons altogether unknown, suddenly became very nervous and frightened and half-inclined to kick, with the apparent notion of getting rid of the carriage behind. The coachman swore again, as he wondered what had inspired so normally sweet a goer to take a head full of bees.

With that sentiment, had he but known it, the coachman's employer might have agreed. A somewhat corpulent gentleman dressed in sober fashion, Quentin Inchquist scowled at his companion and drummed his fingers irritably on one plump and pantalooned knee. Slumped beside him on the carriage seat was a sandy-haired and very freckled damsel of almost seventeen years. She wore a plain, high-waisted muslin dress and pelisse of lilac sarcenet, and a pretty hat trimmed with a lilac riband. Her head was bent, her attention fixed on the little reticule clasped on her lap.

Her refusal to meet his gaze further irritated Quentin. "You are a goose!" he said, not for the first time. "That a daughter of mine should tumble in amours with a mincing Jack-a-dandy who hasn't sixpence to scratch with—Good God, Sarah-Louise! The fellow fancies himself a *poet!* I think you must be all about in your head!" The damsel paused in her fidgeting to glance at her parent. When she raised her head, she looked down on him, for Sarah-Louise was very tall, and her papa was not. Quentin derived further annoyance from that fact. And then what must she do but quiver her lower lip at him? "Mr. Teasdale is a very fine p-poet," she whispered.

This from a damsel who, in the normal course of things, couldn't say boo to a mouse? Things, were in worse case than Quentin had realized. "Poppycock!" he said sternly. "I have had occasion to read some of Teasdale's poetry, if you will recall."

Sarah-Louise did indeed recall the occasion to which her papa referred, although she would have much rather not. She dropped her gaze again to her lap. It had been such a pretty poem, too, that certain sonnet which had been discovered under Sarah-Louise's mattress by an overzealous housemaid, and brought to her papa's attention by his horrified butler.

"Hiding sonnets in your bedclothes!" scolded Quentin, shrewdly following his daughter's thoughts. "It ain't like you to pull such a sly trick. Damned if it ain't all that Byron fellow's fault for putting poetical notions into everybody's head. Corsairs, by God!" He paused to eye his offspring. A gentleman who wielded a great deal of power and influence in certain government circles, Quentin was long on neither patience nor tact, was in fact well known for his ability to mercilessly bully and badger his political opponents into submission. He saw no reason to deal differently with his daughter now. "In case you don't know it, and I do not know how you would *not* know it, it ain't the thing to encourage poets to dangle after you composing sonnets to your nose! You're not up to snuff, my girl, nor close to it! You may be grateful that I sent your precious poet about his business before you came to grief!"

Did she look grateful? A peek at his daughter assured Quentin that she did not. Instead, she wore as stubborn an expression as he had ever seen. "Don't think to go against me in this!" snapped Quentin, and she flinched. Sarah-Louise had never responded well to raised voices, Quentin recalled. Well, if he had raised his voice, she had only herself to blame, and Quentin would take advantage of the opportunity to ensure that she did not likewise err again. "Let us be frank!" he said. "You may be a considerable heiress, but you ain't going to be cried up as a great beauty, what with your freckles and your height. Be assured, that pup who was dangling after you was less wishful to drown in your eyes than dive into the depths of my purse! I had not wanted to mention it, but I had certain inquiries made, and young Teasdale is so deep in dun territory that he will have to contrive mightily to get clear. To give you the word with no bark on it, you have been soundly hoaxed! Teasdale must have a rich wife."

Sarah-Louise pressed her lips together. She was determined not to weep. Of course her papa meant the best for her; that she did not doubt. That her papa had the faintest notion of *what* was best for her, however, Sarah-Louise doubted very much indeed. Timidly, she plucked at her tasseled reticule. "I wish you would reconsider, Papa!" she murmured. "I'm sure there is some mistake. Mr. Teasdale is all that's proper. You do him a great d-disservice—"

"Balderdash!" interrupted Quentin, and brought down his hand upon his knee with such force that Sarah-Louise shrank back. "Teasdale is on the dangle for a fortune, and *you* are such a ninnyhammer that you would give him mine! Not another word," he added, as she parted her lips in protest. "I am very displeased with you, miss! How sharper than a serpent's tooth is an ungrateful child!"

Not surprisingly, a profound and uncomfortable silence descended upon the interior of the carriage after this exchange. Despite her best intentions, Miss Inchquist sniffled, inspiring her parent with the dreadful notion that she might at any moment start blubbering. Like many another acerbic gentleman, Quentin had an aversion to feminine waterworks, particularly those waterworks which he inspired. He was not truly an ogre, Quentin assured himself, but merely a fond parent doing what he must. As for packing Sarah-Louise off like this to Brighton—it was for the chit's own good, and someday she would be grateful to him for removing her from harm's way. If only his wife had not died so young, leaving him with a child to raise. Yes, and here the child was near seventeen already, and tumbled violently in love with a curst fortune hunter, and fancying her heart broke. It made a man feel old. However, if Quentin knew anything at all about the fairer sex, Sarah-Louise would get over her disappointment quick enough and be pestering him for pin money to buy new fripperies. Having thus arranged matters to his satisfaction, if not that of his offspring, Quentin looked out the carriage window and allowed his thoughts to drift to less taxing topics, such as the ongoing hostilities with the French, the riots and machine-breakings in industrial areas, the question of Catholic relief, and the Corn Laws.

Sarah-Louise gazed out the opposite carriage window. Her thoughts were considerably more bleak. Sarah-Louise had long been aware that she was a bran-faced beanpole of a female who would inspire no gentleman to romantical transports. She was all too well acquainted with her reflection in the looking glass, and, as Quentin's daughter, none too naïve about the world in which she lived. Her papa's influence and his wealth would provide for her a husband—but it would not be the husband of her choice. Better to wed a stranger, Sarah-Louise had supposed, than to be left on the shelf. At least she would have a home and family of her own.

But all that was before she had met Peregrine. Sarah-Louise had never dreamed to catch the eye of so handsome and agreeable a gentleman, to be the object of his compliments and smiles. Peregrine didn't seem to mind that she wasn't a nonpareil, had even assured Sarah-Louise that the beauty of her soul more than compensated for any physical lack. Perhaps Mr. Teasdale did not love her yet, but Sarah-Louise dared not hope to marry for love, and believed she and Peregrine might go on together very well. Had he not hinted at as much? Had he not confessed that he found in her presence a serenity that inspired him to take up his pen? Her papa could not be expected to understand the artistic spirit, and therefore he was determined to cut up all her hopes. If only she had the strength of will to stand up for herself. Unfortunately, loud voices terrified Sarah-Louise, especially her papa's loud voice, as did so many things. Despite her best intentions, Sarah-Louise could not prevent a wayward tear from stealing down her cheek. Face firmly averted, she wiped at it with her glove.

Thus distracted from his contemplation of more important matters, Quentin bit back a sigh. Damned if Sarah-Louise didn't put him in mind of a rabbit he had once owned, which upon hearing him approach would cower all atremble in the corner of its cage. She even looked like that wretched beast, with her trembling lip and pink nose. Not that she had whiskers, for which he supposed he must be grateful, considering the chit's other shortcomings. "There there!" Quentin said, and awkwardly took her hand. "I do not mean to be cruel, but you must trust your papa to know what's best! Of course you will marry— some nice, sensible fellow who will value you as he should. Mayhap this business is my fault; I have kept you too well-wrapped in lamb's wool. Little wonder, I suppose, that you should hold such a man as Teasdale in girlish fascination. 'Twas an unfortunate business, but now 'tis done, and we will say no more about it. You will like to stay with your Aunt Amice. *She* will know how you should go on."

Sarah-Louise was not looking forward to visiting her Aunt Amice. Nor did she want to marry some nice, sensible fellow; she wanted Peregrine. "As you wish, Papa," she whispered.

"We need not tell your Aunt Amice about this business; she would be prodigious shocked," Quentin said generously. His sister was devilish high in the instep.

He had no fear she'd tolerate any poetical nonsense, whether or not forewarned. *"If* I have your word that you'll think no more on that twiddlepoop."

Expectantly, Mr. Inchquist paused. Sarah-Louise bit her lip. Peregrine was *not* a twiddlepoop. To dispute further with her papa was to gain nothing more than his increased ill humor. "You have my word, Papa," Sarah-Louise murmured, with crossed fingers and a fervent wish that she might be forgiven for the fib.

Three

Miss Halliday stood in the kitchen of her modest little house. Though not located in a fashionable part of town, this structure had a fine prospect of the sea, as well as curved window bays and low roof parapets. Georgie was not a summer visitor to the seaside, seldom drank tea at the Public Rooms, only rarely put in an appearance at card assembles and plays and concerts, and was not known to display herself on the Steine, although she did have a subscription at one of the libraries, and therefore was sometimes to be glimpsed. Miss Halliday was not enamored of Society, and liked Brighton best of all when Prinny and his raffish friends and all their hangers-on had gone back to London, and the fog had settled on the cliffs, and no one was left to marvel at the oddity of a lady who preferred to eschew polite company of an evening to stay home and read a book. Not that this luxury was often accorded her, due to the demands of the other members of her household.

Currently demanding Georgie's attention was her cousin Agatha, a plump and amiable soul of fifty-odd years with a passion for cooking and household matters, pursuits not suitable to her station in life perhaps but fortunate for all concerned, save the snub-nosed, brown-haired little housemaid who was responsible for a great deal of the work.

"Gooseberries," mused Agatha, who was this day swathed in yellow dotted muslin more suited to someone half her years, as was the flaming red hair arranged in the Grecian style with ringlets hanging down. "Currants, raspberries, and strawberries must be preserved, and jams and jellies made up. Mixed pickle should also now be made." She then explained, with enthusiasm, just *how* mixed pickle should be made, a procedure that involved ginger, mace, shallots, cayenne, mustard seed, turmeric, six quarts of vinegar, and a pound of salt. And then she launched into a discussion of fish—lobster, mackerel, mullet, pike, salmon, trout, turbot—and ended up with carp. "What do you think, Georgie, dear?"

Guiltily, Georgie started, as did the little housemaid who sat at the large elm table turning and mending and darning sheets, which in her opinion was better than her previous task of cleaning marble with a paste of soap lees and pipe clay, bullock's gall and turpentine. Neither Georgie nor the housemaid—whose name was Janie—had been contemplating fish. Janie was wondering how best to strike up an acquaintance with a young footman who'd newly hired into an establishment further along the street. Georgie, however, couldn't stop thinking of kissing, which was exceedingly odd in her, because kissing wasn't something that ordinarily exercised her mind, possibly because no one had ever kissed her as had Lord Warwick that morning, and she didn't know whether she should be cross—or grateful to him. "I think," Georgie murmured, "that you know best about such matters. Agatha, the oddest thing happened. You will be surprised to hear who I met on the beach."

Agatha had scant interest in matters outside her own domain. "Fried cow heel," she murmured thoughtfully. "An asparagus pudding. Rhubarb jam. Liver and parsley sauce. Perhaps we might invite a few people for dinner, cousin. Seeing fresh faces 'twould do Andrew a world of good." She did not wait for a response, but went on to discuss, with great enthusiasm, a receipt she had recently come upon for eels *à la tartare*.

Receipts were Agatha's passion. Georgie smiled. Had she the resources, Agatha would have them sitting down to a formal dinner every night. But they did not have the resources, and Agatha's receipts, while intriguing one in one, seldom fitted together in a palatable whole. Georgie distracted Agatha from her eels with a question about the frenzy of housecleaning that was currently under way. Agatha waxed enthusiastic about the use of gin-and-water, followed by powder blue, and the application of an old silk handkerchief, to best clean looking glass. Janie glowered. Agatha was keeping her as busy as a hen with one chick.

Came an interruption then, in the form of an elderly butler dressed in ancient livery, complete with an old-fashioned white wig. All three women held their breath as he stepped unsteadily onto the stoneflagged floor. "Begging pardon, Miss Georgie," he said, placing a hand on a whitewashed wall to steady himself, in the process dislodging a copper pot, which clattered to the floor. "There's a gentleman as has come to call. I put him in the drawing room." His tone was anxious. "I hope that was right."

Georgie picked up the copper pot and wondered

where else Tibble thought he might put a caller. In
the kitchen, perhaps? "Did the gentleman tell you his
name?"

Tibble screwed up his features in intense concentration. Then he sighed. "Reckon he did, Miss
Georgie, and I misremember what it was. But he was
a gentleman of substance. Everything prime about
him. Civil as a nun's hen." He peered hopefully at his
mistress, as if she might recognize the caller from this
description.

Agatha and Janie also regarded her speculatively.
Georgie was the cynosure of all eyes. All this com-
bined attention had the effect of making her feel very
cross. Granted, she was quite on the shelf, but was the
notion that a gentleman should call on her worthy of
such astonishment as this? "Have the lot of you nothing to do?" inquired Georgie, and turned on her heel.

With her departure, the kitchen was briefly silent.
The little housemaid was the first to speak. "Cor! A
gentleman caller!" she breathed.

Tibble sank down into a chair at the elm table, took
off his wig, and wiped his brow. His eyesight wasn't
what it once had been; times had changed, in his
opinion not for the better, and he lived in fear that he
would do the wrong thing; but it was sure as check
Miss Georgie's caller had been a gent. "All the crack!"
he added. "A well-breeched swell."

"Cor!" said Janie once again. She would have liked
to glimpse this paragon herself. In honor of the
momentous occasion, Agatha brought out her home-
made dandelion wine.

Happily unaware that he was once again the subject
of conjecture, Lord Warwick paced around the drawing room, which was furnished with restrained

classical elegance grown somewhat threadbare. Rosewood furniture upholstered in striped silk, a faded Wilton carpet on the floor. Add to that a doddering butler who had no doubt gotten his name wrong, and an unfashionable address, and Garth could not help but conclude that Georgie had come down in the world. A partially embroidered pair of men's slippers lay on a pretty breakfront writing desk. He wondered if Georgie had been embroidering the slippers, and with a pang, for whom.

Georgie stepped into the room. Since Lord Warwick was glowering in a most forbidding manner at the slippers she had been embroidering, she had a moment to study him. This afternoon he was dressed for riding in leather breeches and a high-collared, double-breasted coat that displayed his crisp, high shirt points and flawlessly tied cravat. In comparison, Georgie's gown was sadly out of style. At least this time she wasn't bedecked with sand. "Hello, Garth," she said. "You're wearing black again, I see."

Lord Warwick's mood, not sanguine to begin with, was further exacerbated by being caught out brooding over half-finished embroidery. Slowly, he turned to face his hostess. "I seldom wear colors, ma'am," he retorted. "Colors seldom suit my mood."

That mood was currently very dark indeed. Georgie crossed the room to stand by him. "'Ma'am?'" she echoed. "So you have come to offer me further injury?"

Lord Warwick had come to do nothing of the sort. Long and sobering reflection had led him to the unhappy conclusion that he had behaved very badly toward Georgie, and the conviction that he must apologize for making a Jack-pudding of himself. Apologizing was not something Lord Warwick did easily or well, and consequently he was visited by a strong desire to either shake Georgie or kiss her again. To do either was unthinkable, of course. "I have come," he said stiffly, "to apologize. I behaved abominably to you."

Georgie had a good idea of what that apology had cost him. Not that she particularly desired an apology for something that she had liked very well. "Oh," she said with interest. "So I was not one of your peccadilloes, then?"

Lord Warwick looked startled. This was not the Georgie he remembered. "Hardly that," he replied.

Georgie wondered what it would be like to be one of Lord Warwick's peccadilloes. And precisely what a peccadillo *was*. "You needn't put yourself in a taking," she said amiably. "It wasn't so abominable as all that."

This less-than-flattering appraisal of his embrace caused Lord Warwick's expression to lighten. "Saucebox!" he said.

Georgie was studying him, head tilted to one side. "I suppose you have had a great many peccadilloes?" she inquired.

Damned if she didn't sound wistful. "You should not ask me that," he retorted, and quickly turned the subject. "Devil a bit, Georgie, what do you expect when you set out unescorted, inviting attentions from reprobates like myself?"

Georgie hoped there was no other reprobate like this one, else she would dare not step foot out of doors for fear of encountering one of them, and subsequently disgracing herself. "Are you a trifle bosky still?" she asked. "Because I don't know otherwise why you should say such silly stuff. I have been looking after myself for quite some time. It won't debauch me to walk along the beach."

Lord Warwick was appalled to realize how much he wanted to debauch his companion. He scowled even more dreadfully. "I know what it is," Georgie said. "You are sorry that you kissed me. No doubt it was an aberrant impulse brought on by an overindulgence in the grape. I assure you that I do not hold it against you. In truth, I am quite grateful that you should show such flattering attention to an apeleader like myself."

Apeleader? Lord Warwick could not help but laugh at this absurdity. As for that aberrant impulse, he was experiencing it again. In search of distraction, he glanced around the drawing room. "Things have changed for you, I think."

So did Georgie look around her drawing room, at the narrow, ribbed mouldings and recessed ceiling panels, the silk-striped furniture and faded Wilton rug. Whatever else it might be, the room was sparkling clean, as she knew very well, having wiped down the walls herself. Not that Lord Warwick, a gentleman of wealth and lineage—a marquess, no less, who owned estates northwest of London and in Cornwall as well as in the Lake District—could be expected to understand her simple satisfaction in a house well kept. "My grandmama's legacy allows me to be comfortable, if not particularly extravagant," she said dismissively. "Don't look at me that way, Garth! I promise you we rub on very well."

The Georgie he had known would have had no consideration for extravagance. Lord Warwick was tempted to tell her she was doing it rather too brown. "You have not married?" he asked, although discreet inquiries had already provided him the answer to that question, as well as the intelligence that she was estranged from her family, for reasons undisclosed.

Georgie did not like the tenor of this conversation, or the direction that it took. "My dear Garth," she retorted lightly, "the marriage mart is glutted with young women of impeccable breeding and somewhat impecunious circumstance like myself. I promise you, I am quite happy just as I am. What of you? What brings you to Brighton? Have you come to take the waters for deafness? Rheumatism? Gout?"

No, and not for any of the other ailments the waters were claimed to cure, from impotence to diseases of the glands. "Cry pax, Georgie!" Lord Warwick retorted. "You are deliberately trying to set up my back."

Georgie sighed. She *was* behaving badly. "Why did you walk away from me like that? On the beach?" she asked. "We used to be friends, I think."

Lord Warwick studied her. Georgie spoke the truth when she said she was well past her first youth; he found her even lovelier than she had been as a girl. The elegant features were more finely drawn; there was a hint of sadness in the remarkable gray eyes, and her hair— Her hair remained ungovernable. Drawn back in a serious style, braided and rolled up behind, wisps had already escaped their moorings to curl on her forehead. "Your family has been no friend to me," he said.

So had they not, which had led Georgie to quarrel with them herself. "Perhaps not," she replied quietly. "Still, you must not tar us all with the same brush."

Lord Warwick's innate perversity asserted itself then. Or perhaps he was moved by her words. Whatever the reason, if indeed he had a coherent reason, he raised his hand and touched Georgie's face.

Her eyes widened. She took a step, not away from but toward him. If she advanced one iota further, he would have her in his arms.

Garth wanted very much to have Georgie in his arms. He dropped his hand and clenched his fists. "Your behavior is imprudent, ma'am."

Imprudent? Georgie supposed she *was* imprudent, but she wanted more than anything to feel those tingles and tremors again. However, it was clear that Garth wasn't going to kiss her. He looked as though he might dive right out the window if she didn't retreat. Georgie sank down on the silk-striped sofa, which was possibly the most uncomfortable piece of furniture in the house. Perhaps the discomfort would distract her from her improper thoughts.

She looked up at him, her pretty lips parted, her cheeks flushed. "*Damned* imprudent," said Garth, and stepped toward her. A knock on the door caused him to reconsider, and Georgie to lean back on the couch.

The dining room door opened. "Beg pardon, Miss Georgie," Tibble said. A young woman brushed past him, almost causing him to lose his balance, which was even more precarious than usual, due to a certain recent indulgence in dandelion wine.

The newcomer paused dramatically on the threshold. That she was a very beautiful young woman was evident even through the heavy veil she wore. Her voluptuous little body was swathed about in black bombazine. Her gloved hands grasped a jet-beaded reticule. "Oh!" she gasped, in throbbing tones. "I interrupt!"

She did indeed interrupt. Lord Warwick, no aficionado of dramatic young women with histrionic tendencies, wished her to the devil. As did Tibble, hovering discreetly just outside the drawing room door. Georgie, however, gasped, "Marigold!"

"You were not expecting me!" Marigold flung back

the heavy veil to reveal red-gold hair, sapphire blue
eyes, a bewitching elfin face. "Did you not get my letter? I made sure you would. Did it somehow go
astray?"

Would Garth have kissed her again if not for this un-
timely interruption? Georgie regarded her oldest
friend with a somewhat jaundiced eye. Then she
winced to recall that Marigold's letter had last been
seen in the beak of a seagull, and immediately forgot.

Lord Warwick cleared his throat. Hastily, Georgie
set about making introductions. "Marigold, I make
you known to my friend, Lord Warwick. Garth, this
is—"

"Mrs. Smith!" Marigold interrupted hastily, and
dropped a pretty curtsey. "I'm pleased to meet you,
milord."

"Mrs. Smith," was it? Here was a clanker, thought
Lord Warwick as he glanced at Georgie's startled face.
"I am *de trop,*" he said, and made Georgie a formal
bow. "I will see myself out."

Silence reigned briefly in the drawing room. Then
"Mrs. Smith" firmly closed the door, causing the lurk-
ing Tibble to abandon his attempts at eavesdropping
and hobble back to the kitchen, there to inform
Agatha that the household was about to be set on its
ear by one "Mrs. Smith," and if that was her real
moniker, he would eat his wig.

Marigold tossed her bonnet carelessly onto the sofa.
"Georgie, I have heard the most astonishing *on-dits!*
Tell me, do *you* think Warwick murdered his wife?"

Four

The remaining member of Miss Halliday's household strolled along the Brighton streets. Accompanying him was Lump, whose normal exuberance was restrained by consideration for his companion's painful limp, which necessitated a slow progress, and the employment of a cane. Andrew Halliday bore a marked resemblance to his sister—not that his sister ever attired herself in nankeen trousers, gleaming boots, brown double-breasted frockcoat; he had the same slender build, classic features, gray eyes, and unruly blond curls. Unlike his sister, however, Andrew's expression was discontent. He had come back from the Peninsula a curst cripple, prey to recurrent fevers which necessitated that he drink copious amounts of cool water, and that his body be rubbed all over with cold water-soaked cloths; that he be fussed over and scolded and made to eat such stuff as barley gruel and calf's foot broth and stewed rabbits in milk. Of course he was grateful to his sister for her care of him, but he knew he could not but be a burden to a household already perilously near *point non plus*. Andrew sometimes wondered if it wouldn't have been better for all concerned if, instead of being invalided out of his regiment, he had stuck his spoon in the wall.

Georgie told him that such fustian was further indication that he was not yet entirely well. Perhaps she was correct. Andrew had to admit that he was not plump currant. Most often he felt fagged to death. Damned if he knew how he'd turned into such a milk-sop. Much as he might wish to put a period to his existence, he lacked the courage to take the necessary steps.

Carriages and vehicles of every description, drawn by superb horseflesh, thronged the narrow lanes and winding streets, wound their way among the well-dressed crowds. Andrew would have preferred to stroll upon the brilliant white cliffs, or along the sandy beach, but his curst leg would not tolerate such exercise. With a firm grip on his companion's leash, he ventured onto the Steine. Shops with piazzas and benches lined each side of the brick-paved walk.

Toys, rare china, lace, millinery, ribbons, chintz and cambric, tea and knickknacks—none of these caught Andrew's eye. His destination was the subscription library, there not to read the London newspapers, or to play cards in the back room, but to fetch his sister a new book. Andrew knew he was being a bloody nuisance. This was his way of making partial amends. He paid no heed either to an advertisement of cocking to be fought at the White Lion in North Street, a pair of cocks for twenty guineas a battle, and fifty guineas for the main—nor to the announcement of a bull bait at Howe, or a military review, or a prizefight. It was not that Andrew had no interest in these diversions so beloved of young gentlemen. His thoughts were many miles away . . .

Bussaco. Coimbra. A city in flames. Terrified prison inmates screaming to be released. The ghastly French retreat that left behind ravines, pits, ditches filled with a shocking collection of skeletons and fresher decomposing bodies, some mangled and half burnt by captors in search of hidden food and wine. A pile of kilts that showed where the pride of the Highlanders had been slain. Albuera, with its dreadful carnage, where Colonel John Colborne's Light Brigade was blinded by a sudden hailstorm, mown down and annihilated by the demon lancers of Poland. Cuidad Rodrigo. Gallant Dan Mackinnon blown up by a mine, and General Robert Crauford of the Light Division buried in the breech where he fell. Colonel Colborne wounded so badly in the shoulder, the gold braid of his epaulette driven so far in his flesh, that he could only bear the ball to be dug out five minutes at a time over a period of months. The terrible dead of the Peninsular battlefields, who lay stripped of their clothes by human scavengers and left to burn naked in the sun until the vultures swooped down from the sky, and the jackals from the hills.

Lump might have liked to investigate a kilt, or chase a jackal; but in their absence, he was bored. Not with his surroundings, which offered countless adventurous opportunities for an enterprising hound, but his master was moving along at a snail's pace. Not that Master Andrew could be blamed for his lack of speed, for he had come home from his travels done to a cow's thumb, which was why Lump trotted meekly at his heels. But Lump was only a canine, albeit an exceptional one, and could not be expected to continue this forbearance indefinitely. Furthermore, he was growing hungry. He looked around at the bustling crowd.

Andrew was wakened from his unhappy musings by a sharp tug on the leash wrapped around his wrist. "Fiend seize it!" he growled. But Lump was already off in quest of adventure. Andrew could only stumble along in his wake. First Lump inspected the fishing nets spread from one end of the Steine to the other, and caused several promenaders to be tripped up by entangling their feet, and several fisherman to shout most colorfully after him. Then he narrowly avoided collision with a military gentleman in a magnificently laced jacket, decorative yellow boots, and breeches with gold fringe. Persuaded by his master that the fringe was not for eating, he next interfered grievously with a young woman selling gingerbread and apples out of a little basket at her side. Lump especially liked gingerbread. With the basket clenched in his teeth, he led his master a merry chase through the crowd, leaving quite a rumpus in his wake.

Among that crowd, a particular young lady caught his eye. Not that Lump was a connoisseur of female beauty, though he thought his own mistress was very fine. And not that the young lady *was* a beauty, for she was taller than was common, and had a generous smattering of freckles across her nose. Nor did Lump care that she looked anxious, or observe the odd circumstance that she appeared to be alone. What intrigued Lump were the tassels dangling from the young lady's reticule. Lump was especially fond of tassels. He let go of the basket and leapt forward with a happy bark. The little gingerbread girl, who had been chasing after him, snatched up her basket and sadly depleted wares.

Not of interest to Sarah-Louise, either, were such fashionable diversions as toys and rare china, tea and knickknacks. She peered anxiously around, wondered if perhaps she might go unnoticed among so vast a throng. Not that Sarah-Louise would be easy to overlook, wearing as she was a straw hat turned up round the front, lined with white satin, a bunch of ribbons on one side; and a walking dress of green striped muslin with long, full sleeves tied up in three places with colored ribbons, and a deep vandyked flounce that also had a ribbon trim. If only she could be certain Peregrine had received her note! She twisted her reticule in her hands. And then Sarah-Louise gasped, for she espied not a handsome poetical profile but a singularly unattractive hound with a pale young man in tow. The hound was making straight for her, despite the gentleman's heroic attempt to hold him in check. In but a trice it would be upon her, its great paws on her shoulders, drooling all over her dress.

Despite Mr. Inchquist's poor opinion of his daughter's mettle, Sarah-Louise did not shriek and run away, or turn faint with fright. Hounds were not among the countless things she regarded with trepidation, for Sarah-Louise had survived considerable exposure to her papa's own hounds, though none of her papa's hounds were so queer-looking as this. "Halt, sir!" she said sternly, and held out a commanding hand.

It was the hand that held the reticule. Tassels swayed. Lump parted his great jaws. "Galumphus!" snapped his master, at the same moment the young lady demanded, "Sit!" Astonished at being addressed in so forceful a manner, Lump flopped down on the bricks, directly in his master's path. Andrew, too, would have flopped down on the bricks, had not the young lady caught his arm. "Oh!" she said. "Sir, are you all right?"

Of course Andrew was not all right. He was mortified by his weakness, and embarrassed that he had been saved from a nasty tumble by a female. Granted, the female was almost as tall as Andrew himself, but it still rankled that his rescuer was a member of the weaker sex. In the proper scheme of things, the boot would have been on the other leg. But he had regained his balance, and with it his manners. "Thanks to you, I am, ma'am," he said stiffly, and glowered at Lump, who lay panting at his feet. "You and I shall have a word later, muttonhead!" Stricken with conscience by the realization that his master was looking queer as Dick's hatband, Lump meekly wagged his tail.

Sarah-Louise could not but smile, so ridiculous did the hound appear, with his tongue hanging out of his mouth, and his great plumed tail waving, and his eyes fixed wistfully on her reticule. "You must not blame the creature for following his nature. Tassels are a particular temptation, I have found." Again she peered into the crowd.

Andrew would not ordinarily have approached a young lady to whom he had not been introduced— would probably not have approached a young lady at all, not being in the petticoat line, and certainly not one who resembled a great freckled Maypole—but Lump had precipitated matters, and now the damsel's anxious demeanor led him to wonder what was amiss. If Lump was unaware of the oddity of a very young lady of obvious breeding being unescorted, Andrew was not. Brighton was a favorite meeting-place not only of fashionable society, and some of those others would not hesitate to take advantage of innocence in distress. Not that she was a likely candidate for some of the worse fates that might lie in wait for an unaccompanied female, being so freckled and so tall. "Permit me to introduce myself," he said, and did so. "That wretched beast groveling before you goes by the name of Lump."

Sarah-Louise blushed. So deep had she been in her own thoughts that she had not realized the young man still stood by her side. Her aunt, not to mention her papa, would hardly approve of Sarah-Louise conversing with someone to whom she had not been properly introduced. But her aunt, and her papa, approved of little that Sarah-Louise could see, and she didn't wish to be rude. "I cry your pardon! I am not usually so skitterwitted," she murmured, and in turn gave him her name.

Andrew shifted positions, leaning heavily on his cane. "I could not but notice—are you looking for someone, Miss Inchquist?"

Sarah-Louise lamented her tendency to blush, even as she felt her cheeks flame again. "Yes! That is, I mean, no. Oh, it is too complicated to explain, and my aunt—"

Andrew understood perfectly. He was being cosseted and doted upon by his sister's entire household, and allowed scarcely a moment's peace. "Escaped your keeper, did you?" he inquired. The young lady looked startled. "A regular Gorgon, I suppose?"

What an apt description of her aunt, and supplied by a perfect stranger. Sarah-Louise felt very much in charity with him. "Lieutenant Halliday, you have no idea," she sighed.

"Sarah-Louise! What are you doing?" snapped a voice behind them. Sarah-Louise started guiltily. Even Lump raised his head. Andrew turned to see a patrician-looking lady of middle years staring icily at him. Her lips were narrow, her nose exceedingly Roman, and her hair blacker than ever nature had intended. "Who is *this*?" she asked, in tones that made Andrew wish Miss Inchquist's Gorgon were wearing tassels so that Lump might knock the rude creature down.

What did it look like she was doing? Sarah-Louise was conversing with a stranger. Determined for once not to cower before authority, she turned to meet her aunt's arctic gaze. "It-it was so close inside that I grew overwarm. You were d-deep in conversation and I did not wish to interrupt, and I d-did not think you would mind so terribly much if I stepped outside for a breath of fresh air."

The Gorgon was not appeased. The ostrich feathers on her bonnet trembled with the force of her outrage. Lump had no notion what a Gorgon was, but the feathers on her bonnet were very fine. Desirous of a more intimate acquaintance with those feathers, he bounded forward, placed a great, shaggy paw on her shoulder, and drooled.

She shrieked. Sarah-Louise bit back a giggle and demanded, "Stop it at once, sir!" as Andrew drew back sharply on the leash.

Lump was surrounded by spoilsports. Sulkily, he dropped back down on the bricks. "It was *my* tassels that he liked, you see," Sarah-Louise explained to her horrified aunt.

Andrew limped forward. "I should have never brought him—or allowed him to bring me—among so many people." The Gorgon favored his lame leg with a startled glance. For the first time Andrew realized how being a cripple might prove to be of some benefit. "Fortunate it was that Miss Inchquist did step outside when she did. She saved me from a nasty tumble. Lieutenant Andrew Halliday of the 88th at your service, ma'am," he said, and made a gallant bow.

Five

Miss Halliday and her visitor had withdrawn to Georgie's bedchamber and firmly shut the door, thereby foiling the efforts of several interested parties to eavesdrop, a case of closing the stable gate entirely too late, for Tibble had already heard enough to astound his audience, if only he could remember it straight.

The bedroom was a pretty chamber furnished with a dressing table made in satinwood and decorated with festoons of flowers painted in natural colors and surmounted by a circular toilet-glass; a tallboy chest of drawers veneered with finely figured dark mahogany lined with oak; a reasonably fine wardrobe with matched oval panels of figured mahogany veneer; a tester bed with carved mahogany posts; and a corner basin stand. If the painted flowers had faded, and the veneer pulled away from its backing, and the wood of the tallboy chest had separated at the joint—well, the muslin window hangings were carefully mended and freshly washed, the faded carpet on the floor newly shaken and swept, the grate and andiron dusted and polished with Brunswick black. Pretty embroidered pictures hung upon the plaster walls. If there were no real treasures in this chamber, neither were there cobwebs nor dust.

Marigold glanced around the room, and then back at Georgie. Although the surroundings were not what she was accustomed to, it would be most imprudent for her to remark, because Georgie's expression was already very stern as she said, "Well, Marigold?"

Marigold's lush limps trembled. "I'm sure I meant no harm! I merely said all the *ton* have been whispering about Warwick, which they have, so you needn't *glower* so. I thought *you* would know the truth, because he is practically a member of your family. Or *was*, at any rate. But I do not mean to flog a dead horse!"

Georgie wondered how Lord Warwick would respond to this description of himself. "Marigold, you are a goose-cap. Warwick never murdered anyone. Now we will hear no more about it, if you please."

Marigold was quite content to speak no more of Warwick. She had not liked the man. Nor had he liked her, which was very strange in him. Most gentlemen took one look at Marigold and responded very differently, at the very least calling her fair fatality, and proffering their hearts.

She sank down on a stool by the dressing table and gazed at herself in the looking glass, watched a practiced tear trickle down one porcelain cheek. "It is very *hard* of you to pinch at me when I am in such a quandary. Oh, Georgie, I don't know what I'm going to do."

Neither did Georgie know what she was going to do, with a household on the verge of revolt. If rebellion wasn't yet in the air, it soon enough would be. Georgie didn't imagine that Janie—even then attacking the guest bedroom with sweeping-brush and dust-pan and moist tea leaves—would be overjoyed to learn that in addition to her numerous other duties, she was about to be asked to serve as lady's maid. Agatha was unlikely to appreciate someone whose palate was not sufficiently adventurous to savor such delicacies as eels *à la tartare* and fried cow's heel. Tibble, though he might be willing, was not sufficiently robust to undertake duties more strenuous than those he already attempted to perform. And Andrew's nerves were not likely to benefit from exposure to a sad shatterbrain like Marigold.

Still, Marigold was Georgie's oldest friend. There was no real harm in her, other than being dreadfully spoiled, which was not surprising in someone who had been cosseted from the cradle and married three times by the time she was twenty-six. Georgie sank down in the faded wing chair and picked up her embroidery. "You still have not explained this quandary of yours. Suppose you start at the beginning," she suggested.

Marigold rose from the stool to pace back and forth across the faded rug. "I wouldn't have to start from the beginning if you had not lost my letter, which was very bad of you, because it took me the longest time to write it all down. Yes, and it was also very *dear* to post! Oh! This is all Leo's fault."

Georgie blinked. Leo had been the first of Marigold's husbands, with whom she had eloped when she was fifteen. The union had been short-lived, due to the disappearance of the bridegroom during his honeymoon. "Have you heard from Leo?" she asked, with genuine interest.

"Oh, that I had!" Marigold wiped away a tear. "Leo

always knew what to do. If only you had met him you would understand. He was so dashing, so handsome, so—romantic!" Prettily, she cast down her eyes. "How different my life would have been had not poor Leo met up with foul play!"

How different Marigold's life might have been had she not been taken advantage of by a man of the world. Beautiful though she might be, Marigold's understanding was not powerful; she was heedless and stubborn and extravagant, a charming, gay butterfly with scant interest beyond the moment and what amusement it might bring.

It was hardly for Georgie to censure anyone's conduct. Only a short time past she had herself been regretting that she was a respectable female. "What do you think happened to your Leo?" she asked.

Marigold pressed her hand to her lush bosom. "Oh, Georgie, it is such a puzzle! I have wracked my brains until I cannot think! Leo would never have parted from me willingly, I vow." From her sleeve she plucked a lacy handkerchief and wiped away another tear. "You know that Papa cut me off after my elopement, for which I suppose I cannot blame him, because much as I doted on Leo, even I must admit that he was not the thing. Oh, but we would have lived a carefree life of dissipation, and he would have taken me to fascinating places, and shown me all manner of forbidden stuff!" She paused, lost in wistful imaginings.

Delicately, Georgie coughed. Reluctantly, Marigold returned to the dreary present. "It was not to be. Leo disappeared, and though I thought I should die from a spasm of the heart, I found I did not. I knew nothing of Leo's family, or even if he *had* a family. And so unaccustomed was I to being purse-pinched that I thought it was only people who became deranged!" She fanned herself with the lace handkerchief. "I would have been in the basket altogether, had it not been for Mr. Frobisher. I did not know where else to turn. Why I didn't think of *you* I can't imagine, other than my senses were so overset."

To say that the flesh crawled on Georgie's bones as a result of this suggestion might be an overstatement, but she did allow her embroidery to drop unheeded in her lap. "Mr. Frobisher would be the theatrical gentleman?" she asked.

"Yes." Arms held out at her side, Marigold spun around, then sank into a graceful curtsey. "He set my feet upon the stage. It was vastly interesting, Georgie! I appeared in-oh-so many productions in the provinces." She had advanced from appearing most often as a supernumerary ordered to play whatever walk-on part was needed, dressed in whatever old costume might be left over in the theater wardrobe, to a leading lady of whom one unkind critic had written that she was "a pretty piece of uninteresting manner, with almost enough ability to speak her lines." The memory caused Marigold's elegant nostrils to flare. What did that critic know of acting? *He* had never trod the boards. Nor played to so discerning an audience as this one. Marigold raised a languid hand to her pale brow. "And then, just when things were going well, poor Mr. Frobisher suffered an accident."

Georgie watched her friend's dramatic perambulations and wondered just how good an actress Marigold had become. That these confidences were leading somewhere, Georgie had no doubt. "What manner of accident?"

Marigold did not deem it of any purpose to speak

of wheelbarrows and pigs and gentlemen who habit-
ually took too much to drink. "A fatal one," she
sighed. "Truly I have *tried* to choose a companion for
life! It is not *my* fault if something happens to them
all. I met Sir Hubert when I was performing at Tunbridge Wells. He had gone there to nurse his gout. It
was a *most* felicitous encounter. Sir Hubert was taken
with me straightaway. And I vow I did not care a
minute if he was quite old, no matter what *anyone* may
say!"

Georgie had not realized, until presented with
these disclosures, how very dull had been the events
of her own life. Marigold seemed to be awaiting some
response. "Good gracious!" Georgie murmured.
"How very bothersome for you."

Had there been a tinge of irony in Georgie's voice?
Marigold could not be sure. The ladies were interrupted then by a tap on the door. "Enter!" Georgie
called.

Tibble tottered into the room, gingerly carrying a
tray. Georgie quickly rose and rescued it from his
trembling hands. "I know you wasn't wishful of being
interrupted," he apologized. "But Miss Agatha would
have it that you'd care for some refreshment."

Georgie was grateful to see that her cousin's notion
of appropriate refreshment was a beverage stronger
than tea. "Thank you, Tibble," she said, and watched
her butler make his unsteady way out the door, en
route to the kitchen, where he would report that Miss
Georgie's hair, always an excellent barometer of her
emotions, currently made her look like an owl in an
ivy bush.

"My cousin's own ratafia. It is very potent." Georgie
presented Marigold with a glass. Ratafia was a sweet

cordial customarily flavored with fruit kernel or almonds. Not one to hedge her bets, Agatha made use of both.

Marigold downed more of the beverage than was prudent. "I *should* have cared about his age," she muttered, and resumed her pacing. "Because he died before changing his will, and left me not so much as a brass farthing, the old coot." She caught her friend's shocked look. "That is, the old dear! It is not true that I am a fortune hunter, Georgie! Sir Hubert was most amiable, and most boring, and I vow I made him a good wife. Perhaps *too* good, I fear! The fact of the matter is that I should have been provided for. That I was not—it was a monstrous, shabby thing."

Georgie wondered just how Sir Hubert had gone to meet his Maker. She did not like to ask. The waters at Brighton were prescribed not only for asthma and ruptures and deafness, but also for agitated nerves. Perhaps Marigold could be persuaded to drink the wretched stuff. "Why are you calling yourself 'Mrs. Smith'?" Georgie demanded. "Let us have the straight of the story, Marigold. Without further roundaboutation, if you please."

Marigold's chin quivered. She drained her glass. "Oh, if only my poor Leo was here!" she wept. "*He* would understand how it is that one can do something that one shouldn't and it seems an excellent notion until the piper must be paid!" Did Georgie feel the least bit sympathetic? Marigold peeked over the edge of her handkerchief, and took a deep breath. "And I'm sure I'm willing to give back the Norwood Emerald, but I no longer have it in my possession, which is entirely Sir Hubert's fault for being such a miserly purse-pinch!"

The Norwood Emerald? What the devil was the Norwood Emerald? Georgie wished that she hadn't drunk her cousin's ratafia. Or alternately, that she might drink some more. Carefully, she set down her glass. "Marigold, you haven't—"

Here was the telling moment. The *pièce de résistance*, the *coup de grâce*. Marigold sank down on her knees in a supplicating posture. "Oh, Georgie!" she whispered. "I do not wish to go to gaol!"

Six

Marigold's forebodings were not without foundation. At nearly that same moment, another conversation was taking place in the private room of a local inn. The chamber was small but comfortable, with a low-beamed ceiling, huge fireplace, shuttered windows, and sawdust on the floor.

This meeting was not of a social nature. Carlisle Sutton had journeyed all the way from Calcutta, India, to deal with the irregularities of his late uncle's estate. He frowned at his uncle's man of business, a self-effacing, bespectacled individual who wore a brown jacket and buff pantaloons, and was the very picture of subdued efficiency, save for the height of his shirt points. "A bit young, ain't you?" he asked.

Mr. Brown was indeed young, all of four-and-twenty, a matter for which he felt apologetic, though one that would soon enough be rectified by time. "Sir Hubert was kind enough to allow me to continue to handle his affairs," he responded stiffly, "after my father died. I do not believe he ever had any complaint about the quality of our service to him, sir."

Carlisle lounged against the fireplace. He had not meant to set up the young pup's back. "Then we will hope I also have no complaint. Tell me about this marriage, if you please. It sounds like a deuced havey-cavey affair."

Havey-cavey was not the half of it, as Mr. Sutton would soon learn. "I believe your uncle met the lady," Mr. Brown said delicately, "when she was performing in a pantomime in Tunbridge Wells."

Carlisle had been attending Mr. Brown with only a small part of his mind; the rest of his considerable intelligence had been focused on Calcutta, and the business that awaited his return. Now he stood bolt upright. "Tunbridge Wells? Pantomime? My uncle married an *actress?*" he exclaimed, incredulous.

Mr. Brown understood this reaction. Mr. Brown had experienced a similar horrified astonishment upon discovering the theatrical background of his octogenarian employer's bride. He held out a playbill, and a miniature portrait in an ornate frame. "It shouldn't be too difficult to find her, sir. Not many females look like this."

Mr. Sutton perused the playbill, which announced the presentation of a pantomime at Tunbridge Wells, featuring in the role of Columbine one "Miss Mary Macclesfield." Then he contemplated the miniature. There had been nothing wrong with his uncle's eyesight, conceded Carlisle, as he studied a lovely, roguish lady with periwinkle eyes and guinea-gold hair. Unfortunately the same could not be said for Sir Hubert's common sense. Had he wed the wench in a Hindu ceremony, she would have taken seven steps around the holy fire, propitiated the goddess Parvati, and then had her nose pierced. Himself, Carlisle was at the moment feeling partial to the four-armed goddess Kali, with her earrings of corpses, necklace of skulls, and protruding, blood-dripping tongue.

As Mr. Carlisle brooded over the miniature, Mr. Brown covertly regarded him. Although Mr. Brown had known Sir Hubert for several years, he had not before met Sir Hubert's nephew, who spent the majority of his time in India. Carlisle Sutton was a ruggedly-built, harsh-faced man of middle years with icy blue eyes, bronzed skin, and long, sun-streaked brown hair drawn back in an unfashionable queue. He looked as though he would be far more comfortable in uncivilized native dress than in the brass-buttoned blue coat, colored waistcoat, buckskin breeches, and Hessian boots he currently wore.

A sojourn with seven hooded cobras, mused Mr. Sutton, as he gazed at the miniature. Confinement in the dread black hole of Calcutta. Exposure to viciously stinging Kashmiri red ants. Not that Carlisle was in general predisposed against ladies who trod the boards. He had known a number of pretty actresses very well himself. Hopefully another forty years would not turn him into such a cod's head as his uncle, who admittedly deserved a great deal of credit for attempting the amorous congress at his age, a startling testimonial to the salubrious effects of Tunbridge Wells, or perhaps not so startling, considering that Sir Hubert had expired in the marriage bed. "Why should we have to look for her?" he asked. "You must know where she is."

Mr. Brown adjusted his spectacles, which were forever sliding down his nose, and wondered how Calcutta employers dealt with servants of whom they had complaint. "The lady was most distressed to learn that your uncle had neglected to alter his will in her favor, sir. She apparently decided to, ah, take matters into her own hands."

The young pup was as nervous as a cat on hot coals. Carlisle saw his longed-for return to Calcutta recede further and further into the distance. *"What* matters?"

Manfully, Mr. Brown screwed up his courage. "The Norwood Emerald, sir."

With these words, Carlisle's forbearance vanished. He cursed. "The Norwood Emerald was smuggled out of India in the early 1700s. It took five years to cut. The family has refused countless offers from connoisseurs eager to purchase the gem. The most recent offer was for thirty thousand pounds. Hell and the devil confound it! My uncle must have been in his dotage to allow such a bauble to be casually worn. By a Cyprian, no less!"

Although it might be unwise in him, Mr. Brown found himself compelled to defend the lady. "I don't think she was a Cyprian, exactly," he murmured. "I have an impression that she was of good birth."

Mr. Sutton snorted. "She was an actress, you nodcock. No, don't fly into the boughs! I meant you no insult."

Perhaps he *was* a nodcock, reflected Mr. Brown, for he had liked Sir Hubert's young wife very well. "I am very sorry to tell you that the lady has vanished, and the emerald with her, sir. We traced her here to Brighton, and then she gave us the slip. However, I have every reason to think that she has not left town."

The Norwood Emerald stolen by an enterprising bit of muslin! Carlisle seethed with rage. Sir Hubert had served his own turn in the service of the East India Company, as had numerous members of the family ever since the early eighteenth century, when an enterprising Norwood—the same Norwood who had smuggled out the missing emerald—began to buy cloth and ship it to Java in exchange for spices which were then sold in London. Soon that first Norwood had owned his own ships, and after twenty years' diligent service and even more diligent trading, had amassed an estate of some several thousand millions, and began to perform small services for the royal family, and to marry his children into the aristocracy. Carlisle had been little less enterprising during his own sojourn in India, although he was of an irascible, argumentative nature that made him highly unpopular with the Court of Directors at Leadenhall in London, to whom he spoke out with embarrassing regularity against such things as the forced cultivation of Indian opium, and the plunder of Bengal. Carlisle couldn't care less for the ignorant secretaries of the Indian Board who didn't know whether the Mahrattas were Mahometans or Hindus. Between the natives and the climate, most foreigners found India a miserable country. So contrary was he that Carlisle liked it very well.

He set down the miniature and the playbill on a table. "You will find her, Mr. Brown," he said. "When you do, you will send me word." He clapped a tall beaver hat onto his head, and strode out into the hall. Mr. Brown paused to wipe his damp brow. Then he collected the playbill and the picture and retired to the taproom, there to inspect the landlord's stock of sack and canary, ale and stout, and initiate his inquiries over a well-earned pint.

Carlisle stepped into the courtyard of the inn, which styled itself The King's Hand, and was one of several establishments in which Charles II was said to have tarried while in flight to France. Carlisle had not wanted to return to England, and put on these curst uncomfortable clothes that made him feel trussed up like a chicken for the pot, and be subjected to the various humbugs that being rich as Croesus entailed. Here in Brighton he was, nonetheless, and in Brighton he would remain. Not that Carlisle had the slightest interest in the town's fashionable pursuits. Even the extravagancies of the Prince Regent could only seem tame to someone who had rubbed shoulders with a Rajah, a Scandial, a Holkar, and a Peshwah. What Carlisle found most interesting about Brighton was its mention in the Domesday Book, with 4,000 herrings paid as rent. Since he must be here, he would probably inspect the shipping and the harbor, and ride out to view the remains of the old Saxon camps. He called an ostler to bring round his horse.

Marry at haste, repent at leisure. The Norwood Emerald must be returned where it belonged. Carlisle contemplated a horse trough filled with clear, fresh water, the ground below it sprinkled with fresh hay. Had Mr. Brown spied his employer at that moment, he might have glimpsed in those normally cold eyes a certain bloodlust. Mr. Sutton's complicated nature thrived on adversity.

It would not be difficult to drive the wench out into the open. Even after so long an absence, Carlisle had access to resources not available to the earnest Mr. Brown. Not as stimulating as a tiger hunt, perhaps, he thought as he swung into the saddle, and certainly not so dangerous, but "Miss Mary Macclesfield" would provide him a diversion all the same. And when the chase was over, the little trollop would come to rue the day she first heard the name Norwood.

Seven

The following morning, because it was her habit—unthinkable that it should be for any other reason—Miss Halliday took her energetic pet for a stroll on the beach, and even went so far as to engage him in a game of fetch with a piece of driftwood. Georgie greatly enjoyed the seaside, though not so much that she might venture out in one of the storms that periodically encroached upon the shore and tore away great pieces of land. She held in great respect a force of nature that swept away embankments as soon as they were built. But she liked to watch the packet boats sail to and from Dieppe, and the fishing fleet, to hear the murmur of the water against the shore, and inhale the bracing air.

That air, just now, was very chill and damp. Georgie pulled her shawl closer round her shoulders and trudged through the sand. Fortunate that Marigold was not an early riser, else even this little bit of solitude would be disturbed with laments about an unkind fate. Georgie did not recall her oldest friend being so prone to melodrama. That would be the influence of the theatrical Mr. Frobisher, no doubt. Georgie wondered which of Marigold's husbands might be held responsible for her current foolhardiness. "Blast and damn!" muttered Georgie, and kicked at an inoffensive seashell.

A large shape loomed up out of the fog. Georgie jumped. "I see that you are again unchaperoned," Lord Warwick remarked.

Georgie gestured, as Lump emerged from the fog with the driftwood in his jaws. "Not precisely. I wondered if I might find you here."

"I have grown accustomed to taking solitary walks." Garth smiled to see the riotous blond curls that escaped her bonnet. "You look like some water nymph sprung up out of the mist."

He looked like a devil, conjured up out of the fog to steal away her heart. Georgie blinked. Appalling, the effect Marigold had on one's imagination. "I am thinking of taking a course of sea-bathing. Perhaps I shall even hire a bathing machine."

Then perhaps Lord Warwick would hire a telescope, like those other gentlemen who sat on the Marine Parade and gazed out to sea, watching not for incoming enemy ships but inspecting the ladies in their flannel smocks as they floundered about in the muddy water. "Ah," he said ironically. "The lovely Mrs. Smith."

Marigold had made no conquest of Lord Warwick. "She *is* lovely, isn't she?" Georgie responded. "One might also wish she had good sense. I must ask you not to mention her presence to anyone, Garth. Pray ask me no questions, because I cannot explain!"

"Come, walk with me before you take a chill." Garth offered her his arm. "Is there nothing I can do? I do not like to see you worrying yourself to death."

He could kiss her, Georgie thought. Not that a kiss would solve any of her problems, but it would feel very nice. "We are at sixes and sevens!" she admitted. "Marigold is the least of my worries, to say the truth."

About those other worries, Lord Warwick had some notion. "You must know that Wellington has been elevated from viscount to earl. Your brother was with Mackinnon at Cuidad Rodrigo, was he not?"

Georgie glanced up at him, startled. "I did not think you had known my brother." Lord Warwick shook his head. "I wonder if Andrew will ever wholly recover. He has recurrent fevers. And nightmares. And gets to raving sometimes about the things he saw there."

Lord Warwick had a clearer notion of the sights of the Peninsula than did Andrew's sister. Scant wonder the boy raved. "I knew Mackinnon. He once impersonated the Duke of York at a banquet and dived headfirst into a punch bowl. Another time, when Wellington was visiting a convent, Mackinnon pretended to be a nun. Wellington was quite taken with the lady, or so the story goes."

Georgie smiled. "I think Andrew would like to talk of him. If you would not mind."

Garth would not mind anything that made Georgie less unhappy. Unless, perhaps, that something involved kissing someone other than himself. "I am at your service. And I will plague you with no questions so long as you promise to come to me if you find yourself in over your head with this business. I have taken a house on the Royal Crescent for the season." He paused. "You will be interested to know that Prinny has now lost not only some fingers, and the whole of his right arm, but also a portion of his nose."

The Royal Crescent, built facing the sea by a West Indian speculator, was a most fashionable address.

The houses there were faced with black mathematical tiles, and in the center of the garden enclosure stood a buff-colored statue of the Prince of Wales. Perhaps Georgie should go inspect the defaced statue, for which either the weather or vandals were to blame. Or perhaps she should inspect the lodgings hired by Garth.

Georgie was rendered strangely breathless by this shocking notion. She pinched Lord Warwick's arm. "It is not kind of you to try and distract me! Or perhaps it is."

Lord Warwick wished that he might distract Georgie all the more. "There is one question I *must* ask. However came you by that nitwit of a butler?"

Georgie gurgled with laughter. "Poor Tibble. He tries so very hard. I inherited him from my grandmother along with the house, and could not bear to turn him out. Although I admit to being tempted the day I found him trying to break the claws of a lobster between the hinges of a dining room drawer." She then went on to divert Lord Warwick with additional tales about her household, including Janie's efforts to attract the attention of the new footman down the street, which took the little maidservant out of doors at every opportunity on the slightest of pretexts, with the result that they now had the whitest front steps in the entire neighborhood; and Agatha's efforts to tempt Andrew's sluggish appetite with mutton cutlets, eel broth, and rice milk. "She is now experimenting with home remedies for which I have even less hope," Georgie concluded. "They include dried toad, powdered mole, and fresh horse dung."

Georgie seemed comfortable with her bizarre household, Lord Warwick mused. Indeed she seemed comfortable with herself in a way now that she had not as a girl.

How dull as ditchwater were his companions. Lump dropped the driftwood that he had been clutching all this time in his jaws. His mistress had ignored him sadly since the gentleman had interrupted them at play. She had not even included in her tales of the household Lump's own discovery in the larder of a sleek and well-fed mouse. A seagull flying overhead caught his attention. He leapt up and barked.

Lord Warwick grasped Lump's collar. "No!" he said. "Sit, you wretched hound!"

What was the world coming to, when he was spoken to so rudely twice in so many days? Lump sank down on the sand.

Georgie clapped her hands in admiration. "How did you do that?" she asked. "None of us can." The wind blew her errant curls into her eyes and she untied her bonnet with the intention of pushing her aggravating hair back beneath its confining bounds. "Although I *have* noticed that gentlemen can sometimes persuade people to obey them just by employing a certain tone of voice."

Lord Warwick could not help himself. "Oh?" he inquired.

"Not that sort of thing!" Georgie made a strong effort to discipline her mind. "You are out early," she added. "Or have you not been to bed?" Quizzically, he looked at her. She sighed. "That didn't come out right."

"Come, let us continue our walk. You must be very cold." Lord Warwick regained possession of her arm. "No, I have not been to bed. We fashionable gentlemen would be appalled at the notion of cutting short our revels before cock crow."

Georgie was not deceived by the lightness of his tone. "I am glad to see you return where you belong," she said. "You were gone from us for a long time, Garth."

Only with great difficulty had Garth rousted himself from the sprawling estate near Penrith where he had been rusticating—or, as some would have it, sulking—for some months. "So I was," he said. "It is almost as good as a play to see the fashionable world watch each other to determine how they must react—for the gossips hint that if I did indeed dispose of my wife, who knows what other dark secrets might lie buried in my past?"

Thus was Georgie confirmed in her opinion of the fashionable world. "Fiddle-faddle!" she said crossly, and slapped the bonnet against her thigh. "You had no previous wife to dispose of, and even the largest chucklehead would find it difficult to credit that you would sooner do away with a tiresome *petite amie* than simply pay her off."

Lord Warwick smiled. "I thank you, my dear, for that vote of confidence. Between you and Prinny, I may yet contrive to hold up my head. Although all the world knows Prinny is hardly a judge of character. Speaking of which, I have been privileged to see Mr. Wyatt's plans for remodeling the Pavilion in the most extraordinary Gothic style. It is expected to cost a minimum two hundred thousand pounds."

Georgie had forgotten that Lord Warwick was an intimate of the future king. It did not place him in exclusive company—the indolent, affable Regent was not notorious for the discriminatory quality of his relationships, among which had been included not only Beau Brummell and Lord Alvanley and the Duke of Argyle, "Poodle" Bynd and "Golden Ball" Hughes, but also the Duke of Queensbury, who for a time retired to the King's Bench Prison for Debtors; Sir John Lade and his wife Letty, once the mistress of a highwayman known as "Sixteen String Jack"; the Barrymore brothers, Hellgate and Cripplegate and Newgate, and their sister, Billingsgate. She, it was said, could be outsworn only by Letty Lade—but it reminded her anew of how great the disparity between them had grown. "The Pavilion is already a house run mad," Georgie remarked. "Domes and pagodas and turrets. Banqueting rooms with twining golden dragons. A China gallery of painted glass. One hears the strangest tales."

"All of them true, I make no doubt. I have seen the new stables myself. They include coach houses, harness rooms, servants' rooms, stables, and an open gallery. The whole structure is lighted through the glazed compartments of the cupola by which it is surrounded. It is some sixty-five feet high." Why the devil was he talking about stables? Garth didn't give a damn for Prinny's stables. He paused.

Georgie was thinking of their first meeting, and what Lord Warwick had said. *When* had he wished to kiss her? He had used the word "still." Had he done so then, would things be very different now? Not that intimates of the Prince Regent were prone to dally with spinsters like herself. Bonnet forgotten in her hand, Georgie looked up at Lord Warwick. Her ribbons dangled in the sand.

They were very tempting ribbons. Piece of driftwood or straw hat, 'twas all the same to Lump. He grabbed the bonnet in his strong teeth, and ran.

The moment was shattered. Georgie sighed, and gazed after her lost bonnet. "I meant what I said, Garth. I am glad to see you resume your place in the world."

She was so determined to think well of him. Garth was touched. "As a gentleman of sinister reputation?" he inquired.

Georgie pushed her windblown hair out of her eyes, and frowned. "You are determined to jest."

Garth grasped her shoulders, swung her to face him. "'Tis hardly a jesting matter. I remind you that the gossips have me accused of murder, ma'am."

Steadily, Georgie met his gaze, or as steadily as she could with her hair blowing in her eyes. "To tell truth, there were several occasions on which I wished to murder Catherine myself."

Garth was aware of some of those occasions. Reluctantly, he smiled. "As did I. All the same, I did not murder my wife. Nor incarcerate her in some dank dungeon. Nor wall her up in a nunnery. I truly do not know where Catherine may be."

Georgie was very conscious of the warmth of his lordship's hands through the thin material of her shawl. "Lud!" she said briskly. "I never doubted that."

Garth was conscious also of Georgie's nearness. He could smell her sweet perfume, see the rapid pulse beat at the base of her throat. He thought that he would very much like to press his lips against that tender spot. He thought also that he was a married man, and one who stood accused of murder, and had much better not.

Lump, meanwhile, had discovered that even the

most enterprising of hounds could hardly play fetch all by himself. Or either hide-and-seek. He couldn't imagine what had gotten into his mistress this morning. Normally she would be chasing over the sand after him, begging him to return to her side. Today, however, she didn't even seem to notice that he'd gone. At any rate, she would be glad to have her bonnet back. Lump bounded forward and presented the trophy to his mistress, then sat down, his wagging tail making semicircles in the sand.

Georgie gingerly picked up the sodden, sandy mess than had once been her straw bonnet. Here was yet another unanticipated expense, because the hat would have to be replaced. "Oh, dear," she said.

Abruptly, Garth released her and stepped back. Georgie looked up at him, surprised. "I am not entirely without scruples," he murmured, "despite what the gossipmongers think." Bedraggled bonnet in one hand, unrepentant hound's collar in the other, Georgie watched him walk away.

Eight

Silence reigned in the Halliday kitchen, at least for a moment, among the four people gathered there, due to Georgie's recent irritable announcement that her gentleman caller had been an old friend merely, and the next person who pestered her about the matter would be turned out into the street.

Georgie sat at one end of the long elm table, frowning over her household accounts. Occasionally she reached into a bowl of peas that stood nearby, peeled open the pod, and popped the raw vegetables into her mouth. The peas were very sweet, and grown by Georgie herself in a little garden out behind the house, a pursuit that was horridly unladylike of her, but immensely gratifying nonetheless. Although grubbing in the dirt was behavior hardly befitting a lady, Georgie looked like one all the same, in a high-necked, figured muslin gown. Agatha, just then thumbing through her receipts, was dressed rather less conservatively in a dress of India muslin with a low neckline and puffed sleeves, her blazing hair tucked under a huge mobcap. At the other end of the long table, Tibble sat polishing the silver, a task in which he was unlikely to hurt himself, and one that would over-task neither his strength nor his powers of concentration, since most of the pieces had already been sold. In front of him marched an array of silverplate, a container holding a paste made of hartshorn powder mixed with spirits of wine, a brush, several soft rags, a piece of dry leather, and his wig. Tibble had already this day trimmed the lamp-wicks and replenished the rapeseed oil; brushed and blacked the ladies boots (and if he left behind his hand-mark on the lining, no one but Marigold would be unkind enough to remark); and very narrowly avoided doing himself serious injury while cleaning the kitchen knives.

"Lord love a duck," muttered Janie, the only member of the little group not seated at the elm table. Janie was bent over a kitchen dresser, attempting to remove the stain from a silk ribbon by way of a mixture of gin and honey, soft soap and water, not with a great deal of success. It was not enough that Janie must dust and sweep and polish and scour; now she must also wash out milady's brushes and clean her combs and arrange her hair, remove stains and grease spots from her clothes, and repair her lace. Not that Janie would mind performing any of these tasks for Mistress Georgie, who was a very good sort of person, as Janie should well know, because she had been on the verge of A Fate Worse Than Death when Mistress Georgie and Miss Agatha took her in; but Mistress Georgie's guest was a far different kettle of fish, shedding crocodile tears and capperclawing and butter wouldn't melt in her mouth until one wished that cheese might choke her and the devil fly off with her straightaway.

Janie finished scouring the soiled ribbon with her mixture. She gingerly picked up the ribbon by its corners and dipped the fabric quickly in cold water. After letting the ribbon drip for a moment, she dried it with a cloth, and ironed it quickly with a very hot iron. Then she uttered a strong expletive because the stain was even worse, thereby rousing Agatha from thoughts of Balnamood Skink, and Georgie from the accounts that refused to add up in an encouraging manner, and Tibble from thoughts of which only heaven knew the nature, because he himself could not have said. "Bless me!" Agatha ventured. "What is it?" Georgie asked. Too confused to put in his own two penn'orth, Tibble dabbed his forehead with the silver cloth.

Janie dropped a little curtsey. "Beg pardon, I'm sure. But Miss Marigold is going to have my guts for garters." She dropped the ribbon on the table, then sat down and ate a pea.

Georgie contemplated the ruined ribbon, which was bound to send Marigold again into her tantrums. "Never mind," she soothed. "I believe I have a ribbon of a similar color. Perhaps if you switch them she won't notice the difference. Go now and fetch it from my room." Armed with the ribbon and another pea-pod, Janie set out on her errand, which would take her by a circuitous route that led out of doors, where she hoped to glimpse the new footman down the street, whose name she had learned was Charles.

Tibble wielded his brush with considerable vigor, and sneezed. "Mad as Bedlam," he remarked. "I seen it before. One day a bee in the bonnet, and the next day, poof! Before you can say Jack Robinson, flying off the hooks and maggots in the brain. Best be shut of the flibbertigibbet, afore she takes it into her head to burn down the house." For emphasis he waved the polishing rag. Then he recollected his surroundings. "Not that it's my place to say so, ma'ams."

The ladies did not think that Tibble spoke of Janie. "Beauty will fade," offered Agatha. "A wise woman lays in a stock of something to supply in its place." She then returned to consideration of what dish would go best with green peas *à la Française*. Potted crayfish, perhaps. Or calf's head soup. Providing that Georgie didn't eat up all the peas beforehand.

Georgie stared at her account book. Everything was grown very dear, for this was the fashionable season, and the inhabitants of Brighton must make up a year's income in but a short time. Lodgings were so greatly in demand that unlet houses now commanded fourteen guineas a week. She wondered what Garth was paying for his house on the Marine Parade, and why. If Lord Warwick wished to reclaim his position in society, what made Brighton preferable to London? The Prince Regent's presence? Was there some other less obvious reason, one perhaps that had to do with Catherine? His wife's disappearance left Garth in a most unfortunate situation, not only because he was accused of murder, but also because a vanished spouse could hardly produce him an heir. And if Garth had not murdered Catherine—and of course he had *not* murdered Catherine—where *was* she? A person didn't simply vanish into thin air. Georgie thought of Marigold. Much as one could wish they might. She looked up as Andrew limped into the kitchen. Lump followed at his heels. "Hello, love," she said.

Agatha looked up also. Andrew appeared in better spirits today, perhaps due to the distillation of flowers of cowslip she'd snuck into his morning and evening drink. Happily unaware of Agatha's efforts in his behalf, Andrew brandished an envelope. "I found this in the hall. When did it arrive?" he asked.

Tibble started, guiltily. "I disremember exactly, sir. Mayhap this morning. Or it could have been yesterday. I meant to give it to you straightaway, but you wasn't here."

Andrew contemplated the shamefaced butler, whose bald head was liberally splattered with silver paste. Then he sat down in a chair and broke open a peapod. Lump looked around the kitchen in hope of a bite to eat. Agatha hissed at him. With a great sigh of canine martyrdom, Lump collapsed against Andrew's chair. "We are invited to join Lady Denham's party for an evening's entertainment in the Promenade Grove, sis," Andrew said.

Georgie pushed away her household books and regarded her brother curiously. Here was interesting news. Not that she and her brother should receive an invitation, for Georgie was Lady Georgiana, though she disliked to use her title, and Andrew was an Honourable, and Wellington's staff officers had a certain cachet. The Hallidays between them had used to receive a great many invitations before they made it clear that they would rather be left to themselves. This invitation, apparently, was different. "How come you to know Lady Denham?" Georgie asked.

Andrew grinned, and patted the great head currently resting on his knee. "Lump jumped on her. Which is no more than she deserves for wearing so many curst feathers on her hat."

Too clearly, Georgie envisioned the event. "Oh, dear. And in return Lady Denham sent an invitation? How very odd of her."

"I suspect it is Miss Inchquist whom we may thank for the invitation," Andrew responded. "*She* had a handbag with tassels." He explained his meeting with Sarah-Louise.

Georgie eyed her pet with dismay. "What a dreadful creature you are!" Delighted to have his mistress's attention, Lump panted and drooled.

Andrew pushed the dog's head away from his damp knee. "Don't make a piece of work of it, Georgie. No harm was done."

No harm? This from someone who claimed that attending social functions made him feel like a performing monkey, or a tame blackamoor? "What is she like?" Georgie asked.

"A regular Gorgon!" retorted Andrew, then saw his sister's startled expression. "You mean Miss Inchquist. An unexceptionable young female, I suppose you'd say. She has freckles, and is very tall. Lady Denham is a bully." He popped another pea into his mouth. "It would be nice for Miss Inchquist if we put in an appearance, sis."

The Hallidays had passed muster. Though purse-pinched, they were still sufficiently respectable to associate with Lady Denham's niece, to whom Georgie must be grateful, because she had apparently caused Andrew to think about something other than corpses and fallen comrades. Perhaps he was developing a *tendresse*. Not that romance wasn't frequently a painful experience in its own right.

Agatha had been following the conversation. "Have you thought," she interjected, "what you are going to do with Marigold?"

Andrew's pleasant expression was replaced by a scowl. "Marigold ain't coming along. Dash it, Georgie,

I know she's a friend of yours, but damned if she isn't the most tiresome, totty-headed, rattlebrained female I have ever met. I swear she must have windmills in her head!"

Georgie glanced at Tibble, who had given up all pretense of silver polishing to eavesdrop. "Not windmills, maggots," she murmured. "We have it on excellent authority."

Marigold walked into the room then, perfectly on cue. "So this is where you are all hiding!" she said, and chuckled, because of course it was absurd to think that anyone would hide from her. "Why are you talking about maggots? Good God, are those *peas*? Because if they are, I won't eat them. I dislike peas of all things!"

Agatha pushed aside her receipts. "I thought it was cauliflower that you disliked above everything," she said.

"Did I say that?" Marigold opened her eyes wide. "If I did, I was mistaken. I'm sure it was peas. Not that I like cauliflower either, so don't think you may feed it to me!"

Perhaps Mistress Pigwidgeon might like a nice dish of powdered mole and fresh horse dung. Agatha got up from the table before she voiced the thought. Tibble's memory might not be what once it was but he could still sense which way the wind was blowing. He clapped his wig on his head and beat a hasty retreat.

Marigold observed this sudden exodus. "Well!" she said. "At least *you* are glad to see me, aren't you, doggie?" She dropped gracefully to her knees beside Lump, and gave him a great hug. Lump was much more accustomed to swats than hugs. He rolled a bewildered eye at his master.

Awkwardly, Andrew got up from the table. Lump leapt up also, causing Marigold to lose her balance and sit down smack on her *derrière*. "Oh!" she wailed.

Apologetically, Lump licked her face. Marigold screeched and flung up her arms to protect her head. Andrew curled his lip at this arrant cowardice. "Down, Lump!" he commanded "I mean it, Georgie. She ain't to come along."

Nine

The Promenade Grove, located between North Street and Church Street, was a favorite meeting place of the *ton*. There, amid green lawns and avenues of elms and flowering shrubs, ladies and gentlemen gathered of a morning to sip tea or chocolate and listen to the strains of a military band, or in inclement weather to sit and read journals in the elegant saloon where concerts were held in the rain. In the evenings, the Grove was illuminated with swags and garlands and festoons of brilliantly colored reflecting lamps. This particular evening's entertainment consisted of an Italian soprano warbling sentimental songs.

The Italians could keep the lady, Georgie thought, as she drew her shawl closer against the evening chill. A pity Marigold *couldn't* have come here in her place, because Georgie would much rather have stayed home with her new book. Andrew, at least, appeared to be enjoying himself, and was engaged in an animated conversation with Miss Inchquist, who was as he had said, very freckled and very tall, and dressed not at all to her advantage in a gown of white gauze striped with blue, and an Austrian cap. Perhaps lack of sartorial discernment was a family failing, for Lady Denham also made a startling picture in a dress of raw

gold silk, a great deal of topaz jewelry, and a satin turban made up in the form of a beehive and finished
with a bow at the top.

From the animated expression on Miss Inchquist's
face, Georgie concluded that her brother wasn't
going on about fiery lakes of smoking blood, or
corpses piled so high they were still warm the next
morning, or carnage so severe that Wellington himself had wept. *Was* Andrew developing a partiality for
Miss Inchquist? Lady Denham would wish to look
higher for her niece. Georgie was hardly helping Andrew's chances by wishing very much to kiss a man
rumored to have murdered his wife, and having as a
houseguest a lady who had trod the boards.

Lady Denham was occupied with another member
of the party. Georgie was free to glance about at the
other visitors to the Grove. Not, of course, that she expected to see Garth. Nor did she wish to see him, and
if she *did* wish to see him she might perhaps find him
upon the beach, but then he would only once again
scold her and refuse to kiss her and then walk away. If
he wished to kiss her, as he said he did, then why then
did he not? Scruples, one supposed. Georgie marveled that she had so few scruples of her own, because
despite everything she wished for Garth to kiss her,
and never mind that he had a wife.

Georgie smoothed her gloves. Here was a conundrum worthy of Marigold! Georgie thought guiltily of
her friend, who had not reacted well to expulsion
from this invitation, had wept and raged and stormed
as histrionically as if she still trod the boards. Never
before had Georgie seen someone wring her hands.
Marigold's sense of ill usage, her strenuous expres-
sions of outrage, had lessened only when Georgie

finally pointed out that a lady attempting to outrun the constable would hardly be prudent to parade herself about out-of-doors. Marigold had reacted to this good advice as might have been expected, scolding Georgie for reminding her of the tiresome troubles gathered round their heads. Yes, and what Georgie was doing to alleviate those troubles, Marigold couldn't see—not that she liked to mention it, because she did not wish to *nag*, but it was because Georgie knew how to *fix* things that Marigold had come to her in the first place. Moreover, if Georgie came home from this pleasure outing to discover that Marigold had died of the dumps, it would only serve her right.

Just *how* was Georgie to fix her friend's predicament when Marigold turned hysterical if pressed for details? Georgie might die of the dumps herself—or become a Bedlamite—if she was exposed much longer to Marigold. If only she felt free to confide in Garth. No doubt Lord Warwick was with his great friend Prinny this evening, enjoying a party at the Pavilion, a card assembly, or a ball, rubbing shoulders with well-bred ladies and others not so well-bred, for Prinny had an eye from the ladies, from actresses to other gentlemen's wives. Having contrived to thoroughly depress her spirits, Georgie sighed.

Although he was not speaking to Miss Inchquist of smoking blood and warm corpses—indeed, had not once this evening thought about going out of the world by the steps and a string—Andrew's conversation with the young lady might be considered provocative all the same. It was not Andrew's side of the conversation that invited censure, however. Andrew merely attempted to acquaint his companion with the history of Brighton, while in low tones Sarah-Louise lamented the unfeelingness of her various relatives, and covertly searched her surroundings for a certain poetical profile. "I am very much afraid that they wish to marry me off!" she whispered, with a nervous glance at her aunt.

Miss Inchquist didn't wish to be married? Andrew made an innocuous comment about an ancient flint dagger discovered in the chalk cliffs. Then he lowered his voice. "Surely you are too young," he said.

This was an unfortunate response. Sarah-Louise's brown eyes filled with tears. "No, I am not! But my papa cannot approve, and so they have sent me here, and I do not know if I shall ever see Peregrine again. He is a poet, did I say? I don't know if you can understand this, but no one has ever written poetry to me before, or probably ever will again." Lieutenant Halliday looked startled. He must think she was a little loony. Sarah-Louise flushed. "Pray forgive me. I should not be talking to you like this. I do not know what has come over me except that I have felt so very much alone."

Andrew could sympathize. He'd felt that way himself. Not over a poet, of course, but the principle was the same. Miss Inchquist was a good sort of girl, and he thought it a pity she shouldn't be permitted to marry whomever she pleased. Although he still wasn't convinced she was old enough to be thinking of marrying anyone. Sarah-Louise clutched his arm. "He came!" she breathed. "Peregrine!"

Andrew saw a handsome profile turned in their direction. The poet, no doubt. He *looked* like a poet, dressed in a startling array of colors, with a shockingly unstarched cravat, and dark hair tumbling dramatically over his pale brow. "Lieutenant Halliday, you *must* help us!" whispered Miss Inchquist. "Please!"

Much as he might wish to, Andrew could hardly refuse his companion's request, or her beseeching gaze. The Gorgon was eyeing them. "There are the remains of a Stone Age camp on the hill overlooking the racetrack," he offered. "Saxons following a chief called Aella secured the hill and made it theirs. Brighton is first mentioned in the Anglo-Saxon chronicles of the seventh century as 'Beorthelm's-tun,' the town of Beorthelm."

'Twas an innocuous enough conversation, although Lady Denham didn't know that she cared to have her niece's mind stimulated by mention of half-clad barbarians. "I have monopolized you for too long!" she said to her companion. "Go and talk to Sarah-Louise. You will find her a good biddable girl. Everything that is proper. Exactly to your taste."

Carlisle Sutton wasn't at all interested in good biddable girls, particularly those who regarded him as if he were the greatest beast in nature. Neither was he interested in further boring conversation with his hostess, with whom he had been long acquainted, for she had been married to a distant relative, who was now happily deceased. His gaze fell upon the remaining member of the party, an elegant, lovely lady dressed in a yellow muslin gown trimmed with white ribbon. Her fair hair, which had begun the evening in a severely classical style, had partially escaped its moorings to curl around her face. She tugged at her gloves.

Here was someone who looked as bored as Carlisle

felt. He excused himself from his hostess and made his way to her side. "There is a tiny village in the Rajasthan Desert that boasts a temple dedicated to the glory and protection of rats," he remarked. "Temple devotees believe the rodents house the spirits of their ancestors, and take care not to injure them, and provide them with a sumptuous meal each day."

Georgie blinked at her accoster, whom she already knew as Lady Denham's distant relative, recently returned from abroad. Mr. Sutton cut a fine figure in his corbeau-colored dress coat, white marcella waistcoat, evening breeches of black Florentine silk. There was something of the barbarian about him. She wondered if he was a reprobate. "You are not impressed with your surroundings," Georgie guessed.

Carlisle snorted. "No more than you, Lady Georgiana. I have observed you fiddling with your gloves. Shall we rebel against convention, you and I? You take off your mittens and I'll untie this damned cravat."

He looked as though he might well do so. Georgie laughed aloud, earning a startled glance from Sarah-Louise, who did indeed consider Mr. Sutton with horror, due less to anything he had done than because her aunt had started dropping very particular hints.

"Much better!" said Carlisle. "You have a very nice laugh, Lady Georgiana. I believe I would like to hear it again. Shall I tell you the strange tale of the Nabob of Oudh? Or describe the feat of fire-walking for the gods? You would not like to hear about Calcutta. It is a pestilential town with few decent roads."

Somewhat to her surprise, Georgie found that she was enjoying herself. And she definitely didn't wish to kiss Mr. Sutton, reprobate or not, which relieved her no little bit. "I think you could make any story amusing, did you wish to, Mr. Carlisle," she said.

"Do you?" Carlisle, too, was enjoying himself, or as much as was possible for him in this wretched country and this absurd Grove with its gawky trees and zigzag alleys and unskilled musicians performing in a wooden box. "Then let us put it to the test. I will tell you about the cent-per-cent rascals of Leadenhall Street." He proceeded to do so, with such ironic vituperation that Georgie laughed again. "You seem to enjoy your life in India," she said.

"Queer in me, isn't it?" Carlisle winced as the soprano strove for a particularly ambitious note. "I only returned to this benighted country to settle my uncle's affairs."

Georgie experienced not so much as a shiver of foreboding as a result of this remark. "Your uncle is deceased?" she said. "I am sorry for your loss."

It was a different female who would be made to feel sorry. "There is no need," Carlisle replied. "My uncle died as he might have wished. He was quite old, and apparently in his dotage. There is some irregularity about his affairs."

Perhaps a little prickling of gooseflesh did visit Georgie then. "Oh?" she echoed.

Only a few days in this wretched country and already Carlisle was become mealymouthed. "To give you the word with no bark on it, the old fool married an actress."

Now apprehension did smite Georgie, like a lightning bolt. "An actress," she repeated.

Well might Lady Georgiana look shocked. "Moreover, the little baggage has made off with something she should not," Carlisle added. "Which I mean to get back if I have to track her to the ends of the earth."

Here was a faint ray of hope. "You do not know where she is, then?" Georgie asked.

Hope, alas, was quickly dashed. "I know that she is in Brighton," Carlisle replied. "I assure you, Lady Georgiana, that I will find her out."

Unfortunately, Georgie could not doubt him. "Is it possible, Mr. Sutton," she ventured, "that this may all be some terrible mistake?"

"No mistake," Carlisle replied grimly. "I'm going to wring her avaricious little neck." He regarded Georgie. "You are not much like your cousin," he remarked.

Despite the abrupt shift in conversation, Georgie had not the least doubt of which cousin Mr. Sutton spoke. "You knew Catherine?"

Now it was Carlisle who was startled. "*Knew* her?" he repeated. "Past tense?"

How well had Mr. Sutton known Catherine, and when? Just because Georgie did not wish to kiss him didn't mean that another woman might feel the same, and Catherine had been a dreadful flirt. "You have not heard the gossip," Georgie said.

Carlisle frowned. "I have little time for gossip, Lady Georgiana. Has something happened to your cousin, pray?"

Perhaps Georgie could help to solve Lord Warwick's mystery. Perhaps as a reward he might kiss her again. "I dislike to repeat the story, but I might as well, since if I do not you will hear it somewhere else." She told Mr. Sutton of her cousin's disappearance, and of the rumors that had persisted ever since. "How was it that you knew Catherine, sir?" she asked.

Mr. Sutton did not think he wished to answer that question. Life in India had taught Carlisle to play his cards close to his vest. "You are very interested in Catherine," he remarked.

"Why should I not be? She was—or *is*—my cousin." Even to her own ear, Georgie sounded defensive.

Mr. Sutton smiled. "We return to the present tense."

Why had Georgie thought she liked Carlisle Sutton? He was the most aggravating man. Or perhaps it was simply in the nature of gentlemen generally to be aggravating. Lord Warwick sprang to mind. "Sometimes I think if I knew where Catherine was, I would throttle *her!*" Georgie admitted. "Although I know I should not say so. The truth is that we were not very close."

Here was more of that damnable English reticence. "Why not say so, if that's the way you feel?" Carlisle asked. "Anyway, I doubt Catherine was bosom bows with any attractive female. She would have seen you as a rival. No, I am not emptying the butter dish over your head. You are a lovely woman, Lady Georgiana."

He complimented her dispassionately, making it a mere statement of fact. Georgie had been complimented before, and frequently, but not for a long time. She found herself sorry that she did not wish to kiss Mr. Sutton. "Thank you," she said, and quickly turned the subject. "Now Garth has come to Brighton," she murmured. "I cannot think how it will all end."

Georgie seemed unusually partial to her vanished cousin's spouse, which did not elevate that gentleman in Carlisle's opinion. "You are certain Warwick is here in Brighton?" he asked.

Of course Georgie was certain. She had not had a

moment's peace since the morning she met his lord-ship on the beach. "I have spoken with him myself. Lord Warwick is an old friend."

Having disposed of one wife, was Warwick already on the dangle for another? Carlisle glanced down at his companion, whose expression was remote. Lady Georgiana's yellow dress was obviously refurbished, and the pearls around her throat far from the first quality. Had the lady access to a fortune, she did not display it on her person. Lady Georgiana's pearls had put him in mind of another, far more valuable, neck-lace. Like Sarah-Louise and Georgie before him, Mr. Sutton surveyed the fashionable throng. His attention was caught by a golden-haired lady in company with a multicolored and singularly ugly dog.

Ten

"Oh, do behave!" said Marigold, and gave Lump's leash a sharp tug. "Come away from that wretched bush, because if they see us, we will be truly in the suds. I do not want Georgie to ring a peal over me, while you—" She regarded the dog with an unappreciative eye. "I wouldn't be surprised if they took away your bone privileges. Or even gave you a bath!"

Bath? Lump knew that word. He didn't like it much. Lump reacted in his usual manner to something he disliked. He threw back his great head and howled.

"Shush!" hissed Marigold, and clamped her hands around his muzzle. Nervously she glanced over her shoulder, but no irate Hallidays looked their way. Marigold was aware that certain members of Georgie's household had taken her in dislike, most especially Georgie's brother, because Marigold knew a Canterbury tale when she heard one—certainly she *should* know one, having spun enough herself—and Andrew hadn't wished her to come along tonight, no matter how Georgie tried to dress up that fact. Which was very bad of him, because Georgie's little house offered little in the way of entertainment, and Marigold had already grown bored. *Childe Harold's Pilgrimage* had not long held her attention, nor the works of Hannah Moore. Briefly she had been distracted by putting together a map of Europe, but when Bulgaria caused her a certain difficulty, she cast that, too, aside. Marigold wasn't certain how it came about that she was both a ladyship and not respectable; she certainly had never *meant* to step foot upon the stage. Now she could not even use her title without drawing unwanted attention to herself. If only Leo had not disappeared! It sometimes seemed to Marigold that her troubles were all his fault. What possible mishap could have beset poor Leo to make him disappear in the midst of a most delightful honeymoon?

These reflections had cast her further in the dumps. Everyone was having fun but Marigold, which was most unfair. But Marigold was not one to sit around repining over her unhappy lot, and after brief reflection had decided that she deserved to join the revelers in the Grove. Not Lady Denham's party— Marigold would take Georgie's advice and draw no attention to herself. Frankly, from this distance, Lady Denham's party looked deuced dull.

Again she was doing something that was not entirely proper, but nothing Marigold did turned out to be proper, even when her intentions were of the noblest, so it seemed pointless even to try. Marigold would only remain in the Grove for a few moments, and return home with no one the wiser, and no harm done. As her protector, foolish creature, she had brought along the dog.

This outing was not proving as interesting as Lump had first anticipated. The strange lady was keeping him on an exceedingly short leash. Clearly she did not understand that a hound needed a certain free-

dom to explore, especially in new surroundings such
as these. There was a ditch in particular that had
caught Lump's attention. He inched closer to the
flowering bush behind which they stood.

What was the wretched dog doing? Marigold
tugged on his leash. If only the Italian soprano
wouldn't dwell so much upon such melancholy topics
as unrequited love and faithless lovers and broken
hearts. Already, at six-and-twenty, Marigold had been
thrice a bride. Sometimes she despaired of ever getting it right. Not that many opportunities for
contracting another marriage were like to be offered
her in Newgate, or wherever it was that people were
sent who lost articles of jewelry that belonged to
someone else. What a muddle Marigold had made of
everything. Perhaps she should simply put an end to
her existence and be done with all the fuss. But
Marigold was at heart an optimist. Surely there must
be some way out of her dilemma. If only she might
meet some generous and wealthy gentleman.

Two things happened then, at once. Lump lifted
his leg and watered the flowering shrub, and a gentleman appeared so abruptly in front of her that
Marigold wondered briefly if she'd conjured him up
out of her need.

The gentleman was not pleased to have been drib-
bled on. He cursed. Lump may not have had much in
the way of manners, but he was aware that it was not
comme il fait to go about indiscriminately dribbling. In
an effort to make himself invisible, he dropped to the
ground.

The gentleman appeared to be wealthy, decided
Marigold, judging from the quality of his clothes.
Wealthy or not, he looked very cross. Which was not

surprising, for Lump's dribble was all over his boot. Despite the scowl, his swarthy features were handsome in a certain style—certainly more handsome than Sir Hubert or Mr. Frobisher had been. No one could ever be more handsome than poor Leo had been.

Marigold was melancholy for want of society. And it was in her nature to play the coquette. Prettily, she smiled and asked the stranger, "Do I know you, sir?"

Carlisle had the advantage over his uncle's widow, whom he had immediately recognized from her miniature, although the painting had not done justice to the wench's magnificent *décolletage*. Perhaps his uncle had not been so deeply in his dotage as Carlisle had thought. With some reluctance, he raised his gaze from her plump bosom. "I'll wager you would rather *not* know me! You little jade!"

Here was no gentleman with designs upon her virtue. Marigold felt sad. It seemed a very long time since anyone had cherished designs upon her virtue, save Sir Hubert, and Marigold had contrived so mightily to plant the notion in his brain that it almost didn't count. "Oh!" she said plaintively. "How dare you speak to me *so*? Are you in your cups, perhaps? Because I have not the most distant notion why you should offer a perfect stranger such grievous insult."

Carlisle did not consider that he had insulted the lady, but merely made a statement of fact. "You might as well give it up," he advised. "You shan't have *me* dancing on the end of your string."

Clearly Marigold would not. The man was a curst cold fish. Furthermore, he stood so firmly in her path that she could not duck around him and escape. "I wish you would tell me why you have taken me in such

dislike," she said. "Because I was already feeling out of
sorts, and I must tell you that you are making my
mood very much worse."

So much for his tiger hunt. Instead Carlisle had cor-
nered a peahen. Lovely, granted, and amazingly
voluptuous, but a peahen all the same. "I will give you
a hint. The Norwood Emerald. You little fool, did you
think your victim had no kin?"

Her *victim?* Marigold disliked the suggestion that
she had entrapped her late spouse. Even more did
she dislike to meet a member of her late spouse's family. "Damn and blast!" she muttered.

"Just so." Carlisle grasped her arm. "I was fond of
my uncle, Miss Macclesfield. I won't allow you to have
made a fool of him. Give me back the emerald, if you
please."

Marigold would have very much liked to give back
the emerald, which had brought her so much bad
luck that she thought it must be cursed. Unfortunately, she could not. She did not think this angry
stranger would take kindly to that disclosure. "Emerald?" she said blankly. "What emerald? I do not know
what you are talking about."

Perhaps Carlisle had underestimated Miss Macclesfield, just a little bit. Not that he was to be deceived by
the brilliant blue eyes peering cautiously up at him.
"Cut the cackle and come to the horses!" he advised,
and gave her a shake. "You are rapidly becoming a
dead bore."

First she was a prime article of virtue, and now she
was dull as ditchwater. Marigold stamped her foot. "I
think that you must be the rudest man I have ever
met."

"And *you* are wasting your time and mine," retorted

Carlisle, with brutal candor. "The emerald, Miss Macclesfield."

Marigold wished he would not call her by that wretched name, which had been Mr. Frobisher's invention, and which she had never liked. Nor did she like that this stranger knew so much about her. "My *name* is Lady Osgood. Who are *you?*" she asked. "If you do not tell me, I vow I shall not say another word."

Unlikely that she could remain silent for upward of a moment. Still, it was mildly intriguing to see what the peahen would try next. Carlisle introduced himself.

Damnation! Now the fat was truly in the fire. "Oh!" Marigold murmured. "The Indian. You should have said so sooner. Not that *you* are an Indian, but you choose to live there, which is very strange, but you must know what you like best. I did not realize that I still had the emerald. It must be packed away." She sniffled. "You will understand that I didn't have the heart . . ." She touched a handkerchief to her dainty nose.

Like a certain critic before him, Carlisle found Miss Macclesfield's performance lacking a certain believability. "Ah, yes," he observed. "You were so distrait with grief that there was no remedy save to go jauntering about. Unusual as it may be to find a grieving widow among the revelers in the Grove."

"How unfair you are!" The widow gave him a withering look. "I am merely *observing*, as you can very well see. My state of mind has been so very melancholy! I wished to distract myself." She raised a graceful hand to her brow. "But now your dreadful accusations—I believe—no, *I know!*—that my nerves are overset. Yes, delightful as this conversation has been, I must leave now, because I am quite unwell." She tried to pull away.

Carlisle held her arm fast. "Cut line, Miss Macclesfield," he said. "You aren't going to convince me that you're a respectable female." His eyes moved assessingly over her body, lingered appreciatively upon her dramatically heaving breast. "'Twould be a pity if you were."

Marigold wished she might give this rude man a knock on the head. She put down her handkerchief, and glared. "I *was* a respectable female. Once! And if I'm not one now, it's not my fault."

Carlisle was briefly distracted by speculation upon how Miss Macclesfield had been first led astray. And upon how many times she had tripped along the pathway to perdition since. "And," she added, "you will be very sorry when I cast up my accounts!"

Was she a sufficient actress to shoot the cat on cue? Carlisle trusted not. "Not so sorry as you," he replied sternly. "My person has already suffered sufficient injury this evening. No, and you needn't think to faint, either, because I will let you fall on the ground. Let us have the word with no bark on it! You thought to lie in clover, but you cobbled it, my girl. Oh, I don't doubt you made my uncle happy enough for a time, even though it was cream-pot love on your part. But you didn't make him happy enough that you deserve to keep the Norwood Emerald. I *will* have it back, Miss Macclesfield."

Marigold wished the man would stop harping on the Norwood Emerald. "I'm sure I don't wish to keep the wretched thing," she said, and again employed the handkerchief. "But you will have to wait until I can bring myself to go through Sir Hubert's effects."

Carlisle's fingers dug more deeply into her arm. "Have you heard of the Hindu custom of *seti*, Miss Macclesfield? A widow is expected to hurl herself upon her husband's burning funeral pyre. It is not necessarily a voluntary act."

All things considered, Marigold thought she would prefer to go to gaol. She stared up into Mr. Sutton's dark face. To think she had deemed him handsome. Did he not regain his damned emerald, this unpleasant man would see her behind bars.

But Marigold did not have his emerald. Somehow she must escape. Covertly she looked around, thereby reclaiming Lump's wandering attention, and causing him to stir.

'Twas a long shot, perhaps, but better than none. Marigold gave Lump's leash a sharp tug, then dropped it on the ground.

Freedom! He was set free! Ecstatic, Lump jumped up. Having anticipated this reaction, Marigold ducked, thus exposing Mr. Sutton to the brunt of the dog's gratitude. Distracted, he loosened his grip on her arm. As Carlisle struggled in the great beast's slobbering embrace, Marigold escaped.

Eleven

Without pleasure, Lord Warwick gazed upon the crowd that thronged the Steine. No dislike of its varied society—sportsmen in their many-pocketed jackets and officers of the Prince's regiment wearing yellow and blue; ladies of pleasure and city *beaux;* merchants and *émigrées;* people on their way to and from the baths, or to drink tea at the Public Rooms; the ubiquitous fishermen—prompted his expression. Simply, Garth disliked to be one of the sights himself.

Across from Mr. Donaldson's library, where the *ton* gathered to read newspapers and gossip, the enterprising Mr. Raggett had established a subscription house where thousands of pounds were daily won and lost. Lord Warwick stepped into the street. No stranger to gentlemen's clubs, he was a member of both White's, with its famous bow window, and Brook's, where a single black ball was sufficient to exclude a candidate, and the name of anyone who joined another club—White's excepted—was instantly removed from the membership list. Garth wondered how the accusation of murder had affected the presence of his own name on that list. There was but one way to find out. He stepped through the door.

A hush fell over the room. Garth was not surprised. Sometimes he felt like a perpetual-motion machine, stirring up all the salons. He looked around. Many of the gentlemen there were known to him. Mildmay and Pierrepoint. Alvanley. Brummell. Magnus Eliot, an unscrupulous rogue who lived entirely off his wits, and was said by some to embody a great many of the less admirable qualities of the age.

The silence stretched out unbearably. Then Brummell arched a brow. "Warwick," he drawled languidly, "I do like that cravat."

So simply was Garth's fate decided. He was not to be outcast. Normal conversation resumed, and jocularity, to the great annoyance of several gentlemen who were attempting to play a serious game of whist, and the disappointment of several others who had hoped to see Lord Warwick given the cut direct. Even while he was aware of the absurdity of a society in which the approval of a Brummell outweighed that of a Prince, Garth was grateful to the Beau. Although Brummell's influence was not what it had once been, due to his championship of Maria Fitzherbert in her altercations with Prinny, he was still a force to be reckoned with.

Lord Warwick joined his friends, and was introduced to the other member of their party, an old acquaintance of Lord Alvanley's family who had recently returned home from India. Garth confided to Brummell that the Beau had been fortunate *not* to listen to Prinny's German musicians perform selections from the latest Italian opera on the Pavilion lawn; and that the Regent had been dissuaded from his most recent brilliant notion to have a palace built on the same plan as his magnificent stable. The Beau recalled that Prinny had once lost several thousand pounds betting on twenty turkeys racing against twenty geese on the Steine. Mr. Sutton—for of course Carlisle was the gentleman from India—remarked that if the Regent's stables resembled an Indian mausoleum, as they were said to do, it was like no mausoleum he had ever seen.

The gentlemen then engaged in discussion of Wellington's progress in the Peninsula, and Mr. Percival's demise on the floor of the House of Commons at the hands of a merchant named Bellingham. Mr. Sutton aired several vituperative remarks about the conduct of the Marquess Wellesley in India, which had culminated in his impeachment on the grounds of, among other things, breaking treaties, squandering his employer's wealth, exercising power despotically, and setting up his own statue in Calcutta after consigning that of Lord Cornwallis to a cellar. In response to a question from Lord Alvanley, Mr. Sutton went on to enlighten his audience about certain Indian sculptures which stood comparison with Greek and Roman statuary in the eyes of connoisseurs of pornography, and to explain the connection between religious practice and sexual enjoyment which so fascinated and repelled visitors to India. Mr. Sutton himself had seen a Hindu holy man, a giant of a figure with a massive appendage to which was attached a golden ring, who was so revered by young married women that they knelt before him and took him in their hands while he stroked their hair and murmured purification prayers. "If that don't beat everything!" marveled Lord Alvanley. The ice among them broken, the gentlemen settled into a not-very-serious game of hazard.

Mr. Sutton studied his companions, most especially

Lord Warwick, who had declined to join the play.
Carlisle had a fair notion of Lady Georgiana's feelings
for Lord Warwick, and a much-less-clear sense of his
toward her. He supposed it would be unsporting not
to give the man the benefit of the doubt. "You do not
like Italian opera?" he inquired. "It seems to be all the
crack. I myself heard an Italian soprano at the Promenade Grove last eve."

Lord Warwick was not much interested in matters
Italian. "Perhaps you would prefer the theater," he
said politely. "I believe a performance of *Hamlet* is
being put on at the Theater Royale."

Did Lord Warwick seek to change the subject? Mr.
Sutton was not inclined to oblige. "I was a member
of Lady Denham's party. Perhaps you are acquainted
with her. Or the Hallidays. The brother seems a bit
of an oddity, but Lady Georgiana is a charming female."

Garth did not care for this conversation, or for the
suspicion that something else altogether underlay Mr.
Sutton's words. Nor did he care to be reminded that
he was in no position to accompany Georgie to the
Promenade Grove to listen to a wretched Italian soprano, or for that matter anywhere, lest the gossips
smear her good name with the same brush as had
blackened his own. "I know of them," he said dismissively, and gestured toward the hazard-players. "You
do not care to join in?"

Here was an odd husband for the volatile Catherine, Mr. Sutton mused. Not that marriage had much
to do with compatibility, from what he could observe.
"I'm not here for the rattle of the dice," he replied.

Nor was Garth present at Raggett's for his entertainment. Not that he would confide his affairs to this

stranger, or for that matter even to his friends. Mr. Sutton's manner puzzled him. Fortunately Garth could not guess that Carlisle Sutton suspected him not only of abusing his vanished wife, but also of wishing to mistreat Lady Georgiana. "Business, then?" he asked.

Carlisle contemplated Lord Warwick. "You might say so."

The tabbies would have also something to say about this conversation, Garth thought. The tabbies had something to say about anything Garth did, which is why he had not sought out Georgie, though he had wished to do so a hundred times. He hoped Mr. Sutton had not entertained Georgie with tales of Indian holy men. "Ah," he said.

Mr. Sutton reached a decision. The peahen had escaped the tiger, and like a tiger Carlisle would track down his prey. He would lie in wait, and then begin a slow and silent approach, until he drew close enough to charge. Then he would leap onto his quarry's back and pin her down with his powerful claws. A pity he could not skin the wench and hang up her pelt. Mr. Sutton, it becomes apparent, had during his years in India grown somewhat uncivilized.

Lord Warwick was quarry more worthy of his mettle. Not that Mr. Sutton had any particular desire to sink his teeth into Lord Warwick's neck. "It is an awkward business," Carlisle said abruptly. "I have been pursuing certain discreet inquiries. It occurs to me now that perhaps I have been asking questions in the wrong places. You are a man of the world, Warwick. Have you seen this woman?" He described his uncle's wife.

Guinea-gold hair? Periwinkle eyes? A voluptuous little person with a flair for dramatics? Garth knew her as "Mrs. Smith." "She sounds an unforgettable sort of female. A, um, friend of yours, perhaps?"

Friend? A *friend*? Carlisle snarled. "She's no friend of mine, but a conniving hussy whom I mean to run to ground. One who possesses a singularly ill-mannered canine."

Lord Warwick's apprehensions, already wakened, stood to rigid attention at mention of a dog. "What sort of canine?" he inquired.

"A damned troublesome canine!" Mr. Sutton did not like to mention that the creature had dragged him through the zigzag alleys and gawky trees of the Promenade Grove until they landed finally in a ditch. "It is also very *damp*, and has an astonishing number of teeth. The beast is nearly as big as a horse, looks like it ran amok through a number of paint pots—or had them thrown at him, which is more likely the case—and possesses not a lick of sense. So far it has terrorized everyone at the inn where I am lodging, from the stableboy to the cook, who was preparing a joint for dinner when he interfered. I expect momentarily to be asked to remove myself."

Garth had no trouble following these disclosures, nor envisioning the mayhem his companion described. "You took the creature home with you?" he asked.

"We locked him in the tack room." Carlisle fervently prayed to all the gods of India that the troublesome hound would stay there. "His mistress will come looking for him, I think."

His mistress would no doubt go looking, but not "Mrs. Smith." Garth's bad mood returned. He had been avoiding Georgie in order not to involve her in his troubles, and in the meantime she had managed to stumble into a pickle of her own. Not that said pickle was of her own making. Garth thought that he must have a word with Georgie about her houseguest.

Twelve

Georgie did indeed go looking for her missing pet the following morning, to no avail; and her Lump-less return was a matter of great if silent rejoicing among her household. The failure of her mission was not, however, as some might have hoped, because the hound had vanished off the face of the earth. Lord Warwick had been moved to take a hand. The dog's liberation from its prison had been no easy task, and had involved his lordship masquerading as a lowly groom, and talking a great deal of nonsense, and paying an amazingly stiff bribe.

Garth still wore groom's clothing. He hoped no one saw him in this rig. Although if they did see him they wouldn't recognize him and therefore wouldn't gossip about him, which would be a nice change. "Yes, yes!" he said to Lump, who he had on a stout string. "I know you're glad to be rescued, but I wish you would try and control these transports. No, you may not lick my face! Look, you wretched creature, here is your home." Quite forgetting his appearance, Garth knocked at the front door.

Tibble opened that portal, and stared, first at the groom-like figure who dared set foot on the front step, and then at the dog. Lump, who had not enjoyed being chased about and yelled at by strangers, drooled happily at sight of the butler. "Oh," said Tibble, without enthusiasm. "You have brought him home."

"Only because it would have caused even more trouble had I not!" retorted Lord Warwick. "Stand aside, you nincompoop, and let us enter."

Tibble did not care to be called a nincompoop, especially by a groom. So he said. He also pointed out that servants, even when returning a lost hound, should more properly present themselves at the kitchen door.

Lord Warwick had been in no good mood to begin with—in point of fact, Lord Warwick had not been in a good mood for quite some time—and to be given instructions in decorum by a butler was more than he could bear.

"It's Warwick, you idiot!" he snapped. "Now stand aside and let me enter before we draw all the neighbors out-of-doors to gape."

Tibble might not know the name "Warwick," but he recognized the voice of authority. He opened the door. Miss Georgie was become quite the rage with all these visitors. First the gentleman whose name he could not recollect, and now a groom. Although Tibble was almost certain that a groom was not quite the thing.

"Tell your mistress that I am in the drawing room!" Lump in tow, Lord Warwick pushed past Tibble, leaving the butler very confused as to how this stranger knew where the drawing room was situated.

Mere moments passed before Georgie entered the chamber to find a groom frowning at her partially embroidered slippers, and Lump sprawled upon the silk-striped sofa, to which he was expressly forbidden access. "Lump!" she cried, and rushed to hug her pet. Lump responded with great enthusiasm, to the detriment of Georgie's coiffure and pale blue muslin dress. Laughing, she detached herself. "I am very glad to see you, too! Now get down from there at once."

So much for his homecoming. Lump would have thought the prodigal's return might result in the relaxation of a few silly rules. Perhaps there was a bone waiting for him in the kitchen. He slid from the sofa to the floor.

"I am very grateful to you, sir." Georgie looked more closely at her Good Samaritan, and gasped. "Gracious! Garth! I wonder if I wish to know why you are dressed like that."

Garth turned away from the dratted slippers. "I'm sure you would much rather *not* know! But I think you must." In a few pithy words, he informed her of Carlisle Sutton's search for "Mrs. Smith," and his possession of the hound.

Mr. Sutton was most diligent. How had he encountered Lump? Marigold was locked in her bedchamber, and refused to allow even Janie admittance. "I had hoped Marigold's troubles would turn out to be a tempest in a teapot," Georgie said. "Apparently they are not. Did Mr. Sutton tell you just *why* he wished to find our "Mrs. Smith"?

At this reminder that Georgie was herself acquainted with Mr. Sutton, Lord Warwick scowled. Not that he experienced a pang of jealousy, of course. And if he did, he had no right to it, so he would pretend that he did not. "Did he tell *you* about Hindu holy men?" Garth asked.

Georgie blinked. "Did who tell me what? Garth, I

haven't the least distant notion of what you are talking about."

Again, he was making a Jack-pudding of himself. "Sutton didn't say precisely why he wished to find her, and I could hardly ask." Georgie wore a guilty expression, Garth thought. "You must tell me what you know about this business, Georgie. After all, I *did* rescue your abominable hound."

So he had. Fondly, Georgie regarded her pet. Lump wagged his tail. "I know very little, other than that Marigold was married to Mr. Sutton's uncle, who inconveniently died and left her penniless." Garth was already frowning, and Georgie decided not to inform him that Marigold feared being clapped into gaol. "And that for some reason Mr. Sutton wishes to wring her neck."

Mr. Sutton was not alone in that sentiment. Garth gripped the back of a silk-striped chair. "What the devil are you thinking, Georgie, to allow yourself to be embroiled in such nonsense? Don't you realize the consequences were the gossips to get hold of this business? You are a woman alone in the world, and must be above reproach. How can you be so careless with your good name?"

Perhaps it was not surprising that Lord Warwick would be so concerned with preserving everyone else's good name, having lost possession of his own. Still, it made Georgie very cross. "Has anyone ever told you, Garth, that you are become very *taken* with yourself? You speak to me as though I were the greenest girl. Which I am not! I do not expect you to understand this, but there is a certain freedom in being a spinster left upon the shelf, and I enjoy it very well. I have my own establishment, and my own circle of acquaintances, and no interest whatsoever in what the world may think."

Lord Warwick found himself accused of effrontery. Since it was perhaps not an entirely unwarranted accusation, he flushed. "Forgive me if I have offended you," he said stiffly. "My words were prompted only by concern that you are entirely too credulous in the matter of "Mrs. Smith." Whatever you may feel about the matter, Georgie, you remain the daughter of a baronet. Your family would not care to hear your name on every lip."

Georgie's temper had not abated. "My *family* may go to blazes! And the scandalmongers with them!" she snapped, and crossed the room to stand in front of Garth. "I don't care a fig about the gossips. What I *do* care about are my friends. Whether you approve of Marigold or not, she is my friend, Garth, as you are, and I will do whatever I may to get her out of this muddle."

She had said more than she meant to. Did Garth realize? Georgie stood so very close to him that she could feel the heat of his skin. Or maybe it was the heat of her own skin. Georgie knew her cheeks were flushed. Did Lord Warwick look as if he wished to kiss her? He did not. Instead Garth looked very much as if he were about to scold her again. Georgie was very tired of being scolded. She stood on her tiptoes, grasped Lord Warwick's lapels, and pressed her lips to his.

It was not a skillful kiss, perhaps, but what Georgie lacked in experience she more than made up for in enthusiasm, and Lord Warwick possessed enough experience for them both. His arms moved to enfold her and draw her close. Georgie melted against him.

It was a most romantic moment. Or several moments. The kiss went on so very long that Lump grew tired of watching and lay down on the faded rug.

At length Lord Warwick's common sense asserted itself. He released Georgie and stepped back, appalled. Garth had come to remonstrate with Georgie about the reprehensible Mrs. Smith, and his own conduct had been much worse. A gentleman of conscience could not pursue a course of action that must only rebound to his discredit and the lady's own.

Still, he wished to kiss her again, and keep on kissing her until they were both nigh senseless with the wonder of it, which made him oddly irritable, because if Georgie had not come so suddenly back into his life he would not have these damned uncomfortable feelings plaguing him.

Georgie did not notice how quiet Lord Warwick had grown, so loudly was her own heart beating in her ears. Good gracious, what a talent the man had for kissing! Georgie looked mistily up at him.

And then he spoke. "My dear, this will not do. I think too highly of you to expose you to such tittle-tattle as must accompany my most casual acquaintance." His smile was rueful. "As yours and mine could never be."

A number of thoughts crossed Georgie's mind. "Pighead," "addlepate," and "paperskull" were among the fore. She wondered if Garth would consider it unladylike were she to box his ears.

But were she honest, Georgie had—or at least *should* have had—similar reservations about her relationship with Garth; and if she had no care for her own good name, Andrew still had his own way to make in the world. Not that this realization made Garth's rejection any easier to bear. "Ah, yes," Georgie murmured. "You thought so highly of me that you married my cousin instead. I think I understand the situation quite well. You may leave now, Garth."

Lord Warwick did not wish to leave, not now when Georgie was so cold toward him. He grasped her shoulders. She scowled. "I deserve that, I suppose," he said. "But know this, Georgie: I *am* your friend, your best of friends, no matter what you think."

What Georgie thought in that moment was that if she didn't remove herself from Lord Warwick's presence she would burst into tears. "I think you do not know me at all," she retorted. "I also think that with friends like you, I do not need enemies, m'lord!"

His face white, Garth released her.

Head held high, blinking back tears, Georgie sailed from the room.

And people accused *him* of being clutch-brained. Lump dropped his muzzle on his paws.

Thirteen

As result of her expedition to Promenade Grove, Marigold had taken to her bed, a very pretty tent-like affair draped in cream-colored muslin, with the intention of remaining there for the remainder of her mortal life. Her refusal to allow Janie entrance was apparent in the chaotic condition of the small chamber. The wardrobe doors gaped open, as well as the drawers of the tallboy, and articles of feminine apparel were strewn everywhere.

A knock came at the door. Marigold burrowed deeper under the coverlet and pulled a pillow over her head. Again, the knock. "Go away! I do not care for company!" Marigold called out. Instead of blessed silence, she heard a key turn in the lock.

Who possessed a key to her bedchamber? Cautiously Marigold peered over from beneath her pillow. Georgie walked into the room, followed by her hound. Marigold was no more delighted than any other member of the household to set eyes on Lump. Her own troubles briefly forgotten, she sat up. "Where did *he* come from?" Marigold asked.

Firmly, Georgie closed the door, and regarded her houseguest, who looked annoyingly lovely *en déshabillé*. "Lord Warwick brought him home. I think it time, Marigold, that you and I had a comfortable coze."

Marigold stared unhappily at Lump. The dog returned her regard. Lump recognized his partner in adventure, who had run off and abandoned him. He didn't hold this shabby treatment against the lady. To demonstrate his lack of hard feelings, Lump gave a great woof and leapt upon the bed.

Marigold shrieked and scrambled out from beneath the covers, struggled into a lacy peignoir. "How did *Warwick* come in possession of the, er, beast?" she asked.

"He stole him." Georgie settled into a stuffed, cabriole-legged chair. "Right from under Carlisle Sutton's nose. Mr. Sutton had been making inquiries about Lump's owner. Don't try and flimflam me, Marigold! You have been pretending and prevaricating ever since you set foot upon the threshold. I'll have the truth now, if you please."

Marigold did not please. Moreover, she thought Georgie was making a great fuss about a silly old dog. "I don't know why you should accuse *me* of contumacious behavior. Gracious, you can't think *I* know how your dog got lost."

Georgie was growing very weary with this dissembling. "I *know* that you lost him, Marigold! Tell me, did we not agree that you were supposed to be hiding in the house?"

Marigold did not recall that she had agreed to anything. She picked up a fan of pierced horn leaves. "I *was* hiding!" she retorted. "It is not my fault that— um! Georgie, you must understand that it is not *healthy* for a person to be always being within-doors."

Holding a reasonable conversation with Marigold

was like trying to push a very large stone along an up-hill slope. Valiantly, Georgie persevered. "But you were not always within-doors, were you, Marigold? And *what* was not your fault, that Mr. Sutton saw and recognized his uncle's widow?"

Marigold was so startled that she dropped her fan and sat down on the bed. Lump gave her a great lick. She stood up again. "Is *that* his name? He is the most obnoxious man. But I do not understand. How do *you* know Mr. Sutton? Did he mention me?"

Her friend's self-absorption was remarkable. Georgie wondered what it must be like to think all things revolved around oneself. "Yes, Mr. Sutton mentioned you. He said that you were an avaricious little baggage, and that he would like to wring your neck. And *I* wish very much to know what you made off with that you should not. No more taradiddles, Marigold! I am *not* in a good mood."

That much was obvious. Georgie's hair stuck out about her head like a wild hayrick. Marigold picked up a ribbon that was draped across the cheval glass. "There is something queer about this ribbon," she remarked. "But I can't think what it is."

Of course there was something queer about the ribbon. The ribbon belonged to Georgie, who thought it might look very nice tied tightly around her old friend's throat. "Marigold!" she said.

Marigold put down the ribbon in favor of a bird-cage bag beaded in blue and green with a floral border, which she clutched to her breast. "Why are *you* so out of curl? *I'm* the one who has been bullied and threatened within an inch of my life. That horrid man did not even render the observances of civility before he began accusing me of the most dreadful

things. It was most unjust!" She looked at Lump, who
had rolled over on his back and now lay dozing, all
four paws stuck in the air. Unthinkable that Marigold
should sleep again on those sheets. "It was very kind
of Lord Warwick to return the dog to us," she remarked, with great insincerity. "I trust he did not also
tell that horrid man where I was to be found."

Lord Warwick would never do something so igno-
ble as to betray Marigold. The resultant scandal might
rebound upon himself. Perhaps she was being a trifle
unfair to his lordship, but Georgie was still out of
sorts. "Never fear," she murmured. "Garth will stand
buff."

Marigold tossed the beaded bag aside. "Do you
know, I think I may have been a little hasty as regards
Warwick. He and I have a great deal in common,
don't you think? My Leo disappeared, and so did Warwick's wife. We are companions in misfortune.
Warwick is very wealthy, is he not? He is certainly a
handsome gentleman."

Georgie wondered how she might add her houseguest to the current rash of disappearances. All she
needed was for Marigold to set her bonnet at Garth.
"No! Lord Warwick *was* wealthy, but he uh, suffered
reverses. The East India Company, you know."

Marigold knew nothing about India, nor did she
wish to, unless it was that Mr. Sutton had returned to
that distant land. "You are bamming me, I think! Warwick doesn't *look* like he is in the basket, and believe
me, I should know, because I have been there myself,
and when one is under the hatches one does not go
strolling about as if one had just come from Bond
Street. Georgie, you are looking very queer. I know
what it is! You are thinking that I said Warwick was

disagreeable, and so he is a little bit, but it is nothing in comparison with Mr. Sutton, who I vow is the devil himself. You must see that Lord Warwick would be the perfect solution to all of my difficulties!"

Georgie saw that a great many females would be eager for Lord Warwick's kisses, tarnished reputation or not. Marigold was probably very good at kissing, with all the practice that she'd had. Georgie contemplated the faded floral pattern that trailed across the cream-colored Brussels rug.

Marigold picked up a white muslin veil with an embroidered leaf border and draped it around her head, looking for all the world as if she fancied herself again a bride. She began to hum. "Marigold!" Georgie protested. "Have you forgotten that Warwick is said to have murdered his wife?"

Marigold *had* forgotten that minor detail. She frowned, then shrugged. "Pooh! I care nothing about that! It's not as though he will murder *me*, you know!"

Georgie thought that perhaps *she* would murder Marigold, did this foolishness persist. "You will not pester Lord Warwick," she said sternly. "He already has quite enough on his plate. Do you understand me, Marigold?"

Marigold understood that a great many people were cross with her these days. Her blue eyes filled with tears, and she sank back on the bed. Lump snuggled closer. "Oh, get away, you—you *chawbacon!*" she snapped, and pushed him to the floor. Wounded, Lump slunk across the room to collapse at Georgie's feet. She gave him an absent pat. The dog wagged his tail and then began to investigate a white kid glove that lay upon the rug.

"I'm not leaving this room, Marigold," said Georgie

with determination, "until you tell me exactly what transpired between you and Mr. Sutton. Without further confabulation, pray!"

Marigold fumbled in her pillows and withdrew a vinaigrette. "Oh, very well!" She recounted her adventure in the Promenade Grove.

If Marigold's conversation with Mr. Sutton was not repeated entirely verbatim, it was still disturbing enough to make Georgie turn pale. "I thought," Marigold concluded, dramatically, "that I should swoon from the shock!" She paused to gauge her friend's reaction to these disclosures.

Georgie was frowning. Lump was gnawing on a sodden mouthful of white leather. "My glove!" Marigold wailed.

"Your glove? What glove?" Georgie despaired of ever persuading Marigold to talk sense. Then she, too, gazed upon Lump's trophy. "I should leave you to your just deserts! This is all about the Norwood Emerald, I'll warrant. You still have not told me how the emerald came to be out of your possession, Marigold."

"That is because I did not want you to *pinch* at me!" Marigold had recourse to her vinaigrette. "And you will *wish* to, but I think that you should spare your breath, because I *know* it was very wrong of me. The truth of it is, Georgie—" She took in a deep breath. "—I lost the emerald at play."

Marigold had succumbed to the lure of the tables. Georgie didn't know why she should be surprised. Marigold had already succumbed to the lure of everything else. "Oh, Marigold!" she sighed.

Marigold unearthed her handkerchief from among the bed linen. "Why must everything be so difficult?"

she wailed. "Oh, Georgie, I wish that we were children again, before any of this happened, before I met poor Leo, and before you—" She peered over the handkerchief. "Well, before whatever it was happened to you, because something obviously did!"

So now she was grown hagged? Despite her exasperation, Georgie could not help but sympathize with her friend. Marigold's life would have been much simpler if not for her tendency to land herself in the suds. As for Georgie's own life—"This is getting us no nearer the emerald," Georgie said.

"That shows all *you* know!" retorted Marigold, somewhat unfairly, because she had done her utmost to keep Georgie in the dark. "We *are* close to the emerald, I think. That is why I came to Brighton, Georgie. Besides my wish to see *you*, that is! I have it on very good authority that the person who won the emerald from me lost it in turn to Magnus Eliot."

Fourteen

Lady Denham's household was not kept smoothly running by a mere cook-housekeeper, butler, and maid-of-all-work. Lady Denham would have been appalled at the notion of attempting to function without a full complement of kitchen and scullery maids, laundry maids, upper and under housemaids, footmen and grooms and coachmen, not to mention her abigail and her French chef, all of whom she kept extremely busy, because everyone knew that idle hands did the devil's work, and Lady Denham would tolerate no such nonsense in her household. Nor were Lady Denham's own hands idle at this moment. In them she held a list.

Lady Denham's busy hands, and the list they held, were ensconced in her drawing room, upon a painted chair with cross-front legs, a carved Sphinx on each arm-post, and rosettes at the base, crowned with twining honeysuckle and yet another rosette. The rest of the furnishings had also fallen under the Egyptian influence, as witnessed by additional Sphinx-head bodies and ornaments, models of mummies, athenaeum friezes and, most notably, a crocodile sofa. Tables, chairs, and sofas were studiously disarranged around the fireplace and in the middle of the elegantly proportioned chamber, in the modern fashion of placing furniture. Arranged in and about that furniture this afternoon were Lady Denham, her niece, and a number of their guests. Mr. Sutton was in attendance, and Lieutenant Halliday. Most splendid of all present, outshining crocodile and Sphinx and mummy case, Miss Inchquist's cherry-striped dress and even Lady Denham's puce muslin gown, was Lieutenant Halliday's companion—*My great good friend! Came upon him quite by accident! Didn't think you'd mind if I brought him along!*—Peregrine Teasdale. Mr. Teasdale was a sartorial wonderment in canary-yellow breeches and polished top boots, a waistcoat broadly striped in salmon and cramoisi, and a long-tailed coat of pea-green. His starched cravat was tied in the Oriental, a very stiff and rigid arrangement with not a visible indenture or crease. Exceedingly high shirt points made it very difficult for him to turn his head. His dark hair tumbled dramatically over his pale brow.

Mr. Teasdale's poetic nature demanded expression in flamboyance. Moreover, he very much hoped to set a style. Truth be told, Peregrine would have preferred to dress in black, but Byron had already been before him, and Peregrine above all wished to be considered an original. Or almost above all. Most immediately, he must catch himself a rich wife, preferably before his tailors' bills came due. Miss Inchquist was just the ticket. Young, malleable—Peregrine had no idea what he might wish to mold her *into*, but malleable seemed like a good thing.

"*But true love is a durable fire,*'" he murmured, for her ear alone. "*Into the mind ever burning./ Never sick, never old, never dread/ From itself never turning.*'"

Sarah-Louise blushed. If she knew those pretty

words had actually been written by Sir Walter Raleigh, she kept that knowledge to herself. "You should not say such things to me," she murmured insincerely, and wished he would not stop.

"*Fair, fair and twice so fair/ As fair as any may be,'*" Peregrine responded promptly, this time borrowing from George Peele. Blissfully, Sarah-Louise sighed. She caught her aunt's eye upon her. "Lieutenant Halliday knows a great deal about Brighton!" she said hastily.

Lieutenant Halliday, who had been brooding upon his part in this dashed irregular liaison—had he been privileged to know Sarah-Louise's papa, Andrew might well have agreed with that acerbic gentleman that Peregrine was a twiddlepoop—responded to his cue. "At the time of the Norman Conquest, Brighton was not entirely without importance," he said, unenthusiastically. "It was one of the Sussex Manors of Harold II, who raised forces here to augment his troops at Sentac." Mr. Teasdale possessed an imagination as fanciful as his flamboyant attire. Were Andrew called upon to compose a sonnet to Miss Inchquist, he could only compare her to an amiable giraffe. Not that he meant the young lady any disrespect.

Peregrine took advantage of Andrew's silence to plagiarize the words of both Mr. Schiller and Pierre de Ronsard. "*What is life without the radiance of love?/ Live now, believe me, wait not for tomorrow./ Gather the roses of life today.'*" Deuced if he didn't like Lieutenant Halliday's cane. The limp was a nice touch. Perhaps Peregrine might adopt a limp himself. He wondered if Halliday would mind answering some questions, about whether the leg hurt all the time, or more so when the weather was damp, and how he managed to get in and out of bed. Peregrine would have to create an interesting story as to how he had come by the limp, but that should be no problem for someone so imaginative as himself. If it wasn't for that damned Byron, he could carry a cane with a skull knob. Then he recalled with disappointment that Byron also walked with a limp, and a couple of ill-tempered dogs.

Miss Inchquist was regarding him expectantly. "*Eternity was in our lips and eyes, Bliss in our brows bent,*'" Peregrine murmured. Lieutenant Halliday looked skeptical, and he hastily added, "Shakespeare."

Andrew didn't think he should be listening to this poetical nonsense. Nor, for that matter, should Sarah-Louise. Surely someone so very tall and freckled shouldn't wear so many stripes? "A rent, then deemed considerable, was paid to the Lord of the Manor by the fishermen for the privilege to dry their nets, and in the winter to haul their boats upon what is now the Steine," Andrew said.

Sarah-Louise liked stripes. To wear them, when she knew they didn't flatter, was her small act of defiance against the world. To defy the world in the matter of stripes was one thing, however, and to run counter to her papa was another. A letter from that acerbic gentleman had come in today's post. Sarah-Louise's papa wished to know how the ladies went on. Sarah-Louise gazed on Peregrine. Truly, she didn't *mean* to be a serpent's tooth. But Mr. Teasdale had seen the beauty of her soul, and she wouldn't even mind living in a garret if she could be his muse. Not that Sarah-Louise was entirely certain what a garret was, but she thought it would be very romantic to dwell in squalor with only a few servants, and perhaps a single coach.

Lieutenant Halliday had ceased to extol the wonders of Brighton. Sarah-Louise tore her gaze away from Peregrine to glance at him. Andrew was looking very pale. His limp was more pronounced than usual, she thought, concerned. "Lieutenant Halliday, are you unwell?"

Andrew disliked the suggestion that he might be in delicate health, though the truth was that he had been racketing himself to pieces, and his bad dreams had returned. "Nothing of the sort! Fit as a fiddle!" he retorted. "In the great gale of 1705 all the houses on the flats below the cliffs were washed away."

At the suggestion that one of her callers might be ailing, Lady Denham looked up from her list. Heaven forbid that someone should disgorge his luncheon upon her expensive Aubusson carpet. Lieutenant Halliday did not look so ill as all that. "I do not think I have ever heard that young man speak of anything but Brighton. It is very odd."

Mr. Sutton had no interest in young Lieutenant Halliday, save perhaps for his sister's sake. Carlisle had reached his own conclusions regarding certain remarks recently overheard. He did not choose to acquaint his companion with those conclusions. Amice was accustomed to having her own way. She had decided that Carlisle would do for his niece— heaven only knew why, the chit wouldn't last in India a fortnight—and it never occurred to her that the parties involved might have other ideas in mind.

Carlisle very definitely had other ideas in mind than the timorous Miss Inchquist, who very plainly had a partiality elsewhere. Did not the girl blanch and tremble each time she was in his vicinity, Carlisle might warn her against wearing her heart upon her sleeve. "You are not attending me, Amice," he protested. "Do you recognize this female?"

Lady Denham glanced up from her list, which concerned arrangements for the grand event she planned in honor of her niece. A great many members of the fashionable world would be in attendance. Hopefully the girl could be dissuaded from wearing stripes. She studied the miniature which Mr. Sutton extended to her. Guinea-gold hair, periwinkle eyes, an admirable *décolletage*—Lady Denham sniffed. "No, I don't know her, and you shouldn't, either! She doesn't look like she's the thing, Carlisle."

That depended on what one considered "the thing." Carlisle found the lady very much in his style. Not that she was a lady. And not that he had lessened in his determination to wring her neck. "What about this dog?" he said, and described Lump.

A great, damp, rude, and multicolored hound? The description sounded familiar. Lady Denham frowned. "I do believe I have seen such a creature. *Where,* I cannot recall. Ah well, it will come back to me, I'm sure! Meantime—" She waved her list. "Dare I invite Brummell, do you think?"

Lady Denham sat as regally upon her Sphinx-arm chair as if it were the Peacock Throne, once property of the Emperor Shahjahan, a stunning construction of gold and jewels surmounted by a golden arch and topped by two gilded peacocks, birds of allegedly incorruptible flesh. How foolish these English were, with their conviction of superiority in all things, their sublime assurance that they knew best. True, Carlisle was English himself, but India had schooled Mr. Sutton in the arts of duplicity to the point where he could outwit the devil himself.

He smiled. "No party is complete without the celebrated Mr. Brummell. If you truly wish to guarantee his presence, you must invite Warwick as well."

Warwick? The name sounded vaguely familiar. Its origins, Lady Denham could not recall. Perhaps it need not be pointed out that Lady Denham had reached that certain age females must dread, when certain facilities begin to fade, and hair and teeth loosen from their moorings, and the wearing of corsets becomes a necessity instead of a fashionable conceit. "Very well. If this Warwick will assure me Brummell, I shall add him to the list."

Among the things Lady Denham had forgotten was that Mr. Sutton was of a sardonic temperament. "I promise you that Brummell wouldn't miss it. Nor would I," he said, and rose to take his leave.

Fifteen

The Marine Parade stretched to a considerable extent along the sea. The buildings there boasted large windows that disclosed wide views of the Channel, and were considered by some to be preferable to the structures on the Steine.

On a fine day, the Marine Parade was an ever-changing panorama. Military music played. Under the colonnades, visitors congregated to read newspapers and watch other members of the fashionable world pass by. If no more immediate entertainment beckoned, the gentlemen might raise their telescopes and inspect the seashore and the bathing machines. In theory, a person desirous of taking the waters could hire a machine, therein to privately disrobe and don the requisite flannel smock. The machine was then pulled into the water by a horse, and the bather descended under cover of seclusion. In reality, because the bathing machines lacked awnings, little escaped the severe inspection of the gentlemen's telescopes.

Among the gentlemen lounging in front of the library was Magnus Eliot. Mr. Eliot was not peering through a telescope—did Magnus wish to observe a female bathing, there were any number who would oblige him, and without the distraction of a flannel smock—but reading a newspaper article about the Turkish practice of shampooing, which consisted of being wrapped in a wet blanket and stewed alive by steam strained through odiferous herbs, and dabbed all the while with pads of flannel, until one was dissolved into a mass of gelatinous cartilage, all of which Mr. Eliot considered so much humbug. He was distracted from his newspaper by the arrival of a slender blond lady in company with a large and ugly dog. She sat down in a chair beside him. "Mr. Eliot?" she said.

The lady appeared ill at ease, as well she should. Magnus was a man of libertine propensities, a gambler and a wastrel, an impenitent and utterly charming rogue who lived on his wits, which were considerable. He was also handsome, in a very wicked way, with auburn hair and laughing green eyes, intriguingly dissipated features, and the physique of a sportsman. Additionally, he possessed a pair of most enchanting dimples that appeared when he smiled. Magnus smiled often, for he had a large sense of the absurd.

The ladies ran mad for him, of course; how could they resist? Magnus was very grateful for their appreciation and prided himself that he seldom left a lady dissatisfied.

He did not think, however, that this particular lady had *amour* on her mind, which was rather a pity, because she was very lovely, and not at all in his style. "In the flesh," he responded. "You seem perturbed. Perhaps you would like to compose yourself by gazing out to sea through my telescope. You may watch the fishing boats come and go."

Georgie doubted very much that Mr. Eliot was interested in fishing vessels. How this conversation had passed beyond her control in the space of a single sentence she did not know. Beneath Mr. Eliot's green gaze, she felt like the gawkiest schoolgirl.

But she was not a schoolgirl, and Mr. Eliot was no gentleman to watch her with such overt amusement. "Fishing vessels, indeed!" Georgie retorted, and wrapped Lump's leash securely around the arm of her chair. "Mr. Eliot, I must speak with you."

She amused him, this so-serious lady. Magnus set his newspaper aside. "You may do with me as you wish, my pet." She flushed, and he smiled at her. "Intriguing as the notion is, I do not think you have come here to get up a flirtation—although *should* you wish to do so, you may come to me any time. How may I be of assistance to you, Miss Halliday?"

Magnus Eliot made a person wonder what it would be like to enjoy unrepentant wickedness so much. "You know my name," Georgie said.

Mr. Eliot quirked a brow. "I know many things, Lady Georgiana. For instance, I know that your brother is named Andrew. And that this beast—" His gaze fell on the dog, which was stretched out at his mistress's feet, smack in the path of passersby. "—is known as Lump. You look startled, my sweet. To a man in my position, knowledge is wealth."

Georgie imagined Mr. Eliot knew all manner of interesting things. He was probably almost as good at kissing as Garth. Perhaps even better. She scolded herself for her improper thoughts. Her companion looked ironic. Surely he could not know what she was thinking. "Truly, Mr. Eliot, I do not wish to be one of your flirts."

Of course she did not wish to become one of his

flirts. Magnus wondered if he might make her change her mind. "I do not have flirts, my poppet. I have *petites-amies.*"

The man refused to be serious. Georgie frowned at him. "Plural, of course," she commented.

There was more to this so-proper lady than had first appeared. Magnus threw back his head and laughed. *"Touché!* Pleasant as this is, you should not be talking with me, Miss Halliday."

Now a rakehell told her what she should and shouldn't do. "I don't think that even *you* will make an attack on my virtue in broad daylight!" Georgie snapped, then flushed. "Oh, dear. I ought not have said that."

Magnus was deriving considerable amusement from inspiring Lady Georgiana to say things that she shouldn't. "You underestimate me," he protested. "Not that I would *attack* you, my poppet. I might *persuade* you, perhaps. And I promise you that, if I did so, you would like it very well."

Georgie didn't doubt that for a moment. Mr. Eliot had a most unsettling effect. Somehow she must steer this conversation into safer waters. "Mr. Eliot, I am *not* afraid of you," she said, feeling as though she were the captain of a vessel headed toward shipwreck.

Of course she was afraid of him, a little bit. Which was not only enchanting in her, but showed a great good sense. "You *should* be afraid of me, Miss Halliday," murmured Magnus. "You should be very afraid, indeed."

His green eyes rested on her. Georgie was surprised by their warmth. A person might almost drown in those deep green depths. Georgie understood how many a lady before her had tumbled violently into

love with this practiced rogue. Georgie, however, unlike those other ladies, would be enticed into no
improper tryst.

Not that this tryst was entirely proper. Georgie was
not alone, precisely, having slipped away from Andrew
and Agatha while they were engaged in a discussion
of the relative merits of haddock and carp. Hopefully,
she would rejoin them before they even noticed that
she was gone. Providing that the wicked Mr. Eliot did
not lure her onto the primrose path! The very absurdity of the notion that a libertine like Mr. Eliot should
regard an apeleader like herself with amorous inclination set her strangely at her ease.

"Palaverer!" Georgie said. "You are coming it rather
too strong. I am hardly the sort of female you might
fancy, Mr. Eliot, and I know it as well as you. As you
have said, that is not why I am here."

Magnus didn't think that there was a particular sort
of female that he fancied above another. Lady Georgiana was, in his not-inconsiderable experience, an
unusual sort of female. Magnus appreciated unusual
females. In point of fact, Magnus appreciated all sorts
of females, from the grandest duchess to old Phoebe
Hessell, who sold bull's-eyes and pincushions and
other articles from a basket on the corner of Marine
Parade and the Steine, and who when young had dis-
guised herself as a boy and served in the army for
several years without being discovered, even getting
wounded in the arm at the battle of Fontenoy.

It was rather refreshing to meet a member of the
gentle sex who didn't hold him in fascination. Not
that Magnus hoped to encounter many such discerning lovelies. "Alas, you spurn me," he mourned. "I
think my heart must be broke. Yes, it is ungentlemanly

of me to tease you, but I could not resist. Now you see that I am serious. Pray do continue, *chérie.*"

Nor was it gentlemanly for Mr. Eliot to address Georgie in such terms. However, if Georgie became embroiled with Mr. Eliot in a conversation about what was and wasn't proper, they would be here all day. He was correct in saying that it was shocking for Georgie to be talking with him at all.

Georgie was rapidly concluding that the things that were most shocking were also the most pleasurable. "I have come in behalf of a friend," she ventured. "It is a very delicate affair."

"It generally is," Magnus said ironically, and leaned back in his chair. "One's friends are the very devil, I have found. Pray proceed, Miss Halliday. I am all ears. But I must warn you that an appeal to my better nature is futile, because I have none." She looked as though she might protest, and he raised a hand. "Truly! You may ask anyone. The whole world will tell you that I am the greatest blackguard alive."

Georgie didn't doubt it. However, she was finding that she liked the blackguard surprisingly well. Not that she considered him at all trustworthy. "The matter involves a lady. And a certain loss."

Why was it that females, bless them, must forever make mountains out of molehills? "Ah," said Magnus. "A loss. I see."

Was the wretched man laughing at her again? Georgie ignored his twinkling eyes and persevered. "The matter poses the lady a dilemma. The item that she lost was not hers, unfortunately."

Magnus saw that Lady Georgiana's reputation would be in tatters by the time she concluded this long, drawn-out tale. He did not wish Lady Georgiana's reputation to be in tatters on his account. At least not without good reason, such as might involve a mutual jaunt along the primrose path. "I do not recall that a lady has lost anything to me recently," he said, with a devilish smile. "At least not anything that can be redeemed."

What an exasperation the man was. Georgie tried to frown. "You are determined to be wicked, are you not? In point of fact, the lady did not directly encounter you. The person to whom she lost the, um, item then lost it to you at play."

Many people lost items to Magnus at play. Magnus's facility with the cards almost equaled his luck with the fairer sex. These two abilities were followed closely by a nose for mischief. Something about this tale smelled deuced fishy. "I am curious," he said. "Why is it you apply to me instead of this lady, Miss Halliday?"

Why, indeed? "Because she is a goose-cap!" Georgie retorted. "You will also, pray, forget that I said that."

Magnus didn't think he would forget a single word of this remarkable conversation. "Your friend sounds like a ninnyhammer," he said. "Not that I dislike ninnyhammers, so long as they are beautiful. Is she beautiful, this ninnyhammer of yours?"

"Beautiful ninnyhammer" precisely described Marigold. Georgie was visited by an appalling vision of her old friend begging a boon of the wicked Mr. Eliot. A boon that he would no doubt grant under certain conditions. Conditions that Marigold would be hard-pressed to resist.

Georgie thought she might be hard-pressed to resist those conditions herself. Given Marigold's propensity for disastrous relationships, she must never be permitted to meet this rogue. "Um!" said Georgie, and looked cautiously around. "The item in question is a certain green-colored, ah, whatchy. Do you still have it, sir?"

A green-colored whatchy? Magnus was intrigued. "Plant? Animal? Or mineral?" he asked.

Just what *was* an emerald? "Mineral," Georgie guessed. "Shiny. Hard. Faceted. Surely smaller than a teacup."

Aha! Magnus realized what Lady Georgiana sought. Wise of her not to name the thingamabob with so many people about. Magnus had been reluctant to part with the emerald, because such extraordinary items seldom came his way. And he had been right to keep the thing, for had he not kept it, he would not be having this equally extraordinary encounter with Lady Georgiana. "I do see that your friend is in a dilemma. I suppose you want the doodad back."

"*I* don't want anything to do with it!" responded Georgie. "But she must return the item where it properly belongs or suffer a dire consequence. In short, she may go to gaol."

Mr. Eliot studied her. The lovely Lady Georgiana wore a flounced gown of spotted lawn and a chip straw bonnet that were several seasons out of date. "I hope you haven't taken such a hubble-bubble notion as to think I'll give the doodad back, because if you have, you might as well give it up. Sympathetic as I am to the plight of your beautiful ninnyhammer, I am *not* in the habit of dispensing charity."

Georgie sighed. She had feared his answer might be something of the sort. "I don't know if you can imagine what it is like, sir, to feel as if you're standing on the edge of a precipice. If you do not help us, I truly do not know what we are to do."

Magnus felt as if *he* were standing on the edge of a precipice at that very moment. The sensation was very queer. Lady Georgiana wasn't going to have hysterics, was she? Magnus disliked hysterics of all things. She didn't look hysterical, however, merely defeated. Magnus was touched. It was a most unique sensation. Magnus didn't think he cared for it.

"I will make you a bargain," he offered, because he could not help but take advantage of a lady in distress. "You may buy the thingamadoodle back from me for twenty-five thousand pounds. Yes, I know that I'm a scurvy rascal who should be condemned for the heartlessness of his conduct, but I have expenses, too, my darling, and I am extravagant and undisciplined to boot, and twenty-five thousand pounds is the best that I can do."

His darling? Poppet and pet, perhaps, even *chérie*, but Georgie could not let "darling" pass. "I am *not* your darling," she said, and stood up from her chair.

Impossible to chasten Mr. Eliot. "Not yet," he said, and smiled. "Do not poker up at me, Miss Halliday! It is a word only." His green eyes twinkled wickedly. "One that saves me the trouble of remembering names."

The man was beyond outrageous. Georgie parted her lips to tell him so. At that moment Lump espied a familiar figure in the crowd passing in front of the library. The figure wore a somber expression, and walked with a limp. Accompanying him was a carrotyhaired woman wearing a gown of white pina-cloth embellished with a veritable garden of roses. She was carrying a package of fish.

Lump jumped up and ran to meet his master. In so doing, he overturned the chair to which Georgie had tied him, and tipped her right into Mr. Eliot's lap. Andrew and Agatha stared in astonishment. "The devil!" muttered Georgie, against what could only be considered a most comfortable masculine chest.

Sixteen

"I do not expect that you will play the coquette," said Lady Denham, "but you might at least try and be civil, Sarah-Louise! I wonder at you, indeed I do!" At least this evening the girl had been bullied into foregoing stripes. She looked almost unexceptionable in a dress of white gauze embroidered with sprigs of bright color, her hair dressed in flower-adorned ringlets.

Unexceptionable, that is, except for her freckles and her height. Lady Denham hissed, "Back with those shoulders! Stand up straight! Stop staring at the floor! I begin to despair of you. This evening is entirely in your honor. Pray try and look as though you are enjoying yourself just a little bit."

How could Sarah-Louise enjoy herself in the midst of a crowd of strangers, none of whom were the slightest bit interested in her save Mr. Sutton and her aunt? Obediently, she raised her gaze from the floor to her aunt's face. Lady Denham was an unforgettable figure in red satin trimmed with multiple frills and flounces, artificial flowers and satin leaves, the bodice molded tightly to her figure, the sleeves short and puffed. Atop her raven curls perched a turban made of fine lace and decorated with additional ribbons and foliage. Lump would have liked that headdress very well, Sarah-Louise thought, and smiled.

"Much better!" Her niece's megrims aside, Lady Denham was in alt over the success of her rout. Brummell had put in an appearance, as had several other of Prinny's friends. And if the Regent himself had not yet stepped through her front door—well, one could still have hope.

Candles glowed. Jewels sparkled. In one elegant chamber, gentlemen tried their luck at cards. In another chamber, an orchestra played. In yet another, a cold collation was laid out. All the public rooms were crowded. The music of the violins could hardly be heard above the din of voices. To Amice would go the highest of all accolades: she had achieved a dreadful crush.

Lady Denham returned her attention to her niece. At least the girl only stuttered when she was nervous. Unfortunately, that was most of the time. "Perhaps you might marry a title. The *on-dit* is that Lord Amblecoat is looking for another wife."

Sarah-Louise dared interrupt her aunt. "Another?" she asked. "How many d-does he need?"

Lady Denham tut-tutted at this irreverence. Amblecoat had already gone through four wives. The ladies had an unhappy tendency to die in childbirth. Unlikely that a gentleman so enamored of the marriage-bed would be interested in her great, gawky niece. Lady Denham crossed him off her list. Many other fish, however, remained yet in the sea. She pointed out various eligibles, and listed their assets and their faults. Baron Letchcomb was a bachelor of the first stare who had an unfortunate weakness for gambling and other vices best left unnamed; Viscount

Taplow was an excellent creature save for a tendency to drunkenness; Hickleton would make a tolerable husband, even if he was a perfect block. Then there was her own favorite candidate, Mr. Sutton, who was rich as Croesus, against whom one could say nothing, and who held Sarah-Louise in the highest regard. "You are but a girl, and must trust me to tell you how to go on!" Lady Denham concluded, and tapped Sarah-Louise's knuckles with her painted fan. "Though I cannot but think you would be the perfect wife for Carlisle, he will want you all the more if he sees you have made other conquests."

Sarah-Louise wanted Mr. Sutton no more than she wanted a case of the spots. Somehow she must try and flimflam her aunt. As she was thinking how to do so, a stir rippled through the crowd. Sarah-Louise quivered as she glimpsed the gentleman she *did* wish to wed. Mr. Teasdale was very splendid in a cerise-colored full dress coat, frilled shirt with lace ruffles, white marcella waistcoat, and black florentine silk breeches, to which he had added yellow silk stockings with large violet clocks, a muslin cravat with ends left afloat, and a quizzing glass.

"What are you staring at?" inquired Lady Denham, and turned to look. Disapprovingly, she clucked. "Heigh-ho! That boy's tailor should be hanged."

"Madam, your servant!" Elegantly, Peregrine bowed. It was only natural that the ladies should gawk at him. He was the very pink of perfection, dressed in the first stare of fashion, all the crack. The whispers which followed his progress only bore that opinion out. From her awe-struck expression, Sarah-Louise appreciated his fine appearance, which was fortunate, because Peregrine's creditors were growing most annoyingly persistent, and he did not fancy being reduced to poverty. "There is a country dance forming. May I have the honor, Miss Inchquist?"

Sarah-Louise glanced at her aunt. Lady Denham waved her fan. "Do not allow yourself to become overheated!" she said, and returned her attention to her guests. The rooms were grown so crowded that a person could hardly move. She wondered if the Regent had arrived yet.

Peregrine led Sarah-Louise into the room where the orchestra was playing. "You are a vision, Miss Inchquist. Behold me dazzled," he said, and bent over her hand. "*'Roses red, and violet blue,/ And all the sweetest flowers, that in the forest grew.'*"

Sarah-Louise wasn't certain what flowers had to do with her appearance. She blushed, all the same. "*'All that in this delightful garden grows,/ Should happy be, and have immortal bliss,'*" added Peregrine. Having depleted his store of Mr. Edmund Spenser's poetry, he raised his quizzing glass to survey the throng.

Mr. Teasdale was magnificent! Sarah-Louise felt honored that so splendorous a gentleman should look with an eye of fondness upon someone like herself. How strange it was to converse with him without Lieutenant Halliday looking on. If only Andrew had come to the rout! He had declined on account of his lame leg. Sarah-Louise frowned. It seemed to her that of late Lieutenant Halliday had not been feeling quite the thing.

Why was Miss Inchquist frowning? Was he not paying her sufficient attention? Peregrine hoped she didn't mean to be one of those *demanding* sorts of wives. If so, he would have to cure her of that habit.

Training a wife could not be all that different from breaking a horse. He would have to ask someone how it was done.

First, Peregrine must get her to the altar. "*'Gather the rose of love,'*" he murmured soulfully, "*'whilst yet is time.'* My dear Miss Inchquist, I beg you will not keep me long in suspense." He slipped a note into her hand.

Surely he could not think she would read it now! Sarah-Louise stuffed the folded paper into her glove, and with Mr. Teasdale joined the set that was being formed. Eight couples stood facing each other. Nervously, Sarah-Louise watched the top couple to try and learn the movements of the dance. Practicing one's steps in the drawing room was a very different thing from performing them in public. With feet so large as hers, Sarah-Louise could not hope that a misstep would go by unnoticed.

The men took hands and fell back a double, forward-turning single, then the women did the same. Right hands across halfway, turn single; second couple, followed by first couple, cast down into a line of four facing up, first couple outside. Forward a couple and back, first couple falling into first place; first couple cast down into second place and cross over, while second couple lead up into first place, crossing . . .

Although Sarah-Louise was not precisely overheated by the time the set was finished, she felt a trifle warm. Then she espied Mr. Sutton walking toward them, and her blood ran positively cold.

He bowed. "Your aunt sent me to fetch you in to supper," he said, and nodded to Peregrine. "Teasdale."

Sarah-Louise did not wish to have supper with Mr.

Carlisle, but was too meek to argue. She swallowed hard. Peregrine bowed stiffly, and thanked her for the dance. Sarah-Louise watched his cerise-colored jacket until it was swallowed by the crowd. Then she returned her attention to Mr. Sutton. "I am n-not very hungry, sir," she said.

Carlisle placed the young lady's hand on his arm and steered her toward the supper-room. Perhaps she might benefit from a gentle hint. "Young ladies your age are sent by their families to India with letters of introduction into circles where they might find a husband, preferably a well-paid officer or official. Those who do not find a husband within a year are shipped home in disgrace. There are fates more unhappy than theirs, Miss Inchquist. As a young woman of considerable fortune, you should take care not to encourage impecunious young cawkers to dangle at your shoestrings."

Sarah-Louise was not attending. She was not even aware that Mr. Sutton offered her advice. Instead she was wondering who else Mr. Teasdale might ask to dance. Certainly there were young ladies prettier than Sarah-Louise. Perhaps even wealthier. "Oh, no! I should never think of such a thing!" she murmured.

Ah well, Carlisle had done his duty. At least the girl's eyes were no longer starting in terror from their sockets, though she did look very glum. "Do try and smile, Miss Inchquist, lest people think your aunt has served up something sour on her refreshment plates. Much better! This sort of affair does not have to be such an ordeal. You need only watch the people around you make monkeys of themselves, and occasionally smile." He left Sarah-Louise seated in a chair as he went to fetch her a supper-plate.

Again, Sarah-Louise thought of Lump. It cheered her immensely to contemplate the havoc the hound might wreak in a setting such as this. She wished again that Lieutenant Halliday might have come here tonight. He was her only friend in London. Perhaps her only friend anywhere. Sarah-Louise was too shy and tall and gawky to make friends easily, too lacking in the social graces, as her aunt was quick to point out. Now she was a wallflower at her own party. Among this gay and glittering crowd, Sarah-Louise felt very out of place.

Mr. Sutton returned bearing a plate laden with sliced ham, a lobster patty, fruited jelly, and a jam tartlet. He handed it to her. "I am not going to bite you, Miss Inchquist! Pray try not to look at me as if I were the wolf and you the lamb." He sat down beside her, entertained her with a description of Indian marriage rituals.

Sarah-Louise did not think she would care to have her husband-to-be place his foot on top of hers, signifying that he should be the dominant force in their life together. Naturally he *would* be her lord and master in all things, but it sounded most uncomfortable to have one's foot trod upon. Mr. Sutton went on to explain that all Hindu ceremonies began by invoking the blessing of Lord Ganesha. "Unlike the other Hindu deities, Ganesha has the head of an elephant. His own father axed off his head, and then replaced it with that of the first animal he saw."

Talk of axing heads quite put Sarah-Louise off her food. She poked at the tartlet on her plate. "India," she murmured, "sounds like a very *uncivilized* sort of p-place."

This was precisely the impression Carlisle wished to

give her. "Oh, it is!" he said, and cheerfully downed a forkful of broiled fowl. "Cows are sacred in India, did you know? The cow is considered one of the mothers of mankind. Confound it, don't goggle at me so! I most seriously and solemnly assure you that I do *not* intend to marry you, Miss Inchquist. However, I don't think we should tell that to your aunt."

Mr. Sutton did not wish to marry her? Had Sarah-Louise heard him right? "Do you mean that, sir?" she asked.

"I promise you, Miss Inchquist, that you need not worry yourself into a fidget on my account. The last thing I wish to acquire is a wife."

Miss Inchquist ruminated over a mouthful of fruited jelly. Mr. Sutton's reluctance was good news. Nonetheless, her Aunt Amice had fallen in love with the idea of a match between them, and Sarah-Louise could not trust that Mr. Sutton would not waver in the face of such stern resolve. If only he might develop a preference for someone else. "Tell me, Mr. Sutton," said Sarah-Louise. "What is your opinion of Lady Georgiana? She seems to me to be a m-most extraordinary female."

Seventeen

Lady Georgiana moved through the glittering throng, pausing to speak with acquaintances, exchanging smiles and nods.

As well as Mr. Teasdale, Georgie was also in suspense, although so far as she could tell the tale of her encounter with a rakehell was not yet public knowledge, because she had not yet encountered knowing glances and barbed remarks. Georgie greatly disliked such affairs as Lady Denham's rout, but it had somehow seemed in Andrew's best interests that she attend. Not that Georgie held out much hope for Andrew's *tendresse*, if *tendresse* he had. Miss Inchquist had seemed very taken with the eye-catching gentleman in the absurd cravat.

Carlisle Sutton appeared before her, so suddenly that Georgie jumped. "Lemonade, Lady Georgiana?" he said, and handed her a glass. "I know the situation calls for something stronger. Madeira, perhaps, or claret. In India we add brandy so that the wine may survive the climate. One should have strong spirits to get through so curst dull an affair as this. But I refrained from bringing you strong spirits—and you must thank me for it—because I had a thought for your good name."

Curious that so many gentlemen should be concerned for her good name. "How kind," Georgie murmured and accepted the glass. What would the wicked Magnus Eliot make of this so-boring rout? Thought of Magnus Eliot—and Georgie thought of Magnus Eliot rather more than she wished—recalled a certain missing piece of jewelry. However was the Norwood Emerald to be retrieved? Marigold hadn't two shillings to rub together, and Georgie could no easier lay hands on twenty-five thousand pounds than pigs could sprout wings and levitate. "I confess surprise, Mr. Sutton, that you would lend your presence to such a 'dull affair' as this."

Carlisle, quite naturally, had his own fish to fry. Behind him lay a lifetime's game of snakes and ladders, after all. "I had hoped that I might encounter you," he said, and raised his own glass. "You are looking lovely this evening, Lady Georgiana."

Georgie knew a clanker when she heard one. She looked well enough in a dress of silver-shot gauze with a square, low neck, but she would wager her grandmama's pearls that Mr. Sutton had not come to this affair to seek her out. "Spare my blushes, sir!" she said, and favored him with a smile. "I take that to mean you are tired of making polite conversation with Lady Denham's other guests."

Mr. Sutton was not accustomed to such plain speaking. He had, after all, just spent considerable time with Miss Inchquist. What a timid chit she was. Lady Georgiana, conversely, was An Original. Whatever had she done to cause Miss Inchquist to hold her in such high esteem? "I wouldn't give a cuss for the lot of them!" he said cheerfully. "Moreover, you have them all beat to flinders. There! Have I now put you to the blush?"

Georgie sipped her lemonade and wished that it were indeed something stronger. Cordially she responded, "Nothing of the sort! I think you are trying to flummery me, sir. If so, I wish you would continue, for I am enjoying it very well."

Carlisle laughed, causing several heads to turn in their direction, and offered his arm. "Would you favor me with your company, Lady Georgiana? Perhaps you might like to dance. I don't know that *I* do, especially, but I will go to any lengths to have so lovely a lady on my arm. I do *not* recommend the supper-room, unless you wish to see the boar's head garnished with aspic jelly, which is enough to put anyone off his feed."

Georgie could not help but appreciate this nonsense. Still, she cast Mr. Sutton a reproachful glance. "I shan't allow you to take a rise out of me, you know."

Mr. Sutton did know it. That was one reason he liked Lady Georgiana so well. "I am teasing you, I admit it," he said as she placed her hand upon his arm. "It is my damnable propensity to become easily bored. I dare not allow myself to give way to ennui. Amice will come after me if I appear neglectful of my duties. You see that I stand in need of rescue, ma'am."

Georgie could imagine no one in less need of rescue than Mr. Sutton. "Piffle!" she said. "Unless—am I correct in thinking Lady Denham means you for her niece?"

Carlisle's smile faded. "Exactly so. Witness me horrified at the suggestion. Amice is a very determined woman. I may have to run away."

Georgie chuckled at this absurdity. "You are joking,

I think." Best for Marigold's dilemma if Mr. Sutton *did*
take to his heels. Perhaps she should encourage him.
"Although I can see that running away would perhaps
be the simplest solution to your difficulties."

Mr. Sutton had no intention of going anywhere
without the Norwood Emerald. He glanced at his
companion's beautiful profile, and repeated to her
the tale of Lord Ganesha's elephant head, and then
mentioned the sacred cow. Unlike Miss Inchquist,
Lady Georgiana laughed.

Damned if he didn't like Lady Georgiana. It was too
bad. "How long have you known Warwick?" Carlisle
asked.

Here was the real reason Mr. Sutton had sought her
out, despite his profuse compliments. Georgie cast
him a searching glance. "I have known Garth since I
was a girl. Our family properties in Cornwall marched
alongside his. My papa sold the land when I was perhaps fourteen, and I did not see Garth again until
some years later in London." She looked rueful.
"Shortly before he met Catherine. It was a case of love
at first sight. Catherine had that effect on many gentlemen."

One puzzle was answered. Lady Georgiana had
been smitten with Warwick at a young age. Carlisle
might have thought the gentleman a fool to overlook
her, had he not himself experienced a similar reaction to Catherine. Fortunately, he had not been so
besotted as to wish to marry her. Not that he *could*
have married her, since she'd already been married
to Warwick. Their relationship had been passionate,
and brief, and ended before Catherine could play
him for the fool. Carlisle probably remembered the
lady with more fondness than she remembered him,

if she remembered him at all. "Lady Georgiana, the emotion that your cousin inspired in gentlemen was not exactly love, although I hesitate to give it a name, lest I cause offense."

Here was a different view of Catherine, as well as of Mr. Sutton, because the gentleman gave no indication of caring who misliked what he said. Mr. Sutton appeared to have known her cousin well. Georgie didn't think she cared to know *how* well. "You are very kind to spare my spinster sensibilities," she said ironically. "Have you had any success in tracking down your uncle's missing wife?"

Carlisle had not, nor had Mr. Brown, who grew more nervous as each fruitless day passed. That young man seemed to fear that, did he fail, his employer would employ some exotic form of Indian revenge. Carlisle had not disabused him of the notion. "Have you ever been on a tiger hunt, Lady Georgiana?" he asked.

Georgie choked on her lemonade, recovered, cast him a reproachful glance. "Mr. Sutton, you are in a very teasing mood. You surely know that I have not."

Certainly Carlisle knew that Lady Georgiana had not been on a tiger hunt. However, he liked to hear her laugh. For Georgie's entertainment, he described the native beaters that moved through the bushes, flushing out deer and wild pigs and birds, the huntsmen riding on the backs of elephants in shooting howdahs, canvas boxes high enough for a grown man to stand and take aim. Elephants were essential in a countryside where tall grasses and dense, low shrubbery made it all but impossible for the huntsmen to see their targets. "There is nothing like the sound of a huge elephant flapping its huge ears. The elephant keeper, the *mahout,* perches on the beast's neck and strokes it, or prods it, with a steel prong. The beast is prone to uproot and eat nigh everything in its path."

Georgie smiled. "I think I should like to see an elephant. From a safe distance, that is!"

Carlisle wished that he might see an elephant himself. He suffered a brief pang of homesickness for the sights and smells of India. Bullocks with vermillion-painted horns. Dancing girls in billowing skirts. Camel-herders and village women with veiled faces. He described to the fascinated Lady Georgiana a contest between two elephants, as staged by an Indian prince for his guests, of whom Carlisle had been one. The visitors arrived at a verandah overlooking an area within a bamboo palisade, from there to observe the hostilities. The war elephants had been fed on a highly spiced diet that kept them in a permanently ill humor, which then reached a pitch of fury when their favorite females were sent into the ring. Enraged bellows and grunts and roars of pain, the clash of tusks engaged—In the end, the beasts could only be separated by fireworks thrown between them. "Indians believe that the world rests on the back of either a tortoise or a serpent," Carlisle added as an afterthought.

"Gracious!" marveled Georgie. "What an interesting life you have led, Mr. Sutton. How dull you must find us here. I wonder that you do not give up your search for whatever it is you search for, and go back home."

Carlisle wondered about that, also. At this very moment he could be wearing a loose robe and smoking a hookah while his well-born Sikh mistress fanned him with a punkah. Somehow he doubted that lady would be waiting for him when he finally returned home. Not that it would be difficult to replace her. Unlike their English counterparts, Indian courtesans understood the nature of pleasure and how it could be achieved.

Carlisle thought of his uncle's wife, and wondered just how much Miss Macclesfield knew of pleasure and its achievement. "My dear Lady Georgiana," he said, somewhat obscurely. "It is never wise to bet against a dark horse." The din around them lessened, then rose again. "Ah. Unless I miss my guess, your friend Warwick has just arrived."

Eighteen

Lord Warwick spent a few moments in conversation with his befrilled and beflowered hostess, conversation which left him none the wiser as to why he had been invited to this function, and further puzzled as to why Lady Denham was at such pains to tell him that Brummell had put in an appearance earlier. Garth had no notion why the Beau should honor so insipid an affair with his presence, nor why he himself should care. Garth's own reasons for attending were simple. He was curious.

Through the Public Rooms he wandered, exchanging a word of greeting, ignoring a snub. He inspected the cold collation, and cast an ironic eye at the sad-looking boar's head; then he accepted a glass of punch, pausing briefly to observe a game of whist. He moved through the crowd to the chamber where the orchestra played. Not that Garth had any especial interest in the dancers. He meant only to make a polite perambulation of the premises, and afterward to take his leave. Suddenly, he saw Georgie approaching him through the crowd.

Georgie at a function such as this? Impossible. Lord Warwick frowned at his glass of punch, which he had not thought so strong.

If a vision, she was most corporeal. Georgie tucked her hand through his arm. "Garth!" she said brightly. "Your sense of timing is superb. I believe I have promised you a dance."

Garth realized that the orchestra had indeed struck up a new tune. He transferred his frown from his punch glass to Georgie's face. "Pray try and not look so *forbidding!*" she said, quietly. "Consider, Garth: if you do not dance with me, you truly will land me in the scandal-broth!"

What she said was true. Reluctantly, Garth led Georgie out onto the dance floor. Apparently she was no longer angry with him, for which he must be glad. However, she had acted precisely as he wished she wouldn't, and publicly allied herself with him, and that caused him unease. "Do you realize what you have just done?" he asked.

"I do," retorted Georgie. "And I promise that if you dare once more to lecture me that I shall box your ears right here in the middle of the dance floor. *That* would give the busybodies something to chew over their chocolate cups, don't you think?"

Georgie thought Miss Halliday had a nice way of turning a phrase. Reluctantly, he smiled. "Much better!" Georgie approved. "Shall we cry pax then, my lord?"

"Considering that you have put your own reputation on the line by championing me, it would be churlish in me to refuse." Several interested observers would later remark upon the particular energy with which Lord Warwick twirled his partner, and dipped her, and swung her around. "It is your own cousin I am said to have disposed of, after all."

Georgie wished her cousin to perdition. Providing

that Catherine was not already there. "I know what it is. You do not wish to be in my debt. I cannot blame you! There is no telling when I may call in my vowels."

"Cut line, my girl!" Garth's smile was genuine now. "Pax it is then, Georgie. At least until I again manage to set up your back. How does the lovely 'Mrs. Smith,' by the bye?"

Mention of her houseguest caused Georgie's own spirits to falter. "It has occurred to Marigold that you are companions in misfortune. She was asking about the size of your pocketbook. I told her you are a pauper, but I doubt she believed me. Well you may look horrified! Marigold has decided that you are very handsome, Garth. Definitely I shall take up sea-bathing. It is said to be most beneficial to the nerves."

With great effort, Lord Warwick refrained from inquiring into the particulars of how "Mrs. Smith" was worrying his companion to death. Not that Georgie looked beset. Garth did not know when he had seen anything so wondrous as Lady Georgiana in her silver-shot dress, her hair arranged in intricate coils and adorned with pearls. "I personally find my nerves most agreeably affected by early-morning strolls along the seashore," he remarked.

"The seashore is very nice," agreed Georgie. "But there is not one handy, and I have grown too warm with the exertion of the dance. I do not know when I have more enjoyed myself. No, I do not require a lemonade. Pray escort me outside. Do not argue, Garth! I might still fly into the boughs. Heaven knows I have seen Marigold do so often enough to have got the hang of it."

"Mrs. Smith" was proving a most unfortunate influence on his companion, thought Garth. He did not

demur, but escorted Georgie into a small but elegant
flower garden embellished with classical statuary and
narrow, flagged paths.

Lord Warwick and Miss Halliday were not the only
of Lady Denham's guests to escape the crush in
search of cooler air, although no other departure
would arouse such interest, or cause so many people
to approach their hostess with scurrilous tidbits of
gossip about the viper she had clutched all unconscious to her meager chest. Garth had a notion of the
tittle-tattle that flourished behind them. "Georgie," he
said, "would you please tell me just what you are
about?"

Georgie had already sat on a rakehell's lap. It would
hardly corrupt her further to stroll around a garden
with Lord Warwick. "Are you still nattering about my
reputation? We are hardly unchaperoned, Garth."

Silently, Lord Warwick escorted her into a dark and
relatively secluded corner of the garden. So much, reflected Georgie, for his care what people thought. He
turned to face her. "*Why* are you doing this?" he asked.

Georgie looked at him. Garth made a very noble
appearance in the black-and-white evening attire
made popular by Brummell. Briefly, she was tempted
to make a flippant remark.

As it turned out, she could not. "Because I cannot
help myself," she said quietly. "You know that. You
have always known that, Garth. I am sorry for what I
said to you the other day. It was most unfair."

Her hair had begun to curl around her face in the
cool night air. Garth brushed an errant ringlet off her
forehead. "I have no right to even speak with you.
Georgie, I was such a fool. I don't know why things
happened as they did."

"I do," Georgie said wryly. "Catherine set her cap at you. There was no resisting Catherine when she wanted something—or someone. I saw it happen time and again." She looked up at him. "Garth, what do you truly think happened to Catherine?"

Even in the shadows, Georgie could see the grimness of his expression. For a moment, she thought he would not reply. "I think that my wife developed a partiality for someone else, and ran off with him," Garth said, at last. "But I do not know the identity of the fortunate—or unfortunate!—gentleman, and I have not been able to trace her one step."

Georgie was more than startled by these revelations. "Garth! You mean that she—uh—"

"I mean that Catherine did not consider fidelity a virtue," Garth responded wryly. "In a husband *or* a wife. I doubt that she was faithful to me beyond the honeymoon, if that. I suppose I should be grateful to her for not providing me an heir, because I should have always wondered who the child's true father was."

"Garth!" Georgie said again, appalled. "Yet you let the world think that—" She paused. "Oh. I see."

"Rather a murderer than a cuckold?" Garth shrugged. "Something like that. To say the truth, I was not altogether certain Catherine was not playing some monstrous practical joke. We had quarreled just before she disappeared."

Georgie tried to assemble her scattered wits. "It was not the first time you had quarreled, I'll warrant."

"You think me high-handed." Ruefully, Lord Warwick smiled. "Truly, Georgie, my intentions were the best. I dreaded the consequences you would face, were your name linked with mine. And I will quarrel with you no more about it. The damage has been done."

What Georgie meant to do, she later was not certain, but she started to move toward Lord Warwick, and her delicate evening slipper slid in the damp grass. Instead of moving toward him, she tumbled right into his arms. Garth caught her up against his chest. Georgie turned her face up to his. He raised one hand and rubbed his thumb along her lush lower lip. Georgie shivered, but not with cold. "Garth," she whispered.

That whisper was Lord Warwick's undoing, such longing did it express. He lowered his lips to hers.

How gentle were his kisses, then how rough. How sweet and strange were the sensations those kisses aroused. Tingles and trembles and shivers—Georgie wasn't certain she could still stand.

Garth inhaled deeply, then he removed her arms from round his shoulders, and stepped back. That kiss—or kisses, to be precise—had affected Georgie no more than they had affected him. Garth wished he might sweep her up into his arms and make sweet, passionate love to her right there in the middle of Lady Denham's garden, and be damned if the entire world was looking on. "My dear, I wish to do much more than kiss you," he murmured. "Prudence dictates that we stop."

Georgie recognized the remote expression that had descended upon Lord Warwick's features. "If you turn away from me now, Garth, I swear that I shall scream! What do you think *that* would do for my blasted reputation, pray?"

Garth regretted that he had put Georgie in a temper. He drew her back into his arms. "Turn away from you? I shall never do that. Oh, my dear, what are we to do about this?"

Georgie knew what she'd like to do—or if she didn't know exactly, had a fair idea. It involved divesting oneself of one's clothing, first of all. Georgie wouldn't at all have minded divesting herself of her clothing at that particular moment, even if they were in the middle of Lady Denham's garden. She snuggled closer to Garth.

Lord Warwick reached a decision. He put Georgie away from him and heroically refrained from planting kisses on the creamy flesh so charmingly revealed by her low-cut gown. "I am going to be absent from town for the space of a few days," he said abruptly. "Much as I dislike to leave you at the mercy of your 'Mrs. Smith.'"

Garth was leaving Brighton? The warmer the embrace, the farther he must distance himself from her, it seemed. Georgie would chew glass before she betrayed her bitter disappointment. "We are not yet at point non plus," she responded lightly. "I daresay we shall contrive. But we have given the gossips enough to jaw about for one evening, don't you think? Let us go back inside."

Nineteen

Andrew was feeling sadly out of curl. Agatha's most recent attempts to physic him, involving as they had cold water and stewed prunes, and snails mashed with mallets, had proven little more beneficial to his nerves than the newspaper accounts he currently perused. Andrew was sorry to read that matters in the Peninsula had degenerated into a waiting game, where the French and British armies were evenly matched, and both commanders waited for the other to make a mistake. While Wellington's officers leisurely explored the city, and Old Douro himself was feted and kissed by Spanish ladies everywhere he went, the troops endured scalding sun and bitter cold, choked down breakfasts of beer and onions after performing outpost work all night, and burned emptied coffins for firewood because no other kindling was to be found in the almost treeless terrain.

Andrew exercised no vast imagination; these details and others were laid out before him in black and white. Leakage of vital military information was an ongoing problem. The croakers, in their grumblings, gave away intelligence to the enemy; and many details of soldiers' letters home were transformed into newsprint to be read by friend and foe alike. Andrew tossed the newspaper aside. As many another soldier before him had discovered, after the heat of battle, civilian life seemed damned flat.

If Lieutenant Halliday found Brighton dull this morning, he was in the minority. Even in the bath establishments created for those individuals who did not wish to dally on the seashore or jostle for a bathing-machine, the most notable of them Wood's Baths and William's New Baths, which stood within a few yards of each other on the south side of the Steine, the atmosphere was gay, and orchestras played. Not that Andrew had chosen to submerge himself in the hot baths or the cold, and certainly he had no curiosity about a method of curing the gout by means of an air pump. He had come merely to drink the waters, not because he had any great faith in their efficacy, although they must surely taste better than stewed prunes and mashed snails. Simply, he had sought an excuse to leave the house. On the floor beside his chair sprawled Lump, who was under strict orders to behave himself. Lump looked most incongruous in these elegant surroundings, which were pedimented and colonnaded, and boasted crystal chandeliers and furnishings in the latest style.

It was that incongruity which first caught Lady Denham's eye. A large, damp, ill-mannered dog with a great many teeth, who looked as though he had been splattered with paint from several different pots—she couldn't think who had been asking her about such a beast. Doubtless she would eventually remember. Just now, she had something in particular to say to Lieutenant Halliday.

"Hah!" said Lady Denham, and deposited herself in

a nearby chair. Behind her, Sarah-Louise hovered nervously. "I wish a word with you, young man!"

Lady Denham looked quite spectacular in a walking dress of Pomona green merino cloth with a stomacher front and a ruff of triple lace; long, full sleeves tied up in three places with colored ribbons; and a frilled edging to the hem. Upon her coal-black hair perched a narrow-brimmed bonnet with a high crown covered in feathers and flowers. Lump perked up his ears and drooled. "No," murmured Andrew, recognizing an incipient canine interest. "If you do not behave I shall make *you* drink the waters. Good morning, Lady Denham. Miss Inchquist." Sarah-Louise was wearing stripes again, he noticed. This day they were orange.

At the suggestion that it was a good day, Lady Denham snorted. "Don't try and change the subject! What do you know of Lord Warwick, young man?"

Warwick? Andrew frowned as he tried to place the name. There had been some business with his cousin Catherine—but Andrew had been in the military then, with scant interest in such stuff. Lady Denham, however, seemed very interested. Cautiously, Andrew said, "I've never met the man."

"Humph!" With the force of her emotion, Lady Denham's feathers swayed. Lump parted his great jaws, and panted. Andrew frowned at him. Thwarted, Lump laid his head back down on his paws. Oblivious to this byplay, Lady Denham continued. "I would not want you to think me a tittle-tattle—I had not wished to mention it—then I decided that I should! I'm sure you will forgive my boldness when you hear what I have to say. To give you the word with no bark on it, you may not have met Lord Warwick, Lieutenant Halliday, but your sister has! She not only waltzed with him, she disappeared with him into the garden for quite fifteen minutes at my rout!"

Andrew followed these disclosures with some confusion. Clearly, Lady Denham experienced a profound degree of emotion, and he failed to understand why. "Beg pardon. Where's the harm in that? Warwick's married to my cousin Catherine, as I recall. Which makes him and Georgie relatives of some sort, I think."

Lady Denham was glad to see that someone else was as ignorant of Lord Warwick's lurid history as she herself had been. "You poor boy! It is positively providential that we encountered you this morning!" Lady Denham proceeded to relate all the tidbits of gossip that had been presented her by her guests, while behind her Sarah-Louise fidgeted and blushed. "Warwick's wife disappeared while on an outing, or so the official explanation goes. Rumor has it that she ran away from home—he must have driven her to it, poor thing!—and Warwick either tracked her down and shot her, or drowned her, or broke her neck himself upon learning she planned to elope. And then he hid her body so well that it has never been found!"

Lady Denham's disclosures were delivered with considerable relish. Some response was required. "Jupiter!" Andrew said.

If Lieutenant Halliday did not faint dead away upon receipt of her confidences, his startled reaction left Lady Denham not dissatisfied. "Your sister should not associate with such a reprobate! You will wish to tell her so. Now you must excuse me for a moment while I speak with an old friend. Sarah-Louise, do stop hovering, and sit down!"

Obediently, Miss Inchquist perched in her aunt's

abandoned chair, reached down to give Lump a pat. "I do not think the matter is so bad as my aunt imagines," she ventured. "She tends to exaggerate. Lady Georgiana appeared to be enjoying herself."

Lady Georgiana was having a prodigious good time of late, reflected her brother. He wondered which she liked better, waltzing with a murderer or sitting on a rakehell's lap. "My sister is a woman grown," he said, with no great conviction. "She must know what she's about."

Sarah-Louise hoped that Lieutenant Halliday was not mistaken. "Have you no family other than your sister?" she asked.

Andrew was still thinking of his sister and her queer behavior. That everything was to be laid at the hen-witted Marigold's doorstep, he made no doubt. "Our parents died in a carriage accident some years ago," he replied. "There are an uncle and some cousins—my cousin Catherine's relations—but Georgie is estranged from them."

"And therefore so are you." Sarah-Louise admired this loyalty. However, mention of family had brought her own to mind. She glanced cautiously around for her aunt, and found that lady deep in conversation some distance away. "I am in a dreadful pucker!" Miss Inchquist confessed. "My papa is coming to Brighton, and once he arrives, my aunt is bound to tell him that she has decided I would make Mr. Sutton a good wife."

Better Carlisle Sutton than Peregrine Teasdale, thought Andrew, but politely refrained from remark. Not that he had ever observed Mr. Sutton so much as talking to Sarah-Louise. "Does Mr. Sutton wish to marry you?" he asked.

"Whyever should he?" retorted Sarah-Louise. "I am hardly in his style. Not that either Papa or Aunt Amice will care for that. Sometimes I wonder if perhaps I was left on my papa's doorstep, because I cannot see any resemblance between myself and any other member of my family. *They* take a notion in their heads, and nothing can stand in their way. I am instead a pudding-heart." She paused to contemplate that unhappy fact. "The only thing I can see for it is that Mr. Sutton should develop a preference for someone other than myself. Do you think—That is, I have noticed that Mr. Sutton seems to like your sister very well!"

Was there a gentleman who *didn't* like his sister? While Andrew had been preoccupied with his own troubles, Georgie had apparently come out of her shell. "No!" he said, so sternly that Lump, thinking he had been spoken to, apologetically wagged his tail. "If Georgie wishes to cultivate Mr. Sutton, it will not be at my request."

Miss Inchquist wondered how she might persuade Lady Georgiana to cultivate Mr. Sutton. If only Sarah-Louise were not of too meek a nature to stand up to her father and her aunt. If only Peregrine were not pressing her to run off to Gretna Green. "I do not wish to elope," she said aloud. "I want a real church wedding. A very *grand* wedding. Perhaps even at St. George's, Hanover Square."

Miss Inchquist did not wish to marry Carlisle Sutton, yet it appeared she'd already made her bridal plans. Andrew despaired of ever understanding the gentler sex. Perhaps it was not Mr. Sutton that Sarah-Louise wished to greet her at the altar in Hanover Square. Andrew wondered what Mr. Teasdale might deem suitable attire for a wedding. The thought gave him a headache. As did the realization that his sister was not so up-to-snuff as he had thought her, as demonstrated by her recent shenanigans in gardens and on laps. Why was it that the ladies seemed to have a susceptibility for gentlemen they should not? Damned if Georgie wasn't every bit as green as Sarah-Louise. Now Andrew must worry about them both. He almost wished that he might be in the Peninsula again, dealing with the bloody-minded French.

Twenty

Marigold had thought and thought, and couldn't think what she was to do. However could she come by twenty-five thousand pounds? If only she had something left to wager, she might win that amount at play, providing that she was very, very lucky, which she had not been yet. Marigold possessed little more than the clothes on her back—figuratively speaking, that is. As poor Janie could attest, Marigold's clothing filled to overflowing both a wardrobe and a portmanteau.

The clothes on Marigold's back, just then, were not what one might expect. "Mrs. Smith" wore no percale or spotted cambric, no embroidered mull or piqué or gauze. Instead she was dressed in baggy breeches, a brown stuff jacket, less-than-pristine linen, scuffed shoes, and had a handkerchief tied round her neck. Her hair was tucked up beneath a felt cap. Although she looked well enough, Marigold enjoyed this garb no more now than when she had worn it onstage. To pass as a boy, her magnificence of figure necessitated the use of considerable camouflage. However, Marigold could hardly jaunter openly around Brighton making inquiries about a certain gentleman from India. Though she may have decided that it was necessary for her to speak with Mr. Sutton, she did not wish him to see her first.

Discovering the gentleman's lodging place was not an easy feat, and dusk had descended on the city by the time Marigold limped into the yard of The King's Hand, past a hay-strewn horse trough and several dilatory grooms. In her wake she had left numerous kitchen maids and potboys with the impression that a certain Indian gentleman was a three-tailed Bashaw, or alternately a Mugwump, guilty of some unnamed but hideous offense, and consequently a-hiding of hisself. None of those worthies questioned Marigold's identity. Her experience on the stage stood her in good stead, and she had liberally laced her vocabulary with such words as "Cricky!", "Hoi!", and "Adone-do!".

Luck continued to be with her now in the person of a little barmaid, who cheerfully confided that Mr. Sutton had a room on the second floor, and was even so helpful as to point out which window was his. Marigold eyed the window, and then a nearby tree. The barmaid returned to her duties. Marigold glanced around, found herself unnoticed, and swung herself onto the lowest limb. Up the tree she scrambled, as if it were the rigging on a stage.

A breeze ruffled the white curtains at the open window. A pity Marigold lacked the wherewithal to gamble, so lucky was she this day. Now she could inspect Mr. Sutton's belongings before he returned home to find her awaiting him, at which time she would be reasonable, and hopefully so would he. In case he was not, Marigold had her little pistol tucked into her waistband.

It never occurred to Marigold that Mr. Sutton might be in his quarters. In Marigold's experience, gentlemen were never in their quarters at this time of day. She swung one leg over the windowsill and ducked into the room. The chamber was much as she had expected—narrow bed and wooden chair, small chest of drawers, water pitcher and bowl on a corner stand—save for the gentleman in the metal bath.

The bathtub was too small for him. His knees protruded through the soapy water like two islands in a sea. "Ah, Miss Macclesfield," he said. "You have recovered from your grief."

From her grief—which admittedly had centered more on her late husband's lack of foresight than the fact that he had shuffled off this mortal coil—Marigold may have recovered, but not from the circumstance of having interrupted a gentleman in his bath. This particular gentleman had the physique of a Greek statue. Marigold was not accustomed to gazing upon so splendid a masculine specimen, her husbands—with the exception of poor Leo—having been past their prime. She experienced a certain difficulty in tearing her gaze away from Mr. Sutton's splendidly bronzed and muscular chest. One would think he went about in the sun half-clothed. Or perhaps unclothed. "Um," she said.

His uncle's widow was perhaps beginning to realize that she had met her match. "I am glad that you have seen the wisdom of coming to me," Carlisle remarked. "Allow me to make myself more presentable. Pray hand me that towel."

Heavens, was the man going to remove himself from the tub *now?* Not that he could stay in it indefinitely without shriveling like a prune. Though Marigold might long to drown Mr. Sutton for the trouble he had caused her, she did not wish for him to shrivel up. She handed him a towel, and then turned her back, a movement that brought her face-to-face with the looking-glass atop the chest of drawers. The mirror afforded her an excellent view of Mr. Sutton as he removed himself from the tub. His lower half appeared every bit as excellent as his upper half had been. Perhaps more so. Marigold scrunched her eyes shut. The odious man had already made it very clear that he would not catch her if she swooned.

What a brazen wench she was, to climb right through his window. Carlisle wondered what she had thought she'd find. Not what she *had* found, he'd warrant. "All right. You can turn around."

Marigold did so, then stared. "Excuse me," she said politely. "I believe you've forgot your shirt."

"Surely a lady of your vast experience isn't going to turn missish at the sight of a man's chest." Carlisle made no effort to retrieve the garment. "We are practically family, Miss Macclesfield. Besides, it's bloody hot."

Marigold would concede the weather. Sweat trickled down her neck, puddled between her tightly bound breasts. If only she could stop admiring Mr. Sutton's muscles. "I've come to talk to you about the Norwood Emerald. Perhaps this is not a good moment. I think that I should leave."

Having lured his quarry into his lair—although he was not sure how he had accomplished this, he would take the credit—Carlisle was not eager to let her depart. Even then she was en route to the window. He caught her by the waistband of her breeches, and tossed her onto the bed.

"Oof!" gasped Marigold, and scooted back against the pillows. "You are no gentleman!"

Admittedly Carlisle was no gentleman. His uninvited guest was even more hen-witted than he suspected if she thought he was. She was also extremely lovely, with her golden curls tumbling down around her shoulders. The felt cap had fallen off when he tossed her on the bed.

Carlisle would have also liked to divest his uncle's widow of the rest of her atrocious costume. The realization did not endear her to him. "I've no ambition to discuss my lack of manners. Have you brought me the emerald?"

Marigold reminded herself that she was going to be reasonable so that Mr. Sutton would respond likewise. She clasped her hands to her sadly diminished chest. "Pray try to enter into my feelings, sir," she said. "Put yourself in my place. There I was, a grieving widow, shocked to my soul by your uncle's demise—"

Carlisle closed the window, lest his visitor think she might still escape. "I don't know why you should have been surprised. You caused it," he remarked.

"I did not!" In her indignation, Marigold bounced on the bed. "Or if I did, I didn't mean to. I—"

"Miss Macclesfield," interrupted Carlisle. "You will catch cold at that. Even a birdbrain like yourself must know better than to ride an old gelding as if he were a colt. Not that I daresay my uncle minded. However, this is all beside the point. You were about to tell me why you have not brought me the emerald."

The man was an unfeeling bully. Marigold's blue eyes filled with tears. "I have come here to fling myself on your mercy!" she wailed. "How can you be so cruel?"

Perhaps he should not underestimate Miss Macclesfield, Carlisle reflected. The white Bengal tigers of

India had blue eyes. And the female tiger was as dangerous as the male.

Carlisle sat down on the bed beside Marigold and grasped her arms. "Give me the emerald, or I shall reduce you to so wretched a state of poverty and hunger that you will be grateful to eat lowly kacchaguccha pods and cakes of wheat kernels and cow dung."

Marigold had never heard of a kacchaguccha pod, but she was fairly sure she wouldn't like cow dung any more than she liked cauliflower or peas. She might have reacted much more strongly to Mr. Carlisle's rudeness had it not been for the proximity of his naked, bronzed chest. As it was, she struggled with an inclination to reach out and trace those splendid muscles. "Cannot you satisfy yourself with the remainder of your uncle's estate? Which is not inconsiderable, and of which I will not see a farthing, since Sir Hubert was so inconsiderate as to not revise his will."

"Doubtless he was preoccupied with other matters." Carlisle was feeling a trifle preoccupied himself. "You have only yourself to blame."

"So you keep saying!" So potent was Mr. Sutton's presence that Marigold was having trouble concentrating her mind. "Anyone with a *smidgen* of compassion would make some provision for his uncle's widow, seeing as she was left alone and penniless and dependent upon the charity of friends!"

Carlisle doubted the widow would remain alone for long. He reached out and touched a finger to the pulse beating in her throat. Wide-eyed, she looked at him. "What are you doing?" she whispered.

Carlisle was not certain. "The Norwood Emerald," he repeated, for want of saying anything else.

Oh, curse the emerald! As well as its rightful owner,

though Marigold did not remove his hand from her neck. "I cannot give you the blasted emerald because I do not *have* it. Still, I know where it is, and you may buy it back for the sum of twenty-five thousand pounds."

Carlisle was not inclined to spend such a sum, although he might have done so easily. However, he was not the one responsible for the emerald having gone missing, and it was not in his nature to let the guilty party squirm off the hook. "I'll hazard a guess. You lost it at play."

Could he like her just a little bit? There was the matter of his hand resting on her neck. Prettily, Marigold pouted. "I admit that I was very foolish. But I am willing to tell you where the emerald is, and then you may buy it back if it is so important to you as all that."

"Oh, it is important, Miss Macclesfield." Carlisle leaned over her, holding her prisoner between his two strong arms. "And I *will* have it back."

If Marigold didn't know better, she would think the man meant to make love to her. Not that she was averse to the notion, exactly, but she disliked the expression in his dark eyes. He was looking at her rather like she imagined a snake might look before it gobbled up a mongoose. Or was it the other way around? Whichever, Marigold didn't think she cared to share that fate. "Whatever are you doing?" she asked, and tried to squirm away.

Carlisle wished she would stop squirming. Damned distracting, it was. "You are asking me to barter," he said. "A good businessman—and I am a *very* good businessman, Miss Macclesfield—makes no bargain without first sampling the goods."

Barter? Marigold didn't think she'd be asked to

barter, though it was very difficult to think clearly with his face—his chest!—so close to hers. Mr. Sutton added, "It would take a great deal of bartering to compensate me for twenty-five thousand pounds."

Good God! *She* was the merchandise Mr. Sutton wished to claim in return for his lost emerald. "Oh! You horrid man! I vow I shall have a spasm!" Marigold gasped.

Mr. Sutton smiled wickedly. "Yes," he said. "I rather think you might."

Marigold was outraged. Rather, part of her was. Another part would have been content to stay precisely where she was and let Mr. Sutton do with her as he would. But Marigold, for all her fecklessness, was not that feather-headed. She wriggled beneath her captor until she could free the pistol from her waistband, and then she jammed it into his ribs. Carlisle, who had mistaken her wriggles for something else altogether, was taken aback. "What in blazes?" he inquired.

"The gun is loaded." Marigold gave his ribs another poke. "I assure you that I know how to use it very well. You will release me, Mr. Sutton. At once!"

Certainly Mr. Sutton would release her. Females were irrational creatures at best. He would not quarrel with a female who held a gun, although more than ever he still intended to have his revenge. "You will recall the Hindu custom of *seti*, Miss Macclesfield," he said as he stood up. "Hurling herself upon her husband's funeral pyre is the only alternative for a widow who is unable to live a chaste life."

The man would have used her as if she were a common harlot. Worse, she had almost let him. Marigold snatched up her felt cap and jammed it on her head.

"You shall have your emerald, damn you!" she snapped.

Carlisle was every bit as angry as his escaping quarry. "Within the week!" he retorted. "Or I will see you hanged."

Twenty-one

Various members of the Halliday household were gathered in the kitchen following a dinner of mutton shoulder, gravy soup, potatoes, and turnips mashed with butter, pepper, and salt. Missing were Andrew, assumed to have stayed away for fear of being subjected to further such delicacies as mashed snails and stewed prunes, and Marigold, thought to be sulking in her room. Andrew's absence was regretted; Marigold's was not. Lump's presence was unfortunate, because he had eaten the entire apple tart that had been intended for dessert, and now lay groaning and belching on the hearth. Tibble was also in disgrace, having broken the soup tureen while washing up the dinner dishes. Gloomily he applied blacking rather too lavishly onto Agatha's boots, then attacked them with a brush.

Janie, meanwhile, was applying a flatiron to one of Marigold's muslin gowns. Janie was not fond of ironing, and her thoughts tended to stray to Charles Footman down the street, whom she had finally contrived to meet, with the result that she had already let the iron sit on the muslin too long, and the material had become scorched. Fortunately, Agatha had a remedy for restoring whiteness to scorched linen—one-half pint of vinegar, two ounces of fuller's-earth, one ounce of dried fowl's dung, one-half ounce of soap, and the juice of two large onions, all boiled to the consistency of paste, spread over the damaged part and allowed to dry—and so the day was saved. Agatha and Georgie sat at the long elm table, savoring cups of hot tea and munching marzipan. Georgie looked unremarkable in a gown of pale sprig muslin. Atop her fiery ringlets, Agatha sported a frilled and beribboned mobcap.

Andrew limped into the kitchen and sat down at the table. Agatha fetched another teacup, and laced the brew liberally with cowslip, because Andrew looked overwrought. Georgie, too, regarded her brother with concern. She knew better than to quiz him about his health. "Where have you been?" she asked.

Andrew shrugged. "Here and there." In point of fact, he had been asking a great many questions, and he didn't like the answers above half. Andrew squinted at his sister over the edge of his teacup. She still looked like the same old Georgie, which just went to show how deceptive appearances were, which Andrew already knew, because although he might look like his same old self, he most certainly was not. Nor was Georgie her same old self, if she was waltzing with murderers and sitting in rakehells' laps. Oh yes, she had said the latter was an accident, caused by Lump—was there ever an accident not caused by Lump?—but she had not looked like she much minded perching there. Nor had Magnus Eliot looked like he minded, either. No doubt Magnus Eliot had females dropping into his lap all the time. Were he not so fatigued by this whole business, Andrew might have found it in himself to envy the man. "What's all this nonsense about Warwick?" he asked.

Georgie should have guessed that rumors about Garth would eventually reach her brother's ears. "You are not to worry yourself about that business," she said soothingly. "Nonsense is exactly what it is."

Andrew didn't know how he was not to worry, although he wished he might. He replaced the teacup in its saucer. "Lady Denham instructed me to tell you that you should not associate with such a curst loose fish."

Georgie blinked in astonishment. "Lady Denham called Garth a curst loose fish?"

Damned if all this to-ing and fro-ing hadn't given him another headache. "No," Andrew admitted. "I added that. She only said that he did away with his wife, although she wasn't certain precisely how it was accomplished. It seems to me that the gossips might have less to say if the man defended himself, or at least said *some*thing, but it seems that he has not." He reached for a piece of marzipan. "Do you think Warwick did for Catherine, sis?"

Georgie looked around the kitchen at the various faces turned raptly in her direction. Agatha and Tibble and Janie had all paused in their various chores to stare. Only Lump had no interest in the conversation. Lump's sole interest was in his distended belly. He rolled over on his back and groaned.

Tibble put two and two together. Warwick—the groom who had insulted him—"Nincompoop!" he announced.

The others ignored this revelation. "I think," Georgie said very clearly, "that Garth had nothing to do with his wife's disappearance. Or so he says, at any rate, and I have no reason to disbelieve him. Now may we please speak of something else?"

"Could hardly blame him if he had." As Andrew

drained his teacup, he caught his sister's startled expression. "I never could abide Catherine myself. Tell me, *do* you like Carlisle Sutton, sis?"

Georgie disliked the seemingly erratic nature of her brother's thoughts. "Mr. Sutton is a very interesting conversationalist. He has told me many intriguing things about his life in India. Yes, I would say I like him well enough. Why do you ask? What has Mr. Sutton to do with anything?"

What Andrew might have said in explanation—surely he would not have confessed that Miss Inchquist wished his sister to act the coquette with Carlisle Sutton and thus provide her a smoke screen—must remain unknown. Marigold burst into the kitchen. Since she was still clad in masculine attire, her appearance caused a considerable sensation. Janie abandoned all thought of her footman, Agatha choked on a swallow of tea, and Tibble dropped his blacking-brush.

"Carlisle Sutton is the greatest beast in nature, and I should know!" Marigold announced. She was momentarily distracted by sight of Lump lying on the hearth with all four paws extended straight up into the air. "Is he dead?" she asked.

"No," said Georgie. "He ate an entire apple tart and is suffering as he deserves. Marigold—"

Marigold flung her hands into the air. "Everything is going as badly as possible! I am cast quite into despair! Since you like Mr. Sutton so well, *you* should talk to him, Georgie. Which now that I think of it, is an excellent idea! Because he certainly won't offer *you* a slip on the shoulder like he did me!"

Georgie supposed she should not be startled by this revelation. And why should a gentleman *not* offer her a slip on the shoulder, pray? Certain people did not think she was such an antidote. "I have already talked to Magnus Eliot. That was quite enough."

Marigold could only be disappointed by this ungenerous attitude. "Mr. Sutton refuses to buy back the emerald from Magnus Eliot. He says he would rather see me hang." She wrinkled her nose. "What's that smell?"

These shocking disclosures had so further astonished Marigold's audience that several members quite forgot themselves. Tibble found that he had been polishing his knee instead of Agatha's boot. Janie quickly snatched the flatiron off the ironing board, and whisked Marigold's singed dress out of sight.

It was not burning muslin that had caught Marigold's attention, however. "Turnips!" she announced. "You have been eating turnips. I detest turnips of all things."

Agatha rose from the table. "God strike me blind!" she muttered, and went in search of refreshment more appropriate than tea. Andrew tried to make sense of the situation. "Does this have anything to do with Georgie sitting in Magnus Eliot's lap?" he asked.

Marigold paused in her agitated gape to stare at Georgie. "You sat in his lap?" she echoed, and then clapped her hands. "How very clever of you, Georgie! I would not have thought of that! Or I would not have thought of it for *you!* Tell me all about it! What was it like?"

"Magnus Eliot is a rascal and a rogue," Georgie replied honestly. Then she quickly added, "You would not like him one bit. And I have already told you what he said. He will not let the emerald go for less than twenty-five thousand pounds."

Thoughtfully, Marigold toyed with her knotted handkerchief. "You did *not* tell me you had sat upon his lap." Perhaps if Marigold sat upon Mr. Eliot's lap it would be more effective. Marigold had considerably more experience with lap-sitting than did her friend.

Georgie had by this time gained a fair understanding of how Marigold's mind worked. "No! You are *not* to approach Magnus Eliot yourself. We will think of something else."

Tibble was trying very hard to follow this conversation, during which he sat rapt and open-mouthed. "Tap his claret!" he interjected helpfully. "Mill his cannister! Break his head!"

"Tsk!" said Agatha, and placed a cup of negus—a mixture of wine, hot water, sugar, lemon juice, and spices—on the table in front of him. Tibble abandoned all thought of costard-smiting and napper-cracking to pick up the cup and drink instead.

Andrew's mind was also a considerable jumble. One thing, however, stood starkly out. *"What* emerald?" he asked. "Why the devil are you dressed like that?"

Now Marigold was truly in the suds, because Andrew already didn't like her above half, and she didn't imagine any more fondness would be engendered by the tale she had to tell. "I don't know why everyone must blame me!" she cried, and burst into tears that abated only when Lump elevated himself from the hearth to come lick her cheek and burp gently in her ear. It was left to Georgie to explain Marigold's plight as best she could.

Lost emeralds, stage actresses, irate nephews—Andrew was appalled by this imbroglio. "Hang it! That's why you were talking to Eliot."

Georgie eyed her sodden friend, who was huddled with Lump on the flagstone floor. "Would you rather I had sent Marigold?"

Andrew shuddered at the suggestion. "I would rather you had sent me if anyone was to be sent anywhere!"

That notion had not occurred to Georgie. Were she honest, she must admit that she had wanted to meet Magnus Eliot herself. Wicked gentlemen did not in the normal course of events come in Georgie's way.

Georgie did not tell her brother that she had longed to meet a rakehell. "I did not care to involve you in this imbroglio."

Marigold didn't feel that her predicament was engendering a properly sympathetic emotion in her companions' breasts. Too, the focus of attention had too long been turned away from herself. "I could always disappear," she suggested nobly. "Disguise myself and take up another name."

Andrew was not impressed by this enactment of the martyr. "You already tried that!" he snapped. "Need I point out that it didn't serve? You are to do nothing, Marigold. Nor are you, Georgie! I will deal with this."

Marigold, who nurtured an admiration for the military, and an appreciation for anyone who took the onus of responsibility from herself, applauded this masterful attitude. Georgie was less impressed. She did not like to see Andrew so flushed and feverish. However, she supposed his efforts would do no harm. And then conversation ceased, as Lump divested himself at last of the remnants of the purloined apple tart.

Twenty-two

"Stand up straight! Don't slouch!" said Lady Denham. With her niece and two parcel-laden footmen, Amice was enjoying a shopping excursion along the Steine. Thus far she had inspected a cap of embroidered mull trimmed with lace and tucks, rejected a pair of front-laced half-boots, purchased an India shawl, a fan of pierced horn leaves, and a number of knickknacks.

"Poundstock is well enough if you don't mind that pendulous belly, and those jowls, and the fact that he is quite old. Whateley is very handsome, and a baronet as well, but I cannot bring myself to repeat the tales I have heard about *him*. Trewhitt is eligible enough, even if he is said to be touched in the upper works, although I do not believe he has yet taken to addressing oak trees in Hyde Park like poor King George!" For this excursion, Lady Denham had chosen to adorn herself in a day dress of chintz with a dark ground, and a silk bonnet trimmed with feathers; she had badgered her niece into wearing a green dress and a soft-crowned bonnet with a turned-back brim. If in the costume the girl bore an unfortunate resemblance to a great freckled shrub, at least she was not striped.

"You will not use this information but in the most discreet manner!" she continued. "I merely wished to give you a word to the wise." Lady Denham was not being entirely truthful. What she really wished to do was to get her niece safely tied-up, thereby sparing them both the agony of a London season. Or seasons, because Amice couldn't imagine that Sarah-Louise would *take*. Not that Lady Denham wasn't fond of her niece, because of course she must be, but there was no denying that the chit had no social graces whatsoever. She could not carry on even the simplest conversation without stammering and blushing and staring at the floor, which made her look rather like a wind-bent tree, because she was so very tall. Fortunate that Sarah-Louise was an heiress, because there was nothing else remarkable about her, or remarkable in a good way. Having roundly denounced every eligible gentleman of her acquaintance—save Carlisle Sutton—as madmen and villains and worse, Lady Denham deemed it proper, according to tactics, to fire a shot of some caliber. "Mr. Sutton, on the other hand, is much relished by everyone who knows him well. You may wait for me out here while I just step into this little shop."

Sarah-Louise was relieved to be spared further embarrassing revelations. Very difficult it was to be in the practice of daily dissimulation with her aunt. She sat down on a bench in front of the corsetiere's shop. The hovering footmen looked hot, laden down as they were with her aunt's purchase. Sarah-Louise suggested that they might also have a seat. The footmen were shocked by this suggestion, and grateful, but it wouldn't be at all proper for them to do such a thing. "Fiddlesticks!" said Sarah-Louise. "I don't see what difference it makes, so long as my aunt doesn't see. Frankly, considering what type of shop this is, I should think she'll be there for some time!"

The younger footman snickered. The elder silenced him with an elbow in the ribs. With Miss Inchquist, they gazed upon an apparition mincing in their direction. "Oh!" breathed the young lady. The footmen exchanged glances, and looked the other way.

Mistily, Sarah-Louise gazed upon her suitor—despite Lady Denham's machinations, her *only* suitor so far as she could tell. Mr. Teasdale wore a bright lime-green double-breasted tailcoat with square-cut skirt tails that reached below his knees, its sleeves gathered at the shoulder seam and finished at the wrist with a side slit, three buttons, and a stitched-down cuff. He had added a high-collared orange marcella waistcoat, faultless cravat, freshly pleated ruffles, pantaloons, and Hessian boots.

Peregrine paused by the bench. Damned if he'd sit down. Her green clashed with his. "Miss Inchquist!" he said, and swept her a bow. "*What is this vision before me that I see?*' I have been looking for you everywhere, since I had your note. Has the time come? Do you wish to, er—" He glanced at the wooden-faced footmen, who were staring with rapt fascination at something across the street. "*Flee as a bird to your mountain*'?"

Her mountain? Sarah-Louise could not imagine what Mr. Teasdale was going on about. Then she blushed as she realized he referred to Gretna Green. "Oh, no! That is not what I meant at all. The thing is, my papa is coming to town!"

Not an elopement? After Peregrine had spent as

much time dressing as if for a ball? And very success-
fully, it would appear, for did he not create a sensation
everywhere he went? Including among his creditors,
alas? The import of Sarah-Louise's words struck him,
and clashing greens forgotten, he sat down beside her
on the bench. "Then time is of the essence! *'The best
day . . . is the first to flee'!*"

Gracious, but his jacket was blindingly green seen
up so very close. Sarah-Louise twisted her reticule in
her hands. "Peregrine, please do not ask me to do
that. I have t-told you I cannot. I wished to tell you
that because Papa will be here—you see that we must
be discreet."

Peregrine saw a most terrible vision of his creditors lined up at his door, prepared to divest him of
all he owned. No longer would he be a Tulip of fashion, smug and spruce in his attire, but reduced to
poverty, clad in rags or worse. But all was not yet lost.
"When will your papa be here?" he asked.

Was Mr. Teasdale angry? Sarah-Louise feared he
was. "I do not know, precisely. When he can get away.
I am sorry, Peregrine, but you know that Papa does
not approve of my relationship with you."

No, nor should he. Peregrine could not imagine
himself a papa, but if he were one, it was deuced certain no daughter of his would marry a fellow so mired
in debt as himself. However, he was *not* a papa, and his
affairs were in a terrible muddle, and Peregrine
would be damned if he whistled a fortune down the
wind. He abandoned the Bible in favor of Mr. Shakespeare. "I am not angry, but disappointed. *Fly away,
fly away, breath; I am slain by a fair cruel maid!'* I fear that
you think more of your papa than myself."

Sarah-Louise was shocked. Naturally she loved her

papa—did not everyone love their papa?—and of course she understood that her papa thought that he knew best. But Peregrine—why, Peregrine was a deity descended to earth who deigned to speak with her, and she wished only that he would not be so *insistent*. "Once Papa sees that all is well, he will g-go away."

Sarah-Louise was all blushes. Her red cheeks and green dress gave her somewhat of the aspect of a holly bush. Peregrine was so provoked that he could not think of a single line of poetry. Her chicken-heartedness exceeded all belief.

"You *are* angry." Sarah-Louise studied her reticule, which she had twisted into a tangle of wire and mesh. "I was afraid that you would be."

"You are afraid of your own shadow!" hissed Peregrine, mindful of the footmen. "I suppose it is too much to hope that you might display some backbone! Or perhaps you have grown tired of my presence. You no longer regard me as a novelty—a poet, after all! One who saw you as his muse! One who was willing to forego all other heir—all other females!—and devote himself to you. I see how it is. You have been *toying* with me, and now your papa's arrival gives you the perfect opportunity—the perfect excuse!—to cast me aside."

Sarah-Louise gazed at her admirer in astonishment. So did the footmen goggle, because Mr. Teasdale's voice had risen with the force of his indignation, until the elder poked the younger and they stared again across the street. "I never!" she said.

Peregrine realized that he was glaring at the young woman about to be responsible for him going naked in the street, and adapted an amorous look instead.

"Forgive me. I was carried away by the force of my emotion. '*Crushed in the winepress of passion!*'" He raised her gloved hand to his lips.

Sarah-Louise snatched her hand away. "Pray remember where we are! My aunt is just inside the shop."

Hang it, but she was a coward! Peregrine reminded himself of the pecuniary advantages of marriage to so meek a little—large—mouse. "*It is no longer a passion hidden in my heart; it is Venus herself fastened to her prey,*'" he said. "Miss Inchquist, please say that you will be mine."

All this passion stuff sounded uncomfortable to Sarah-Louise. In one moment, Mr. Teasdale loaded her with vows and protestations, and caresses if she would let him, and in the next got to dagger-drawing and ripping up at her. "I already have quite enough people scolding me," she said aloud.

Oho! Here was some spirit. Peregrine found he didn't care for it. Unless he wished to bungle the thing completely, he must keep that opinion to himself. Miss Inchquist would be obliged to knuckle down soon enough once they were wed. "Forgive me," he repeated, and reached again for her hand. "It was the thought of losing you that unhinged my tongue. I know I am but a mere poet, and surely you could look higher, but believe me when I tell you '*Passion is a sort of fever in the mind, which ever leaves us weaker than it found us.*' Dear one '*Let me to thy bosom fly!*' You have quite stole my heart."

Sarah-Louise pulled back her hand before Mr. Teasdale could press it to his chest, perhaps in proof that beneath all that marcella and starched linen a heart did indeed beat. She did not wish to give offense, and so did not tell Mr. Teasdale that she wished he would go away, not permanently, but just for a little bit. It was very difficult to think clearly when the object of one's affections was going on about winepresses and bosoms and birds in flight.

Miss Inchquist was not alone in thinking the conversation had gone on long enough. The elder footman cleared his throat. "My aunt!" murmured Sarah-Louise. Peregrine leapt up from the bench as if bee-stung.

When Lady Denham exited the corsetiere's shop, followed by a little clerk, she saw only a retreating lime-green back. Impossible to mistake that sartorial sense, that prancing step. "Was that the fashionable fribble?" she asked, as the clerk loaded down the footmen with further parcels. "Did he speak with you? Teasdale is a vain, silly fellow, but harmless, I suppose. What have you done to your reticule, girl?"

Was Peregrine vain and silly? Sarah-Louise looked at her reticule. "I do not know."

"Shoddy workmanship! Never mind, we shall buy you another." Lady Denham linked her arm through that of her niece. Her ladyship was in an excellent mood, result of her recent purchase of a Shield For The Bosom, which promised to enable the wearer to display the most graceful form imaginable, and a new Short Stay which she was anxious to apply once she got home and lay down on the floor so that her abigail might place a foot on the small of her back to gain sufficient purchase to draw the laces tight. Too, she flattered herself that she had most artfully furthered the notion of marriage with Mr. Sutton to her niece.

Sarah-Louise might be tall and freckled, and as well

very shy, but she could not be said to have more hair than sense. Before Lady Denham could reintroduce her favorite subject, Sarah-Louise spoke. "I think Mr. Sutton may have a partiality for Lady Georgiana. He *did* pay her particular attention at your rout."

As had Lord Warwick paid the wench attention. Lady Georgiana was revealing herself as a very *greedy* sort of female. Odd, she was not at all what one would think of as a *femme fatale*.

Lady Denham frowned. Sarah-Louise dared to hope. "Pish tush!" said Lady Denham, thus causing further disappointment. "Sutton was only amusing himself. You look distressed, niece. It is the way of gentlemen to amuse themselves, you must know that. And if you do not know it, you *should* know it. Come, we shall have an ice, and I will tell you all!"

Twenty-three

The wicked Magnus Eliot went about his customary business, flirting with the ladies, and rather more than flirting with his mistresses of the moment; winning heavily at hazard, and proving rather less lucky at piquet. As was his habit, Magnus ended the evening with more funds in pocket than when he had begun. Whatever else he might be—blackguard, philanderer, seducer—Magnus was also a coolheaded gambler with a great deal of nerve and common sense. Unlike the majority of his fellow players, Magnus knew to stop before Lady Luck turned against him, and he lost what he had won.

That moment came earlier than usual this evening, and Magnus bid his *adieux* to the select gambling club which he had chosen this evening to grace with his presence, and his clever hands. Thought of further revels did not appeal, and Magnus turned his footsteps toward home. He had hired a house in the fashionable part of town, for which he paid rather less than fourteen guineas a week, the owner of the establishment having been so ill-advised as to play with him at cards.

Magnus climbed the polished stone steps, entered the Palladian front door, handed his manservant his

hat and gloves and topcoat. Then he made his way to
the library. Later, he would claim that premonition
prompted him. The truth is that Magnus wished to
savor a glass of his fine, smuggled French brandy before he turned in for the night.

The library was a fine chamber, with book-lined
walls and heavy oak furniture and stuffed leather
chairs. In one of those chairs, a gentleman sat. In one
hand he held a brandy snifter, in the other a dueling
pistol. The pistol was pointed straight at Magnus's
heart, and the hand which held it was not entirely
steady. Perspiration beaded the intruder's forehead.

Magnus closed the door behind him. He might
have experienced more concern had he not recognized the intruder, although he did not like the sight
of that gun. The Hallidays had most unique ways of
striking up conversations. "Have you also come to
speak to me about the whatsis?" he inquired.

"The what?" Andrew was confused.

"The whatsis," Magnus repeated. "That is what your
sister calls it, at any rate. Or perhaps you wished to appeal to my better nature. Your sister might have told
you to spare yourself the effort."

Andrew swallowed a gulp of his brandy. "I do not
wish to talk to you about my sister," he said, in tones
that were somewhat slurred. "And to blazes with your
better nature, and for that matter, with you! I came
here to steal the emerald—whatsis!—back, but I can't
seem to find the blasted thing. Or perhaps I *could*, if
I got up from this chair, but I've hurt my blasted leg."

Magnus recalled that young Lieutenant Halliday
walked with a limp. He glanced around the library,
which was in considerable disarray. "You didn't find
the thing because I am not so addlepated as to have it

here. My man didn't tell me I had a visitor. How did you get in?"

Andrew waved the pistol toward an open window. "If the bubble-brain could do it, then why shouldn't I?" he said obscurely, causing Mr. Eliot to try and remember if any lovelies had scaled the walls of his rented house to enter through a window, which would have been very strange behavior, in light of the fact that he would gladly welcome them properly through the front door.

Andrew was still talking. "Even with a curst lame leg. 'Twas nothing like scaling the walls of the fortress at Badajoz. Huge ochre walls and angular bastions thirty feet high. Kestrels nesting in the castle towers. Frogs croaking nearby. Did you know that Badajoz was wrested from the Moors in 1229?" The room swam around him. Why was he sitting in this chair? Andrew remembered that his leg had given out. "I had to break the glass."

Magnus didn't make the mistake of thinking all that ailed his visitor was an overindulgence in fine brandy. The boy looked very ill. Magnus didn't underestimate the danger of the pistol, not because he feared its owner, but because Lieutenant Halliday's hand was shaking so badly that the damned thing might go off by accident.

Magnus removed himself from the line of fire. "How long have you been here?" he asked.

Andrew shook his head, which was grown very heavy. "We sacked the town. Men dressed themselves up in silk gowns, garlanded themselves with strings of pretty Spanish shoes, carried off hams and tongues and loaves. Where have you been, Eliot? I wondered if you would ever come home."

Magnus fervently wished he hadn't. He very much disliked the wild manner in which his uninvited guest was waving that pistol about. "Having failed to rob me, you decided to talk to me instead?" he asked.

Andrew frowned in an attempt at concentration. "Something like that."

"Good!" Magnus availed himself of some badly needed brandy. "In that case, do you think you might put away that damned barking-iron? It's a trifle disconcerting to look at you over a gun barrel." He quirked an eyebrow. "Unless you mean to call me out for conversing with your sister the other day?"

Andrew put down the pistol, which he had forgotten he was holding. "I don't want to call anybody out. It's a bloody stupid custom. If people wish to kill each other, they should go to war. Although war is like a duel, isn't it, only it's between countries. This war started because the Spanish Royals were quarrelling among themselves, and Napoleon stepped in, and look at us now." He raised his empty hand to wipe perspiration from his face. "Anyway, I daresay it wasn't *your* idea to speak with my sister. Knowing Georgie, she probably spoke to you first."

"So she did." Magnus glanced at the brandy snifter which his guest still held, and looked like he might momentarily drop. "I don't think you should be drinking that."

Andrew, too, glanced at the snifter. "Why not?" he asked. "You might be surprised at some of the things I've drunk. Not now, but in the Peninsula. Why—"

"Never mind!" Magnus was less interested in the Peninsula than in his uninvited guest's obvious ill health. "Dammit, man, you're as sick as a dog."

Dog? Andrew peered around for Lump, who he

didn't think he'd brought along. Lump could hardly have scaled the fortress wall. Maybe he had left the beast outside. No, that wouldn't serve. Lump would have raised a ruckus before now. Maybe the dog had run off. Georgie would be made very unhappy if she lost her pet again. Therefore, Andrew was very sure he hadn't brought him along. He shook his head. "No. No dog," he said.

His guest had let go of his pistol. Prudently, Magnus pushed it aside. "You meant to rob me," he remarked.

Had he? Andrew could not remember. "That would be dishonorable," he said, just before he closed his eyes and slid unconscious to the floor. Magnus swore a great oath, and rang for his servant, and ordered his carriage brought around.

Thus it came about that Tibble was roused so abruptly from his slumbers that he answered the front door clad in his night shirt and cap to find yet another strange gentleman demanding to see his mistress. Tibble was shocked. Surely Lady Georgiana and her admirers must know it wasn't at all the thing to be knocking up a lady at this hour of night.

"Cut the cackle!" snapped the stranger, and strode toward his carriage, to return with the semi-conscious Andrew under his arm. Tibble abandoned his apprehensions, along with his nightcap and his dignity, and helped the stranger carry Andrew into his chamber, and lay him on the bed. "I'll get Mistress Georgie!" he said, and ran to do so, and awaken the rest of the household.

And thus it also came about that Magnus Eliot met with Miss Halliday in a bedchamber, his clothing in disarray, and she in her nightrail. Under other circumstances Magnus might have enjoyed the encounter very well. However, they were not alone. Tibble and Agatha and Janie, each in nighttime attire, clustered around the bed. Tibble held a basin of cool water, while Janie wrung out damp cloths, which Agatha applied to Andrew's feverish brow. Lump, recovered now from his adventure with the apple tart, had to be restrained from leaping on the bed. Only Marigold was absent, not only because Tibble had omitted to inform her of this latest disaster, but also because Agatha had liberally laced her negus with laudanum. "I've sent for a sawbones," Magnus said to Georgie. "You can't deal with this yourself."

Georgie agreed. She had never seen Andrew so ill. "I don't understand. How did you come to—" Her gaze flew to Magnus's face. "Oh, no. He didn't—"

"He broke into my house looking for that damnable doohickey." Even in his current frame of mind, which was made up of equal parts annoyance and exasperation, Magnus could not help but appreciate the manner in which Miss Halliday's hair curled wildly around her head. She looked as though she had just got out of bed. Yes, and so she had, and Magnus would like to get back into bed with her, and not because he was so very tired.

This was hardly a fit moment in which to be thinking of such matters, but Mr. Eliot was incorrigible. "It is very fortunate for young Lieutenant Halliday that I hold his sister in such high regard," he said, with a hint of his dimpled smile. "Else I would have had the young whelp up before the magistrates. He meant to rob me."

What had Andrew been thinking? Georgie stared at the still figure on the bed. "He was also talking a great deal of nonsense about the Peninsula," Magnus added. He held out the dueling-pistol, which caused no small consternation in the room, and recalled to Tibble his desire to knock down a certain gentleman's applecart.

"Stubble it!" said Magnus, and handed the gun to Georgie. "I assume this is yours. Your brother also mentioned twelve-pounders and limbers and caissons."

Georgie sighed, and accepted the dueling pistol, which was one of a set that had belonged to her father. "Yes, I know. Corpses that stayed warm all night. Fiery lakes of smoking blood. I don't know what we are to do for poor Andrew. Nor do I know what to say to you about my brother's behavior, Mr. Eliot. Had Andrew been in his right senses he would never have tried to—to do what he did! I offer you my apologies, sir, in his behalf. And I thank you for returning him to us. If there is anything I can do to make it up to you—" Magnus's blue eyes twinkled. Georgie recalled to whom she was speaking. "Never mind!"

Regardless of the audience, Magnus clasped Georgie's bare hand and raised it to his lips. "I am a marvel of discretion, my darling," he murmured softly, against her palm. "When the stakes are high enough." The doctor arrived then, and Mr. Eliot took his leave.

Twenty-four

Upon his return to Brighton, Lord Warwick paused only long enough to remove his travel-dirt and take a bite to eat before proceeding to Miss Halliday's house. The streets were crowded with pedestrians and traffic, and his progress was slow. Therefore he arrived on Georgie's pristine doorstep in an exasperated mood.

Tibble opened the door. Lord Warwick prepared to explain yet again who he was. Instead, the butler—whose wig was perched rakishly to one side—greeted Garth as though he were an old friend. "Lor', sir, it's that glad I am to see you! Master Andrew has come within ame's ace of turning up his toes. No need to go on the fidgets—he ain't gone off yet to kingdom come, for all the sawbones' brains are in his ballocks, or so Agatha says! I'm afraid we'll have the quacksalver back here for Mistress Georgie afore long, because she's fretting her guts to fiddle-strings. Maybe *you* can get her to take some rest afore she wears herself down to a nubbin!" So saying, Tibble led the visitor to Andrew's bedchamber, and threw open the door.

The room was small, dominated by a heavy wooden wardrobe and a large, carved four-post bedstead. Despite the warmth of the day, a fire burned in the hearth, and the windows were closed. The air smelled of juniper oil and peppermint. A young man lay sleeping—at least Garth hoped he was sleeping—on the bed. Georgie sat watching him from a chair by the window. Lump sprawled like a great deflated pillow in one corner of the room.

Upon glimpsing her visitor, Georgie rose. "Garth! You have come back," she said, and then grasped Lump's collar before the hound could launch himself at the newcomer, whom he recognized as his liberator from the small tack room at the inn. "Lump, lie down!"

The dog collapsed again into a dejected posture. Georgie hurried across the room and flung herself into Garth's arms. He held her to him and frowned at the goggle-eyed butler. Reluctantly, Tibble withdrew and repaired to the kitchen, where he would tell Agatha and Janie that Mistress Georgie was apparently falling arsy-varsy in *amours* with a lowly groom.

Georgie clung to Lord Warwick as if he were the only stable force in an increasingly chaotic landscape. Andrew had been terribly ill, and she had been very much afraid. Through the night he had alternated between unconsciousness and periods of wakefulness that were almost more terrible, because he raved about the Peninsula. Fuentes, Almeida, Wallace and the wild Connaught Rangers, the sudden hailstorm at Albuera—all were as distinctly in Andrew's memory as if he were still there. And also as vividly in Georgie's imagination, alas, for she could have happily foregone the experience of going into battle with bayonet drawn, and regiments with not enough men left alive to bury their dead. Nor would she herself ever have

imagined a breakfast of beer and onions. She pressed
her face against Lord Warwick's chest.

If Georgie did not look, as Tibble might have put it,
like a death's head upon a mop-stick, her gray eyes
were still shadowed, and her lovely features drawn.
"My dear," Garth murmured, "I am so very sorry that
I had to leave you alone." This was clearly no fit moment to tell her of the reasons for that departure,
though he longed to do so.

This comment, unfortunately, reminded Georgie of
the reason why Lord Warwick had left town, which in
her mind had to do with Lady Denham's gardens, and
the kissing they had done there. Here she was, clutching at him like she was drowning. Did she not let go,
Garth would probably leave town again. Georgie did
not want Garth to leave town again, even if he was determined to keep her at arm's length. She removed
herself from his chest.

"There was nothing you could have done," she said.
"Andrew has been prey to recurrent fevers ever since
he came home from the Peninsula, though I have
never seen him so ill as this. I confess that I have been
frightened almost out of my wits." She gazed at the
bed. "The doctor has bled him, over Agatha's
protests. Agatha does not approve of the application
of leeches. She prefers her own remedies, such as
lemon water and sage tea and borage syrup, and
heaven knows what else. The doctor was most insistent, and so I agreed. Andrew's illness is prone to
recur when he is distressed. Garth, I cannot help but
blame myself for this."

"Don't be absurd!" Georgie had not moved so far
away from him that Garth could not draw her back
into his arms. He did so, and smoothed down the wild

mass of curls that tickled his nose. "It was good you had the sawbones in."

It was also good that Georgie had so comfortable a chest to rest against. "That was Magnus Eliot's doing," said Georgie, and then could have bit her tongue, because she felt Garth stiffen. "Don't bother to tell me I shouldn't know Magnus Eliot, Garth, because as it so happens I do know him already, and Andrew was, er, with him when he became so ill, and Mr. Eliot was very kind!"

Garth had not reached the point of scolding, yet. He was still in shock. "Your brother was with Eliot?" Surely young Lieutenant Halliday wasn't such a flat as to fall into the clutches of a Captain Sharp. "Georgie, what has become of your family's fortune? Your father was a wealthy man. Although I know it is not my place to ask."

"The money is in trust for Andrew. So that he may have the means to someday set up his own household." Reluctantly, Georgie stepped away from Garth. "If you are thinking Andrew a pigeon for Mr. Eliot's plucking, you misjudge them both. For one thing, I have not yet told Andrew of the trust, because I know he will cut up stiff, and insist I share the money with him, which I will not do. For another, Andrew has no taste for gaming. If you must know the truth, Andrew was attempting a robbery. Mr. Eliot could have had him up before the magistrates, but instead he brought him home."

"Attempting a *robbery*?" Garth sat down abruptly in the chair. "Let me guess! This is to do with the bird-witted 'Mrs. Smith.'"

"Lower your voice!" Georgie gestured toward the bed. "It was not Marigold's doing, precisely. Andrew came up with the notion all on his own, which makes sense if you think about it, because the idea of robbing Magnus Eliot is clearly the workings of an overheated brain, and that Marigold has a brain at all we have come to doubt!" She sighed. "I should not have said that. Truly, I do not wish you to concern yourself with this nonsense, Garth. You have enough troubles of your own."

So he did, and Georgie was chief among them. Soon enough his name would be again on every tongue. Garth had made up his mind that the devil might fly away with the gossips, so far as he was concerned. Georgie, however, was another matter. He did not wish that she should see her dirty linen aired in public, as his had been and was about to be again. But while he was trying to shield her from the consequences of their relationship, she had involved herself first with Carlisle Sutton, and now Magnus Eliot. Magnus Eliot! Garth had no doubt why Mr. Eliot had not had Georgie's brother dragged off to gaol, and it wasn't from the goodness of his heart. "If Mr. Eliot has something that belongs to Marigold," he reasoned, "why doesn't she just ask him to give it back?"

Georgie shook her head. "Now *you* are not thinking, Garth. Marigold and Magnus Eliot? Speak of a pigeon for the plucking! I have gone to great lengths to prevent that meeting taking place. And it is not that he has something that belongs to her, exactly."

If "Mrs. Smith" did not know Magnus Eliot, how came he to have something that was hers? Before Garth could ask, Andrew tossed and mumbled on the bed. Among other incoherent utterances, Garth could have sworn he heard, "Twenty-five thousand pounds."

Georgie had heard it also. She flinched, but Andrew said no more. "Is this whatever-it-is why 'Mrs. Smith' has gone into hiding?" Garth asked.

If only "Mrs. Smith" had hidden herself better on numerous occasions! "Indirectly," Georgie said. "She is avoiding Carlisle Sutton. You already know that it was Mr. Sutton's uncle to whom Marigold was wed. Thank God he has not discovered that she is staying here. Pray ask me no more questions! I have already said more than I should."

Garth did not consider that Georgie had said half enough. There remained, for instance, the matter of her feelings for himself. He would have liked to hear her say that she had missed him just a little bit.

Not that this was any fit moment to press her about such trifles. "You are very loyal to your friend," Garth said, and rose from the chair. "A great deal more loyal, I think, than she would be to you."

Georgie could not refute the truth of this statement. "Just because Marigold is faithful only to herself doesn't mean I have leave also to go back on my word."

Garth did not respond, but walked closer to the bed, and stood gazing down at Andrew. Lump raised his head and snuffled. The fire crackled in the hearth.

Georgie did not like it that Garth had grown so silent. She had wished, unfairly, that he would tell her that her troubles were nothing in comparison with his own. Or alternately that he would take her by the shoulders and force her to confess precisely what those troubles were. The fact that he did not do so annoyed her. Too, though she had taken the time to change out of her nightclothes, Georgie had not slept and was consequently very tired. "Has the cat got your tongue?" she inquired. Then she had to stop and persuade Lump that he must lie back down, because there was no feline intruder in the room with them. "Or is it that you have nothing to say if you cannot lecture me?"

There were a great many things Lord Warwick wished to say to Georgie, none of them appropriate in that moment, unless it was to comment that she was behaving like a fishwife. He was not going to be drawn into a brangle so that she might vent her spleen. "I wish that you might confide in me," he said merely. "Since you cannot bring yourself to do so, I will impose myself upon you no longer. Clearly you have more urgent matters with which to contend. Should you change your mind, you know where you may find me, Georgie." He paused at the doorway, hoping that she might ask him not to leave. She said nothing, and he walked out of the room, to go downstairs and vent his own spleen by scolding the remaining members of Georgie's household for allowing their mistress to wear herself to the bone.

Georgie stared at the empty doorway. Why had she not confided in Garth when she had the chance? If anyone could untangle this coil, it was Lord Warwick, but pride had stopped her tongue. Georgie could not forget that every time Garth kissed her, he then drew away. This time she had not let him kiss her—now that she thought on it, he had not seemed to *wish* to kiss her, which further deflated her spirits—and he had gone away all the same. The fact that she had *sent* him away was quite beside the point. A gentleman who cared about her even just a little bit would not have paid attention to her nonsense. Georgie stomped on a burning ember that had fallen on the rug.

Twenty-five

As a result of Lord Warwick's scolding, Marigold was feeling very guilty. Marigold did not lack a conscience, merely needed periodic reminding of what was and was not right. Lord Warwick had reminded her of these things so forcefully that Marigold had decided, despite all they had in common, that she and his lordship wouldn't suit. It was a pity; Warwick was a handsome gentleman, and so very rich that he wouldn't miss a paltry few thousand pounds. He was also so damnably high in the instep that one would never ask him for a loan. At least Marigold would not. Perhaps Georgie—

No. Georgie would never ask to borrow money she had no hope of paying back. Perhaps Lord Warwick would just *give* Georgie the money if he knew she needed it. Marigold toyed with the idea, then cast it aside. Georgie was too frugal to fall so deeply under the hatches, and Lord Warwick was most unlikely to haul Marigold's own coals out of the fire. He had made it very clear that he thought this entire muddle was entirely Marigold's fault, which was most unfair of him, because it hadn't been Marigold's idea that Andrew rob Magnus Eliot. Although now that she thought on the notion, it had a certain appeal. If she could steal the accursed emerald, she could then give it to Carlisle Sutton without having to part with twenty-five thousand pounds. Or she could take the emerald and keep it for herself and make a speedy departure from town. An enterprising lady could live for quite some time on the proceeds of a bauble worth twenty-five thousand pounds.

As Marigold thus cudgeled her brain, she paced around Georgie's drawing room. She was not alone in the chamber. Andrew was ensconced on the uncomfortable striped couch, with a blanket over his legs, and an assortment of Agatha's medications—flea-wort mixed with rosewater and a little sugar candy, good to cool the thirst; sage tea with which to gargle; syrups of borage and endive—on a nearby table. Lump was stretched out on the rug in front of the sofa. Not trusting Magnus Eliot's sawbones, Lord Warwick had sent over his own man, and if that worthy didn't pronounce Andrew as fit as a fiddle, he assured them that the worst was past. Marigold took leave to question that. Andrew in his convalescence was as cross as crabs, driving everyone to distraction with his demands and his fidgets, with the exception of herself, because she wasn't listening to a word he said.

Of those words, there were plenty. Andrew had taken it upon himself to relate to his companion the entire history of the Peninsular War, not because he wished to elevate her mind, but because he hoped if he bored her to distraction, she might go away. Andrew was tired of being fussed over by well-meaning people, and although he could not help but be grateful to them for their efforts, he wished they would cease to try and coddle him. He was a grown man, was he not? Even if he had made a cake of himself as regarded Magnus Eliot. Now he would have to thank Mr. Eliot, as well as ask him to please not encourage Georgie sitting on his lap. Like Lord Warwick before him, Andrew had no doubt as to why Magnus Eliot had brought him home instead of before a magistrate. He paused in his explanation of how Napoleon had driven Queen Marie out of Portugal, thereby dominating the Peninsula himself. "I shall never understand females!" Andrew remarked.

Not unreasonably, Marigold thought Andrew still spoke of Queen Marie of Portugal, and so did not comment. She stepped over Lump, and sat down in a straight-backed chair. Marigold could not deny that her presence here had caused Georgie a great deal of trouble. Maybe she *should* just disappear.

Marigold was not listening to him. This circumstance irritated Andrew. "There's no point you being here if you're going to sit there air-dreaming! Because to say the truth, I'd just as lief be by myself."

So would Marigold rather be by herself, but Georgie had gone to fetch some medicine, and Marigold had promised in her absence to tend the invalid. Personally, she thought everyone was making a great fuss over nothing. No one enjoyed perfect health all the time. "Yes, and so would I!" she retorted. "But neither one of us is going to get what we want in this instance, because I vowed to Georgie that I would not leave you alone. You know, it is no wonder you are in such low spirits if all you think about is such dreary stuff as piles of warm corpses and bloody lakes! I do not scruple to tell you that if you continue to go on like that I shall be sick of the mulligrubs myself."

Andrew was startled that anyone would remonstrate

with him about his reminiscences. "You wasn't there!" he said.

"No," retorted Marigold, "but I have been a great many other places, and not all of them were *nice!* And though I may not have seen my comrades fall in battle, I *have* lost three husbands. And I was fond of them all, in my own way. Though I know you think I am a shatterbrain, it is not true that I don't *care*. I care about Georgie and about you, because you are her brother, even though I know you don't like me above half." She looked at Lump. "I even care about that confounded dog! It is very selfish to be always thinking of oneself, Andrew, and I should know, because I have been told it often enough. It is plain to me that between the two of us, we are worrying Georgie half to death, and though I do not know what to do about it, it still makes me feel very bad."

Andrew didn't know how to respond to this scolding from so unexpected a source. Since a great deal of what she said was true, he could hardly take offense. "I allow," he muttered, "that I've been in a bad skin."

Marigold didn't see why she should be the only one to feel guilty. Besides, it was time Andrew was served up some home truths. "You have been as surly as a bear," she informed him. "A crosspatch who has everyone tiptoeing about as if they trod on eggs. All because some bad things happened to you in the past. Bad things happen to everyone, Andrew. It is as though your wagon is stuck in the mud, and you are sitting in it feeling sorry for yourself, instead of making an effort to get *out* of the mud and discover what lies further down the road." Herself, Marigold had always wished to discover what lay further down the road. Providing that those things didn't involve being clapped in gaol, or hanged.

Andrew, like everyone else, considered Marigold a goose-cap. Now it appeared that even goose-caps might possess a grain of common sense. What she had said about his experiences in the Peninsula rang painfully true.

Perhaps Marigold might shed some light for him on another matter. "Maybe you would explain something to me," Andrew said. "If you were a female—I mean, of course you are a female, but if you was very young—"

Andrew must still have a fever. Marigold rose from her chair to ungently slap a cool cloth on the invalid's brow and force lemon water down his throat. "I have not yet," she said in freezing tones, "grown long in the tooth."

"Beg pardon!" When he had done choking, Andrew pushed aside the cloth that Marigold had dropped over his eyes. "That ain't what I meant. If mean, if you was *really* young, say about sixteen."

Once she got past the suggestion that she was an old ewe dressed lamb-fashion in a confection of sea-green, Marigold was intrigued. She nudged Andrew's feet aside and perched on the edge of the couch. "I remember what it was like to be sixteen. I was already married. Proceed!"

She had been already married? Maybe sixteen wasn't so young as Andrew had thought. "What I wanted to know was, do you think you would be wishful of running off with someone who wrote sonnets to your nose?"

Marigold wondered whom they were discussing. She didn't think it was herself. Since Andrew was not well, Marigold didn't tell him that she *had* eloped, not that poor Leo had written sonnets to her nose. Leo had written her no sonnets at all, but he had done other things wondrously well.

At the thought of those other things, Marigold felt sad. Never again would someone make her feel like her poor Leo had. "I don't think I should wish to run off to Gretna Green," Marigold said kindly. "It sounds vastly uncomfortable, does it not?" She might have continued, had not a sound come from the open doorway. Marigold turned. Tibble stood there, and a very tall, very freckled young lady dressed in muslin striped with lilac, a white bonnet tied under the chin with a ribbon bow.

"I am so sorry to interrupt!" said the young lady, as Tibble cleared his throat. "We had heard that Lieutenant Halliday was ill, and wished to pay our respects."

In that same moment, Tibble found his voice. "Miss Inchquist and Mr. Sutton come to call," he announced.

Oh, heavens! Carlisle Sutton *here?* As the gentleman appeared in the doorway, Marigold dived behind the couch. It was hardly an adequate hiding place. Her sea-green skirts clearly showed between the bottom of the sofa and the rug. Marigold crawled under the sofa, grabbed the hem of Andrew's blanket, and tugged it down closer to the floor.

Sarah-Louise deduced from the lady's strange behavior that their arrival had interrupted a lovers' tryst. Her cheeks flamed. "Pray forgive our intrusion. We have come at a bad time."

Miss Inchquist looked deuced uncomfortable. And Mr. Sutton about as pleasant as the pains of death. "Not at all!" Andrew said weakly. "As you say, I have been ill. But I'm feeling better now." Beneath him, he felt a thump on the couch. "That is, I am not yet plump currant! In point of fact, I'm feeling downright sickly! You won't wish to come closer for fear you might catch what I've got."

Carlisle Sutton was angrier in that moment than he could ever remember having been before. He was also well aware of who crouched behind the striped couch. No wonder Lady Georgiana had been so curious about the progress of his search for his uncle's widow. She and her brother had been hiding the fugitive all along. "You think you are feeling sickly *now,*" he said in menacing tones, as he advanced into the room.

That threatening voice was familiar. Lump raised his head and surveyed Carlisle. He recognized the gentleman with whom he had enjoyed a splendid adventure in the Promenade Grove. The same gentleman who, after that adventure, had locked him away in a tack room. An easy-going, amiable creature in most instances, Lump drew the line at being locked away. The appearance of this gentleman in this place made Lump think he was going to be locked away again.

He wouldn't have it. Especially not in his own house. Since no one else made any effort to defend him, Lump leapt to his feet and bared his teeth. "Lump!" said Andrew, without conviction, because he felt his headache coming back.

Growling, stiff-legged, Lump advanced toward the door. "Pardon, sir," observed Tibble, "but he don't seem to like you much. And I can't say as he don't bite, 'cause though he hasn't yet it's sure as check that he may do so at any time!"

Carlisle recognized the dog also, and with no more

fondness than Lump regarded him. The perfidious
Lady Georgiana gave shelter also to this wretched
hound? Mr. Sutton must have a word with her ladyship as soon as he settled his account with her
houseguest.

Still, the dog advanced, his wicked teeth a-gleam.
Still, Carlisle Sutton stood his ground. Matters were at
an impasse.

What was it about gentlemen, that they must strut
and snarl? Not that Lump was a gentleman, far from
it, but still he was male. "You, sir, sit!" Sarah-Louise
said to Lump. Startled by her tone, the dog paused in
mid-stride. She grabbed at his collar. "And you, Mr.
Sutton, leave while you may!" Tibble hurried to open
the front door.

Reluctantly, Carlisle obeyed. Sarah-Louise sighed in
relief. But no sooner did Mr. Sutton pass out of his
sight than Lump barked, jerked away from Miss
Inchquist, and set off in pursuit. "Stop!" cried Sarah-
Louise, and ran after the dog.

Cautiously, Marigold emerged from her hiding
place and shook out her rumpled skirts. Andrew sank
back on the couch and pulled the damp cloth down
over his eyes.

Twenty-six

Quentin Inchquist deposited himself gingerly upon one of his sister's carved-Sphinx chairs, an article that had not been designed for a gentleman of his girth. Unlike Lady Denham, Quentin had no fondness for the current Egyptian craze, and did not see why Napoleon's ill-advised attempt to weaken England's hold in India by taking Egypt should be commemorated in the furniture on which he sat. Himself, Quentin wished that the Corsican Upstart would march into Russia, and get lost. It was not a matter of international politics that had brought Quentin to Brighton, however, but guilt attendant upon having willy-nilly shipped his daughter off to visit her aunt. Quentin was genuinely fond of his daughter, great rabbity freckle-faced damsel that she was; and for her he wanted only the best. However, he also had a fair notion of what that best might be. Sarah-Louise was no beauty, and her papa wasn't such a flat as to let her be married off to someone who valued only her pocketbook. *"Conquest?"* he repeated, because his sister had just informed him that Sarah-Louise had a most eligible gentleman dangling at her apron-strings. "Bring your head down out of the clouds, Amice. A good biddable girl Sarah-Louise may be, but not one to inspire Cupid to let loose his darts."

"That shows all *you* know!" Lady Denham smoothed the sleeve of her pale yellow spotted morning dress. "I have no doubt that Mr. Sutton may be brought up to scratch. Sarah-Louise is with him even now. They have gone to look in on a friend who is ill. A military gentleman."

Quentin didn't know that he liked the notion of his daughter associating with a military gentleman. Some military gentlemen were better than others, however. "He ain't with Prinny's Regiment, is he? Because if he is—"

"Mr. Sutton?" Lady Denham arched her plucked brows. "Carlisle isn't in the military at all. He is a very wealthy gentleman—a relative of mine by marriage, so I should know!—who has made a fortune in India. He will be a steadying influence on Sarah-Louise."

Quentin didn't know that his daughter needed steadying. She already had about as much backbone as a spinach leaf. "Has Sarah-Louise developed a partiality?" he asked.

Lady Denham tittered at this absurd suggestion. "A partiality! What has that to do with anything? It is not as though people of our class marry for love. Carlisle is old enough to know his own mind."

His sister liked this Carlisle fellow very well. Quentin thought she might wish to marry him herself. "*How* old?" he asked.

"In his early forties, I should think." Lady Denham frowned. "Why do you ask?"

Quentin did not answer. Privately, he thought he did not wish to send his daughter off to India with a nabob of almost his own age. His sister was an entirely different matter. But he would give the fellow the benefit of the doubt. "Who's the military gent?"

"Lieutenant Andrew Halliday. Of the 88th, I think it was. He was wounded in the Peninsula, and invalided out of his regiment. The family's antecedents are well enough, but I doubt there's money there." Memory of her rout tugged at her brain, and Lady Denham frowned. "There is some scandal attached. Lieutenant Halliday is not a pretender to your daughter's hand, however, but merely a friend. Sarah-Louise has made many new friends. Beside Lieutenant Halliday, there is Peregrine Teasdale—"

"Teasdale!" Quentin bounced so forcibly in his chair that it creaked in protest. "A posturing popinjay who goes about spouting the most nonsensical drivel? A fashionable fribble? A *twiddlepoop?*"

Lady Denham had to agree that her brother's description wasn't far off the mark. Still, she protested, "I thought the young man unexceptionable enough."

With some difficulty, Quentin pried himself out of his long-suffering chair. "That just goes to show," he said acerbically, "that females shouldn't try and *think!* Where did you say Sarah-Louise is now? Because I have a great deal to say to that young miss!"

It was perhaps fortunate for Mr. Inchquist's blood pressure, already elevated by mention of the twiddle-poopish Mr. Teasdale, that his sister could not reveal his daughter's precise present whereabouts. In point of fact, Sarah-Louise did not know her precise whereabouts either, other than that she was somewhere in Brighton, for in her efforts to contain Lump she had become quite lost. At least she had caught up with the hound—or he had allowed her to catch him—and so she was not entirely by herself. In an attempt to prevent him running off again, Sarah-Louise had fashioned the ribbon from her bonnet into a makeshift leash. Should Lump try and escape, the ribbon would hardly restrain him, but she hoped it might put some notion of compliance into his head.

The streets were crowded, for this was Race Week, and all the city was *en fête*. The Pavilion was crowded with Prinny's guests, and well-dressed crowds sauntered through the streets. The races attracted all Brighton, visitors and residents alike, as well as a great crowd of people who came especially for the yearly event. Not that Lump had led Sarah-Louise to the race course itself, a horseshoe-shaped affair about two miles in length, situated to the east of town, within sight of the sea. Instead, though Lump had not planned it, they had come to steep North Street, lined with coaching offices, and abustle with traffic.

Sarah-Louise had never before been in such a place. She gazed with astonishment at the flurry of vehicles all around her, from high-perch phaetons and Royal Mail coaches to a strawberry vendor's cart. The clatter of iron-shod hooves and wheels filled the air, along with varied cries and shouts.

None of the busy pedestrians paid the least attention to a lone, bewildered-looking young female. Sarah-Louise took hold of Lump's collar, just in case. She did not fear the dog would run away from her so much as she feared someone would steal her from him. Sheltered though she may have been, Sarah-Louise had heard tales—mainly from her papa—of what dire fates awaited young misses who did what they should not. Definitely, Sarah-Louise should not be wandering around Brighton unattended. Although it was hardly her fault that she could not find

Mr. Sutton. However, it *was* her fault that they had
gone to visit the Halidays, for she had persuaded Mr.
Sutton to escort her there. For one thing, Sarah-
Louise had hoped that by so doing she might
encourage Mr. Sutton to further his acquaintance
with Lady Georgiana. For another, she had hoped to
assure herself that Lieutenant Halliday was all right.
As apparently he was, because Sarah-Louise had overheard him asking a lady to elope. A most lovely lady,
the sort of lady Sarah-Louise could never hope to be
herself. No doubt the lady would have accepted, had
their sudden interruption not caused her to dive behind the couch. A queer thing, that, or perhaps not,
if one was the sort of lady prone to romantical high-
flights.

Sarah-Louise hoped that Lieutenant Halliday would
not elope. Not that it was any of her affair, but Sarah-
Louise didn't think the lovely couch-diving lady would
suit Lieutenant Halliday very well. As for who *would*
suit Lieutenant Halliday—Sarah-Louise bit her lip.
Being in love was not at all what she had expected.
She didn't feel at all like dancing on air, or bursting
into song, and birds didn't trill sweetly when Mr. Teasdale came into view. Perhaps this was because she had
to contrive so mightily to see him. Sarah-Louise was
not designed for intrigue and subterfuge. And then
she glimpsed a certain curricle weaving its way
through the crowd. Once seen, the curricle, drawn by
two gleaming black horses, was not soon forgot, for it
boasted a violet base and a vermillion chassis, and
blue iron-work. Sarah-Louise waved her bonnet and
called out, "Peregrine!"

From his perch atop his curricle, Mr. Teasdale—
returning from the race via a circuitous route that he

hoped would forestall any encounter with his creditors—saw Miss Inchquist. 'Twould have been difficult *not* to see Miss Inchquist, so tall was she, and striped with lilac, and waving a bedraggled bonnet. Where had she got that monstrous dog? Peregrine slapped the reins on his horses' rumps, and steered his curricle through the crowd. "Sarah-Louise! Miss Inchquist!" he cried.

He had seen them. Sarah-Louise sagged in relief. "Thank goodness! I had almost given up on Lump finding his way back home."

Peregrine was relieved also. He had sensed that Miss Inchquist's affections toward himself were cooling of late, which simply would not do, because her papa was so well to grass. Perhaps Sarah-Louise had forgotten that he had scolded her. Perhaps she had realized that someone so tall and dowdy-looking could not but expect an occasional scolding, if not worse. Perhaps she had snuck away in hopes of meeting him today—"Miss Inchquist!" Peregrine said again, and gracefully leapt down from his curricle. Lump, who had grown bored with just standing about, inched forward to familiarize himself with the vehicle's great wheels.

Fortunately, Mr. Teasdale did not notice the manner in which this acquaintance was accomplished, involving as it did the canine marking of territory by lifting a back leg. "Miss Inchquist, I find you in high bloom. *'Where're you tread, the blushing flow'rs shall rise/ And all things flourish where you turn your eye.'*"

Miss Inchquist didn't think Mr. Alexander Pope had such a female as herself in mind when he wrote those lines. Furthermore, she very much feared that she—or Peregrine—was making a spectacle, while

Lump was venturing entirely too close to the horses, inspiring them to snort and dance nervously about. "Never mind the flowers!" Sarah-Louise said, somewhat ungraciously. "Do you think you might take me—us!—home?"

Peregrine was chagrined to realize that he had excited no admiration in the object of his, if not affections, then intentions. Doubtless this lack of appreciation was the result of his bland attire. Due to the unhappy circumstance that his creditors had begun to exhibit a distressing insistence upon being paid, and he wished consequently to avoid drawing their attention to himself, Peregrine had dressed today in raiment considerably more subdued than customary for him: a brass-buttoned blue coat with buckskin pantaloons worn with Hessian boots, enlivened only by a vivid purple-and-green-plaid waistcoat. It was not a mistake that he would again soon make. Not that he cared a groat for Sarah-Louise's opinion. Had she any sense of fashion, she would not bedeck herself in stripes.

Why was Mr. Teasdale staring at her in that strange manner? Whatever had possessed him to don that atrocious waistcoat? "Are you going to take us up in your carriage?" Sarah-Louise inquired, impatiently. "Or leave us standing in the middle of the street?"

Peregrine could not care for her tone of voice, nor for the suggestion that he take a mangy dog up in his splendid curricle. He raised his quizzing glass. Magnified, the hound was that much more appalling. Damned if his teeth weren't big.

"No," said Peregrine, and let the glass drop. "No hounds. Not even for you will I have that—that creature!—in my rig."

Critically, Sarah-Louise eyed her admirer, who was proving himself appallingly poor-spirited. Perhaps she didn't wish to dwell in a garret with him after all. "Then I shan't get in your carriage, either," she said coolly. "In which case you are impeding us in our progress—not to mention holding up traffic!—and I wish you would go away." Sarah-Louise did not exaggerate. A number of carriages were lined up behind Peregrine's halted curricle. Those drivers who did make their way around him were inclined to curse.

Go away? Peregrine was horrified, not only by this sign of independent spirit in his intended wife, but also by the vision of her papa's plump pockets slipping out of his grasp. "Didn't mean it!" he said quickly. "*Where'er you walk, cool gales shall fan the glade./ Trees, where you sit, shall crowd into a shade.*'"

Sarah-Louise hoped the trees that crowded into Peregrine's carriage would leave room for her and Lump. "Very well, sir. You may take us home. You will know how to find my aunt's house."

Certainly, Peregrine could have found his way to Lady Denham's house, did he intend to go there, which he did not. Gallantly, he assisted Miss Inchquist into his curricle, and wedged her less-than-eager canine companion in after her, and behind them closed the door.

Twenty-seven

Mr. Sutton was indeed furthering his acquaintance with Lady Georgiana, although not in the manner Miss Inchquist had hoped. Georgie returned home with Andrew's medicine to find her little household turned upon its ear. Tibble met her in the hallway. His wig had by this time slid to the back of his head. "There's the right devil to pay, Miss Georgie!" he announced, and pointed a trembling finger toward the drawing room.

Georgie could not think what to make of this cryptic remark. She pulled off her bonnet and hurried into her drawing room, where she found Carlisle Sutton pacing the chamber like a caged beast, and Andrew stretched out on the sofa with a cloth over his face. Suspecting the worst, Georgie dropped her bonnet and the medicine, and hurried to his side. "Andrew!" she cried. "What has happened to him, Mr. Sutton? Has the doctor been sent for?"

Carlisle Sutton scowled at the lady whom he had once admired, and who was now revealed as having played the concave-suit. "The devil with the doctor! I should call in the magistrates instead."

Why should Carlisle Sutton be threatening to call the magistrates when it was Magnus Eliot whom Andrew had attempted to rob? Georgie felt her brother's brow, which was surprisingly cool. When she lifted the damp cloth from his face, Andrew grimaced. "He saw Marigold."

"Damned right I saw her." Mr. Sutton looked around the room. "And I don't see her now. Where has the little baggage gone?"

Andrew reclaimed the damp cloth, and draped it across his brow. "How should I know? She flew out of here as if the hounds of hell was in pursuit."

Marigold might well have preferred the hounds of hell to Carlisle Sutton. Georgie would herself. She turned to face her irate visitor. "So you have found us out. Truly, it was not my intention to deceive you, Mr. Sutton. When we first met, I had no idea of your connexion with my friend. And by the time I realized it—" Helplessly, Georgie shrugged. "There was little I could do except hope matters would somehow resolve themselves."

Matters *would* resolve themselves. Carlisle would see to that. "Spare me another of your Canterbury stories!" he snapped. "And tell me where you have the Norwood Emerald hid."

Scant wonder Andrew was playing possum. Georgie wished she might do so herself. "I do not recall that I ever told you a bouncer," she protested. "As for the ah, emerald, I have never seen the horrid thing. Nor do I wish to! Is there anything else you wish to ask me before you take your leave?"

Carlisle had no intention of departing before he got what he had come for, although in this particular moment he could not have said precisely what that was. In demonstration of his intention, he sat down in a striped chair. "I am staying right here until you tell me where you've hid Miss Macclesfield."

"Miss Macclesfield?" Georgie echoed blankly, for she had never heard Marigold's stage name. "I do not think I know a Miss Macclesfield, sir."

Mr. Sutton could sit still no longer. He leapt to his feet. "As you never saw that wretched dog? Just how the devil did you steal him out of that tack room?"

"I have stolen nothing and no one!" Georgie was losing patience with her ill-mannered guest. Reminded of her pet, because she wished he might bite her visitor, she looked around the drawing room. "Where *is* Lump?"

"Run off," said Andrew, from beneath his shroud. "Like Miss Inchquist and Marigold."

That Marigold had run off didn't surprise Georgie. Or Lump. "What has Miss Inchquist to do with anything? I thought it was a Miss Macclesfield—Heavens! Do you mean Marigold? Miss Macclesfield, I mean, not Miss Inchquist."

So well did Lady Georgiana play the ingenue that perhaps *she* should go upon the stage. But Miss Macclesfield had not been Carlisle's only reason for returning to this house. "Sarah-Louise has not come back here?" he said, frowning. "Or that blasted dog?"

In the doorway, Tibble cleared his throat. Beside him stood a short and portly gentleman clad in a somber fashion and wearing a tremendous scowl. "Beg pardon," Tibble said. "Mister—Begging your pardon, sir, what did you tell me was your name?"

"Inchquist! Quentin Inchquist!" Quentin pushed the butler aside. "I heard what you people was saying. What's this about my girl? I must tell you that I know

Sarah-Louise has been sneaking off to meet that twiddlepoop, abetted by the residents of this house!"

This was Sarah-Louise's papa? No wonder the girl was so timorous. "I have just returned home myself and know nothing of this matter," murmured Georgie. "Someone else will have to explain."

"Seven hundred men fell at Cuidad Rodrigo," volunteered Andrew, from beneath his damp cloth. "At Badajoz, nearly five thousand died. One regiment lay dead in their ranks as they had stood. Fuentes, Almeida, Albura. Combra." His voice trailed off.

Georgie was fairly certain that her brother was shamming it. "Now see what you have done!" she said, and sat down beside him on the couch.

Mr. Inchquist was not easily bamboozled. He stepped closer to the sofa. "Is *this* the military gentleman my sister was talking about?"

Heaven only knew what Lady Denham had said. "Perhaps we should introduce ourselves," Georgie suggested, and did so. "Over there by the fireplace is Mr. Carlisle Sutton. No doubt Lady Denham also mentioned him to you."

Quentin was briefly distracted from the Hallidays. He scowled at Carlisle Sutton instead. Damned if the fellow didn't look like a barbarian, with that long hair and dark skin. "I hear you have a partiality for my girl. Don't mind telling you that I am not yet convinced that you'll *do!*" he said.

Was there no end to Lady Denham's conniving? Carlisle cast a somewhat spiteful glance at the Hallidays. "Witness me crushed! Anyway, from all that I can see, your daughter is in the process of developing a marked preference for someone else."

"Aye, and don't I know it!" Quentin ran a hand

through his thinning hair. "A mincing Jack-a-dandy whose pockets are to let. Sarah-Louise is a considerable heiress. That blasted fortune hunter was why I packed her off to Brighton. Now I find out he followed her here." He moved closer to the sofa. "You must know Teasdale, Lady Georgiana. Amice said your brother brought him to her house."

No wonder Andrew was hiding beneath his handkerchief. Georgie entertained some very uncharitable thoughts. "I don't believe I was ever properly introduced to the gentleman. Are you certain that he is interested only in your daughter's fortune, sir?"

Mr. Inchquist was damned certain. "Teasdale was in Queer Street when this business first began. By now the gull-gropers will also have got their talons fast in him." He turned to Carlisle Sutton. "Thought I heard you say you brought Sarah-Louise here. Where is she, then?" He looked back at Georgie. "Have you got her hidden away somewhere? What the devil is going on?"

Georgie couldn't answer that question. "Mr. Inchquist, I wish I knew."

Carlisle could not stand still. He began to pace the floor. "I did bring Sarah-Louise here, and then I lost her. The last I saw she was chasing that wretched hound."

The last Andrew had seen of Carlisle Sutton, Lump had been chasing *him*. Curiosity prompted Andrew to peer out from beneath his damp cloth. "How did *you* get away from Lump?"

Mr. Sutton's expression was sheepish, his person disheveled. "I climbed a tree," he confessed.

Mr. Inchquist was interested in none of this. He looked as though his temper might explode. Andrew forestalled the outburst by saying, "It was Sarah-Louise who introduced Teasdale to me. She begged me to help them. It wouldn't have been gentlemanly in me to refuse. Beside, she said Lady Denham was a Gorgon, which she *is*, and I'd no reason to doubt that Teasdale wasn't also everything she claimed. Until I met him, that is, and then I just thought he was a poetical rasher-of-wind."

Georgie didn't like her brother's pallor. She dampened the cloth and placed it again upon his brow. "Please, gentlemen. You must see that my brother is ill. It was perhaps remiss in him to go along with your daughter's charade, Mr. Inchquist, but I'm sure he meant it for the best."

Andrew wasn't sure how he had meant it, but it was clear that he'd been paper-skulled. Now that he realized Miss Inchquist was an heiress, and that her poet was on the dangle for a fortune, a great many things were explained. Peregrine Teasdale was hardly the first young man to attempt to marry a rich heiress. Andrew should probably have been hanging out for one himself. But only the most beggarly of louts would take advantage of an innocent like Miss Inchquist.

"Most extraordinary!" said Mr. Inchquist, in tones that were almost admiring. "Never did I think my girl would have the brass to pull such a sly trick!"

"Ahem!" Tibble appeared again in the doorway. Behind him hovered a slender, bespectacled young man. "Mr. Brown!" announced Tibble, then glanced at the visitor. "Did I get it right?"

"Right as a trivet!" said the newcomer, comfortingly, then stepped into the room. "Pardon my intrusion, but I have come in search of—" His gaze fell upon

Carlisle, and he blanched. "Mr. Sutton, sir!" he gasped.

Carlisle knew perfectly well why his uncle's man of business had come here, and it hadn't been in search of him. "You tracked the Jezebel to this house."

Mr. Brown, thought Georgie, looked as though he wished to sink right through the floor. She could sympathize with the young man. "I was going to tell you," said Mr. Brown. "Truly I was, sir."

"Right!" retorted Carlisle. "After you told *her!* Good God, why is it that every man who meets that little vixen loses all common sense?" The exception, of course, being himself. "I arrived at the same conclusion before you, Mr. Brown, but the chicken appears to have flown the coop."

Janie appeared in the doorway, and elbowed Tibble aside. She carried a cup of restorative apple tea sweetened with honey and liberally laced with brandy, courtesy of Agatha, who thought that Andrew might need reviving, and also wished a clearer account than Tibble could deliver of what the deuce was going on.

Conversation halted as Janie walked across the room. "Thank you, Janie," Georgie said, as she took the cup. Janie turned to leave in the same moment as Mr. Brown removed his spectacles to polish the fogged lens. Janie saw a pleasant-faced young man who looked as though he would never keep a damsel on the dangle, or whisper the same sweet things in her ear as he did a number of other young women, unlike a certain footman that she knew. In his turn, Mr. Brown saw a brown-haired, snub-nosed angel with—due to his myopia—a halo around her head. "Cor!" said Janie. Mr. Brown swallowed hard.

Because he had a damp cloth across his eyes, Andrew

alone remained unaware that, smack in the middle of the drawing room, Cupid had let his arrow fly. Andrew was in a quandary, because he had made it possible for Miss Inchquist's poet to come calling, and could not now abandon her to her fate. "Never mind Marigold! She can take care of herself," he said, and then realized the absurdity of his remark. "Marigold can take care of herself better than Miss Inchquist, at any rate! Have none of you thought that Sarah-Louise is out there in the streets somewhere, alone unless she has found Lump? Somewhere out there also is Mr. Teasdale, who you say is a fortune hunter, and unless I very much mistake the matter, because Sutton here wouldn't do such a cravenly thing—I think!—Teasdale has been pressing Sarah-Louise to elope!"

Reaction to this announcement varied. Mr. Sutton and Mr. Inchquist looked at one another, then hurried together out the door. Mr. Brown and Janie tarried longer, exchanging such mundane information as their names. Andrew cursed because his injured leg would not allow him to join the rescue mission. Georgie stared at the cup that she held, and drank the brew straight down.

Twenty-eight

Lord Warwick returned from a bracing horseback ride along Brighton's white cliffs to be informed by his butler that a visitor awaited him in the peach salon. Because the butler was even-more-than-usually impassive, Garth concluded that his visitor was not quite the thing. Curious, he divested himself of top hat and gloves and riding crop, and proceeded down the hallway.

The peach salon was called so for very good reason; that color predominated in wall hangings, furnishings, and rugs. It was not a color that flattered the sole occupant of the chamber, who was pacing about in so energetic a manner that, if not interrupted, she might well wear a pathway around the perimeters of the room. Lord Warwick moved quickly toward her. "Georgie!" he said.

Lady Georgiana paused in her perambulations. "Don't dare mention my reputation! Or remonstrate with me for coming here. I already know that I must come under the gravest censure for visiting the quarters of any gentleman, let alone one to whose name a disagreeable stigma is attached, and that my conduct must give rise to just the sort of scandal-broth which must be abhorred." Lord Warwick had reached her side, and she looked up at him. "Have I got it right? I wished you to know that I am perfectly conversant with the civilities."

Georgie was still determined to quarrel with him, it seemed. So much so that she risked her reputation by coming to his quarters. "I might have said," Garth admitted, "something of the sort."

"Excellent!" Georgie pushed her tangled hair out of her face. "I have saved you working yourself into a fidget by saying it first."

Lady Georgiana was disheveled, flushed, her blond curls all a-blowze. Garth thought she had never looked lovelier. "My dear, what is it?" he said gently. "Is your brother worse?"

At this kindness, Georgie blinked back tears. "No, not Andrew, but everybody else. You told me once that I should come to you if I was in trouble, Garth. Well, I am in trouble. Unless you can help me, we shall be truly in the suds. Things are in such a muddle that I do not know where to begin."

Garth disliked to see Georgie so pulled-about. He took her hands in his. "You have decided to go back on your word."

Georgie wrinkled her pretty nose. "I wish you would not phrase it in quite that manner. Anyway, I do not see that I have a choice. If anyone can straighten out this tangle, it is you."

Lord Warwick smiled at her. "I appreciate your vote of confidence, I think. Do go on, my dear."

Here was the telling moment. Georgie screwed up her courage. "No," she said.

"No?" Garth echoed, startled.

"No," Georgie repeated, firmly. "I wish that you would kiss me first. We are not at odds at the moment, and I wish to savor the sensation, because I fear that we soon shall be again."

Georgie was acting most unlike herself. Was that *brandy* Garth smelled on her breath? "Georgie, have you been drinking?" he asked.

Now that Lord Warwick mentioned it, Georgie did feel a little odd. "I didn't mean to, but I may have done. Agatha made a tisane for Andrew, and I swallowed it instead. Please, Garth, I do wish that you would kiss me—but only providing that afterward you do not run away."

"Run away?" Lord Warwick caught Georgie by her shoulders. "Is that what you think, that I have run away from you?"

Georgie fought back tears. It was the fault of Agatha's potion that she was grown so weepy, she told herself. "You kiss me, then you say you shouldn't, and then you play least-in-sight. After the last time you kissed me, you went out of town."

Georgie looked altogether adorable, with her reddened nose and tear-filled eyes and wildly tangled hair. Lord Warwick told himself it would be unwise to smile. "My dear," he murmured, "what do you think brought me to Brighton in the first place?"

Georgie blinked. "I do not know. I thought perhaps it was because Prinny was in Brighton. Or that it had something to do with Catherine."

"Nothing of the sort." Garth rested his hand against her cheek. "Prinny's presence was an influence, but I had learned that you were here. I would have gotten up the courage to call on you, Georgie, had we not first collided on the beach."

Georgie was speechless. Or almost. "Me?" she whispered. "Oh, Garth!" And then, because she looked so adorable, and because he was so very tired of being honourable, and because both were so overwhelmed by their mutual admissions, an interval of kissing ensued. When that interval concluded, Lord Warwick was seated on a peach-colored sofa, with Georgie on his lap. "Before we forget ourselves altogether," he murmured, "I think you should tell me about this coil you wish me to untangle."

Georgie sighed, and removed herself from Lord Warwick's lap, lest in reaction to the tale she was about to tell him, he dump her on the floor. "Did you know that Carlisle Sutton was acquainted with Catherine?" she asked. "He was asking me a great many questions about you, and her. I had the impression that he knew Catherine fairly well."

Carlisle Sutton and Catherine? Garth was intrigued. Not as intrigued as he was jealous of Georgie's own association with the man, which was unworthy of him, because Garth did not imagine that Georgie had sat on Carlisle Sutton's lap. "Continue," he said.

"Mr. Sutton has found out that we sheltered Marigold, and is very angry." Georgie resumed her pacing around the room. "He also offered her a slip on the shoulder, and so *she* is very angry with *him*. Lump is lost, and Miss Inchquist, and Andrew has hurt his leg—" She burst into tears.

Garth could not bear to see Georgie cry. As a result, she found herself back in his lap. "You said Catherine developed a partiality for another gentleman? Could it have been Carlisle Sutton?" she asked, when she was done sniffling.

"Doubtful," retorted Garth, as he mopped her face with his handkerchief. "A man like Sutton would not have danced long to Catherine's tune. Tell me something, Georgie, just who are you embroidering those damned slippers for?"

Slippers? Whether due to Lord Warwick's proximity, or Agatha's potion, Georgie couldn't think. "Oh! Andrew, of course."

There was one burning question answered. "And why are you estranged from your family?" Garth inquired.

Georgie lowered her gaze to his cravat, which was sadly rumpled, as well as tear-stained. "We could not agree on a certain matter," she murmured.

Lord Warwick had little doubt of what that matter was. Another interval of kissing ensued. "Let me see if I have got this right," he said, at its conclusion. "Your Mrs. Smith, who is an actress, lost a certain gem at play. Magnus Eliot has that gem. Carlisle Sutton wants it back. Your brother tried to steal it from Magnus Eliot. This conundrum has brought your brother to a state of nervous and physical exhaustion, which causes him to mumble incoherently about twenty-five thousand pounds. And Miss Inchquist—who the devil is Miss Inchquist? No, don't tell me—has run off with a fortune-hunting twiddlepoop."

Georgie sighed. "Something like that."

Garth set her aside and stood up. "I suppose I need not point out that did you wish to subject your family to another round of notoriety, you could not have come up with a muddle that would fascinate the gossips more."

Surely she was not going to cry again! Georgie blinked back tears. "You promised you would not lecture me."

"I am not lecturing." Garth paused in front of a looking-glass to adjust his cravat. "I am mystified as to the reason why you should think that I might wish to lecture you. Granted, I have lectured you in the past. Unfortunately, it is my tendency to treat you as though you were still a girl, which demonstrably you are not, but I cannot treat you as I truly wish to, and therefore fall back on my old ways."

Georgie wondered how Lord Warwick truly wished to treat her. "You are in an odd mood," she said.

Garth turned toward her and arched his brow. "Missing emeralds. Vanished heiresses. Actresses and rakehells."

Georgie winced. "I take your point. Garth, you said you would never turn away from me. Have you changed your mind?"

How forlorn she looked, huddled on his peach sofa. "I promise that I shall neither turn away nor run away from you," said Garth. "Now go home and wait for me."

Georgie didn't know that she wanted to return home. Heaven only knew what additional disasters might await her there. "What are you going to do?" she asked, as she got up from the couch.

"I don't know what I may do!" responded Garth. "Talk with Magnus Eliot, I suppose. I'll say this for you, Georgie: you pick the devil of a way to call in your vowels!"

Twenty-nine

Lump was greatly enjoying his first curricle ride. Since this pleasure took expression in a great deal of barking, drooling, and leaping about, his fellow travellers were less enthused. Like Mr. Teasdale, the horses liked Lump no more in the curricle than they had out of it, and became increasingly nervous and hard to control, a circumstance that Peregrine was not equipped to repair. Unlike a more experienced horseman, who would have known to hold the horses' reins in his left hand, and in his right the whip, Peregrine held the reins in both his hands, and up around his nose.

A cow-handed whipster, nervous horses, and a barking dog; a sharp turning, a wheel caught on the corner of a bridge—the result, a broken axle, and a tumble into a ditch. By the time everyone had climbed out of the ditch, and calmed the horses, and found an obliging blacksmith, no one was in a good mood, save Lump, who considered this the grandest adventure he had enjoyed in quite some time. While repairs were being made, the small party retired to a nearby inn.

It was a very rustic inn. Sarah-Louise looked with some dismay around the private parlor that Peregrine had procured for them. The room had more the dimensions of a warming closet, with low ceilings and a small fireplace and a very dirty floor. Even the air smelled stale. "Where *are* we? This d-does not seem to me to be the way to Aunt Amice's house."

Nor was it, but instead the road to Gretna Green. Peregrine lifted the tankard of ale that the landlord had provided them, along with a cold pigeon pie. "There is no reason it should seem familiar. We are taking a short cut." This did not seem the moment to inform Sarah-Louise that she was to be a runaway bride. Not that Peregrine expected her to protest. He was doing her a favor, was he not? It wasn't like she might expect to make a love match. Miss Inchquist was unlikely to marry at all, if not for her papa's rolls of soft.

Matrimony, in that moment, was also on Miss Inchquist's mind, not as a grand aspiration, but as something she didn't think she wished to do. Not with Mr. Teasdale, at any rate. Mr. Teasdale had not displayed himself particularly well during the past hour, yelling at Lump, and at her, and letting his horses get out of hand. Scant wonder they had wound up in a ditch, which hadn't improved either Mr. Teasdale's temper, or his appearance. Peregrine's clothes were mud-spattered, his boots scratched and dirty, and he had lost both his hat and his quizzing-glass.

Why the deuce was Sarah-Louise staring at him? It put a fellow off. Peregrine hoped she didn't mean to gawk at him like that every morning over the breakfast cups. Gawking was a small enough price to pay for a fortune, he supposed. Peregrine drained his tankard, and broached the pigeon pie. It was not edible. He put down his fork, and decided he might as well get on with the business. *"O'er her warm cheek and rising bosom move/The bloom of young Desire and purple light of Love.'"*

Sarah-Louise was in no mood for this nonsense. "Thomas Gray," she said. "Tell me the truth, Peregrine. *Were* you going to take us home?"

The word "us" reminded Peregrine of that blasted hound. He glanced down to find that Lump had disposed of the pigeon pie. Miss Inchquist was frowning. Peregrine called her his *"bright particular star."*

"Shakespeare!" retorted Sarah-Louise. "Answer me, please! Where were you planning to take us, sir?"

Peregrine cast about in his mind for an appropriate reference to marriage. Neither *"Marriage is a noose"* (Cervantes) nor *"Wedding is destiny, And hanging likewise"* (Heywood) seemed appropriate. *"'As may arrows, loosed sev'l ways, Fly to one mark,'"* he ventured. "Dear heart, we are flying to Gretna Green."

Mention of Gretna Green recalled to Sarah-Louise an earlier overheard conversation. Gretna Green was going to be overridden with eloping lovers at this rate. Sarah-Louise didn't think she wished to be among them. "You bamboozled me," she said.

Peregrine sincerely hoped so. Ladies who had been bamboozled were much more compliant than otherwise. "Not a bit of it! I'm devoted to you! Give you my word!"

Devoted to her? Rather, devoted to her papa's pocketbook. "Fiddlestick!" said Sarah-Louise.

The normally meek Miss Inchquist looked as though she was about to spit fire. "Nonsense!" Peregrine soothed. "You are fine as fivepence!" Perhaps that reference was imprudent. "Top of the trees!"

Sarah-Louise did not care for this reminder of her

height. "You have never written a single word of your own poetry, unless it was that silly sonnet about my nose, or if you have, I have never heard it, so I can hardly be your muse. Papa was right. You only wish to marry me because your pockets are to let."

Peregrine didn't see that it was any of his bride-to-be's business if his purse was empty. And she *was* his bride-to-be, whether she liked it or not. "You are making a great deal of fuss over nothing!" he said crossly. "I wish that you would stop. So what if I pretended to write something that I didn't? You liked it well enough at the time."

So Sarah-Louise had, because she thought he liked her, and now she clearly saw that he did not. The realization of her folly made her very sad. It also made her want to damage something, preferably Peregrine. "I thought I wouldn't mind being married for my papa's money. Now I find I do. I no longer wish to marry you, Mr. Teasdale."

Peregrine smiled, unpleasantly. "A pity," he said. "Because now even your father will agree that you no longer have a choice."

Sarah-Louise couldn't imagine her papa agreeing to any such thing. "You must be all about in your head. My papa doesn't even like you!" she retorted. "And neither do I!"

Peregrine moved around the table. "Think, Sarah-Louise. You are alone with me. Unchaperoned. You have been for some time. Your father will be grateful to me for marrying you, now that your good name has been compromised."

Compromised! So busy had Sarah-Louise been with all her other worries that she had not considered that her good name might be besmirched. What Mr. Teasdale said was true. She should not be alone with him. "Oh, *botheration!*" she cried.

There was more than one way to lead a horse to water. To clinch the matter, Peregrine would see that the young lady was compromised in truth. He moved closer. Sarah-Louise backed away. Lump watched with interest, curious about this new game. Mr. Teasdale and Miss Inchquist circled the small chamber until she came up smack against the fireplace. "Hah!" said Peregrine, and reached for her.

Mr. Teasdale might have done well to recall the remainder of the adage about leading horses to water, to wit that once arrived at the puddle one still had to encourage them to drink. Sarah-Louise grasped the fireplace poker and swung it at his head. Peregrine ducked and cursed. Sarah-Louise screamed, loudly. Lump threw back his head and howled.

The parlor door flew open. Mr. Sutton and Mr. Inchquist burst into the room. Sarah-Louise flung down the poker—narrowly missing Peregrine—and ran to her father. "I am so glad to see you, Papa! How did you find us?"

Quentin regarded his daughter, who did indeed look glad to see him, and rather the worse for wear. "There aren't many violet and vermillion and blue curricles about. Teasdale wasn't hard to trace. But what's this? You *wanted* us to find you?" he asked.

Sarah-Louise suffered a moment's horrid fear that her papa would do as Peregrine had predicted. "Please don't make me marry him!" she cried. "I know I have been foolish, and disobedient, but please, please, *please* don't make me do that!"

Quentin hugged his daughter, somewhat awkwardly, because she was taller than he, and also distraught. "You aren't wishful of eloping, puss?"

Sarah-Louise shuddered. "I never wanted to elope, even when I thought I liked Mr. Teasdale, which I do not anymore. Oh, Papa, if only I had listened to you, none of this would have happened, because all along you were right. Peregrine was everything you said he was. Can you ever forgive me?"

"There, there!" Quentin gave his daughter's arm an awkward pat. "It's partly my fault. I shouldn't have sent you off to your aunt. But if you weren't wishful of running off with him, then why are you here?"

Sarah-Louise explained the accident. "I only got into his curricle because he said he would take Lump and me back to Aunt Amice."

Quentin's eye kindled. "The scoundrel kidnapped you. I'll give him his bastings, that I will." He paused. "He didn't, er—"

Sarah-Louise wasn't sure quite what "er" entailed. "He has never so much as k-kissed me, Papa."

Mr. Teasdale was not only a knave, but a knucklehead as well. "What a paltry fellow," Quentin soothed. "You'll want Sutton, then."

Sarah-Louise glanced at Mr. Sutton, who looked as appalled as she felt. "I do not wish to marry Mr. Sutton! Nor does he wish to marry me. Besides, he is quite old."

Quentin frowned at this pronouncement. It was clear that Sarah-Louise needed a husband, the sooner the better; Sutton would make Sarah-Louise a better husband than the mincing Peregrine. Still, if the girl didn't want him— "That settles it! I don't care if you *are* rich as Croesus! I shan't have my girl taken off to India, and there's an end to it."

Carlisle was happy to disabuse Sarah-Louise's papa of this bloodcurdling notion. "Your sister's match-making aspirations are so much moonshine, Inchquist. The furthest I agreed to escort your daughter was to the Hallidays, and even that has proved to be a large mistake."

Things had gone from bad to worse. Peregrine wished only to escape. He picked up the fireplace poker. Unfortunately, the only exit was the doorway, where Mr. Sutton stood.

Lump grew bored with watching Miss Inchquist and her papa clutch each other. Clearly, nothing interesting was going to happen there. He looked around the room for further entertainment, or perhaps another pigeon pie. Then he espied Mr. Sutton in the doorway. Lump remembered Mr. Sutton, and the tack room. Growling, he advanced.

Carlisle Sutton was not about to wind up this wretched day getting either dog-bit or brained by a fireplace poker. Therefore, he did the only thing he could. With a kick and a swish and a thump he divested Mr. Teasdale of his weapon, knocking him unconscious in the process, and with the poker held off the dog. "Get back, you cur!"

Thus distracted from their hugging, the Inchquists turned to look. Sarah-Louise hurried forward to grasp Lump's collar. "No! Mr. Sutton is a friend!" she said. "If you wish to bite someone, bite Mr. Teasdale!"

Lump did not wish to bite Mr. Teasdale, or, for that matter, anyone. The pigeon pie was not sitting well with him. He parted his great jaws, and belched.

Mr. Sutton looked at Peregrine, stretched out unconscious on the floor, and suggested that they take their leave before the gentleman awoke. Ungently,

Mr. Inchquist prodded the body with his boot. Much as Quentin would have liked to dress the rapscallion's hide neatly, prudence dictated otherwise. Unless he wished to be clapped in irons for attempted kidnapping, the twiddlepoop would bother them no more.

Thirty

Georgie lay on the drawing room sofa with a damp cloth upon her forehead. Andrew had moved with his blanket to a chair, his lame leg propped up before him on a stool. "If that potion is what Agatha has been physicking you with," moaned Georgie, "no wonder you were ill."

Andrew had no idea what concoction Georgie had swallowed in his place. "I'm just as glad you drank it instead of me," he said. "Though I'm sorry for your headache."

Georgie pushed back the damp cloth. "You were shamming earlier, weren't you, Andrew? When you were talking about Cuidad Rodrigo and Badajoz? You are not still feeling ill?"

Only of the mulligrubs, as Marigold would say. Her words, and the truth of them, still stuck in his mind. "No, sis. I'm not feeling ill. I just wished to throw Mr. Sutton off the scent." Could Andrew have paced the floor, he would have. Instead, he drummed his fingers on the arm of his chair. "I wish the devil I knew what was happening."

Georgie wished she knew where Marigold had got to. Her guest was nowhere in the house. Agatha entered the room with a tea tray, to inform them that

Mr. Brown was still in the kitchen with Janie, the pair of them sitting at the kitchen table munching freshly baked almond cake and talking a blue streak. She placed the tea tray on a table. Georgie eyed it doubtfully. "Pray take no offense, Agatha, but what is in that pot?"

"Just some nice tea," soothed Agatha, failing to add that she had added a bit of borage to expel pensiveness and melancholy, and clarify the blood.

Gingerly, Georgie sat up, and allowed Agatha to pour her a cup of tea, which she then spilled all over herself and the sofa, because Lump bounded into the room and leapt into her lap. Lump was much too large a dog to fit comfortably upon anybody's lap, but Georgie didn't mind. She hugged him. Lump licked her face. Agatha tsk'd and set about mopping up the spilt liquid. Andrew looked anxious.

At a less excited pace, Mr. Inchquist and his daughter also entered the drawing room, followed by Tibble, who had given up trying to monitor the parade of people in and out of this house. "Inchquist!" he announced, belatedly, before Agatha shooed him back to the kitchen to act as Janie's chaperone.

"You have found Lump! I am grateful to you." Georgie studied her pet, who was now sprawled across the sofa, as well as her lap. "He doesn't look well."

"I think it was the pigeon pie," offered Sarah-Louise, looking not at Lump but at Andrew, who was likewise staring at her.

Agatha paused in the doorway, en route to fetch more teacups. "Georgie, set that dog down at once! Before he casts up his accounts."

Damned if this wasn't a chaotic household. "He's

already done that," Quentin said, as he settled in a chair near Georgie. "All over my coachman."

Georgie buried her fingers in Lump's thick fur. "I am so sorry, Mr. Inchquist. We Hallidays have caused you a great deal of trouble, sir."

"Nothing of the sort!" Quentin squelched an impulse to pat Lady Georgiana comfortingly on the knee, so disheveled did she look, with her hair every which way, and her dress stained with tea, and that great hound stretched across her lap, staring up at her soulfully. "You Hallidays have *spared* me a great deal of trouble, because if not for your brother I would not have reached my girl in time. We'll say no more on it! Save that I, Quentin Inchquist, am in your debt."

Georgie wondered if Quentin Inchquist might wish to donate twenty-five thousand pounds to the cause of retrieving a certain emerald necklace, then cast aside that unworthy thought. "I am glad all has ended well," she said.

Andrew was less certain that all had ended well. "You *didn't* wish to elope with Teasdale?" he inquired of Miss Inchquist, who perched upon another stool drawn up by his chair. "I'm sure you said you did. You liked that he was a poet. Wrote sonnets to you, and such stuff."

"Yes, but he didn't!" explained Sarah-Louise. "None of those words were his. Mr. Teasdale was a mere *pretender*, and I changed my mind."

Andrew was trying hard to understand. "Sutton, then. I wouldn't wish to go to India myself, but you must know what's best." Sarah-Louise protested that she didn't wish to go to India, either, which further confused Andrew. "Dash it, I was sure you wished to elope with someone!"

"No, I didn't!" Sarah-Louise's cheeks were pink. "Or if I did, it was none of them! Anyway, *you* were the one who was going to run off to Gretna Green!"

"I was?" Andrew set down his teacup, and wondered if Agatha had doctored it again, because this conversation was making no sense. "No, I wasn't! I never would have done such a thing."

"Why is it that gentlemen must be forever telling whoppers?" In her frustration, Sarah-Louise so forgot herself as to strike Andrew on the leg. "I had not thought that *you* would treat me so. With my own ears, I heard you ask that pretty lady if she would like to elope, just before she hid behind the couch!"

"Pretty lady?" Andrew clutched his injured knee and stared at her, appalled. "You mean Marigold. Miss Inchquist, I would allow myself to be captured and tortured by *Afrancesados* before I ran off with a featherhead like Marigold."

"Oh," said Sarah-Louise, in a little voice. "I must have misunderstood."

"Yes, you did," retorted Andrew. "I was asking Marigold why *you* would wish to elope."

"Oh," Sarah-Louise said again.

Mr. Inchquist and Lady Georgiana looked at one another. "As I live!" Mr. Inchquist remarked. Said Lady Georgiana, "Which reminds me, where *is* Mr. Sutton? He did not accompany you here."

Quentin was still watching her brother and his daughter. The girl had some gumption after all. "Sutton said he had some business to attend to. I hope you will forgive my boldness, Lady Georgiana, but your brother is not well?"

Mr. Inchquist's boldness was quite understandable, considering that his daughter and Andrew were casting sheep's eyes at one another. "It is only a fever that he brought back from the Peninsula, and which sometimes recurs," Georgie said. "The doctor thinks those episodes will grow less and less frequent with the passage of time."

"The Peninsula," Quentin repeated judiciously. "Connaught's Boys. The Devil's Own. Nothing wrong with that. But still—"

Georgie interrupted. "Mr. Inchquist, you have seen us at our worst. Under normal circumstances, we are so unexceptionable as to be positively dull. All this muddle is the fault of Marigold—"

Now Mr. Inchquist interrupted. "The lady behind the couch?"

"I was not here to see it," admitted Georgie, "but that sounds like Marigold. She would have been hiding from Mr. Sutton, because she was married to his uncle, and has something in her possession that he wishes her to return. Except that it *isn't* in her possession anymore."

Mr. Inchquist was fascinated. "Extraordinary," he said.

Extraordinary, indeed. "You know how you do not wish to talk about the circumstances in which you found your daughter?" said Georgie. "That is how I feel about Marigold! As for my brother, I should perhaps explain that he is not exactly on the brink of poverty, despite the simple way we live. He has his prize money, of course. As well as property in Devonshire. My uncle is overseeing it until such time as Andrew wishes to shoulder the responsibility. Additionally—" She explained her father's trust.

Quentin frowned at her. "And what of yourself?"

"I have my dowry," retorted Georgie, who was wearied beyond measure by all this fuss about finances. "My father discussed it all with me before the papers were drawn up."

Lady Georgiana's papa would have assumed she'd marry, and thus be provided for. Quentin wondered why she had not. Thought of daughters recalled to him his own, who showed signs of growing positively fickle, he thought.

Andrew was experiencing a similar notion. "Then who did you wish to elope with?" he inquired. "If not Teasdale or Sutton, who else was dangling after you?"

Sarah-Louise blushed even brighter at the notion that someone should dangle after her. "No one!" she protested. "I am not—That is—Oh, g-gracious, it was you! Not that you were—Of course you couldn't—A great freckled beanpole like myself! But I—Oh, *drat!*"

Andrew was moved by this pretty speech. "Of course I do!" he said. "But I cannot—" And then he spoke a great deal of nonsense about honor and unworthiness, and she had grown very precious to him, and he would much rather she was a beanpole than a nonpareil, and curst cripples who did not dare think of such happiness.

Again, Mr. Inchquist and Lady Georgiana exchanged glances. Georgie was relieved to see that Mr. Inchquist looked amused. "Tell me, boy," he interrupted. "Would you like to marry m'girl?"

Now it was Andrew who flushed. "More than anything!" he said. "But—"

Quentin held up his hand. He was a gentleman who believed in cutting to the chase. Someone needed to take the responsibility of Lieutenant Halliday off his sister's shoulders. The boy needed stiffening up. A wife and family would do that for him. And a determined papa-in-law. Quentin had never shied away from a challenge. "No buts! If not for you, Sarah-Louise might have come to such grief as would make it impossible for her to honorably marry anyone. *And* she's showing signs of turning into a shocking flirt, so we had better get her married off. Don't poker up, puss! I spoke in jest. Are you sure you wish to marry this young man?"

Sarah-Louise's cheeks had by this time achieved the rosiness of a ripe tomato. "Yes, Papa!" she said.

"That's settled, then!" Quentin announced. Sarah-Louise and Andrew stared rapt at one another. Mr. Inchquist turned back to Lady Georgiana, who looked dazed. "I'll warrant they'll run along as well together as two ducks on a pond. More important, he'll do right by my girl. I wouldn't see her married to someone who would not." Now that they were practically related, he did pat Lady Georgiana's knee. "I had not wanted to mention it earlier, but Amice said something about some sort of scandal, not that it will signify. We have just narrowly avoided a scandal of our own. I was curious merely as to what she spoke about."

"Scandal?" Georgie wondered for a moment if Lady Denham knew she had sat on Magnus Eliot's lap. "She must have been referring to Garth. Lord Warwick was married to our cousin Catherine. Or *is* married to her. She has disappeared."

"Oh, if that's all!" said Quentin. "And you had it right the first time. The only remarkable thing is that Warwick waited so long to apply for a divorce. Naturally, there will be talk, but there already *was* talk, so it seems to me that he's done the right thing."

Garth had applied for a *divorce?* Georgie was nigh speechless. In her agitation, she pushed Lump off her lap and onto the floor.

Lump whined. "Quiet!" said Mr. Inchquist, so sternly that Lump sat abruptly down. Quentin regarded Lady Georgiana with some concern, so strange was her expression. "Ma'am, are you unwell?"

"Divorce!" Georgie managed to whisper. "Mr. Inchquist, are you certain of this?"

Quentin was more than certain. He had just come from Town, and the *ton* was all abuzz. "Sure as the devil is in London," he said cheerfully, as Agatha returned to the drawing room with additional teacups.

Thirty-one

Wearied and more than a little exasperated by the day's events, Carlisle Sutton returned to his lodgings to find his uncle's widow waiting there. Again she wore boy's clothing. Carlisle glanced at the window, which was closed. "The innkeeper let me in," said Marigold. "I said I was your nephew."

She looked like no one's nephew that Carlisle could imagine. Her hair was tumbled down around her shoulders, because she had taken off her cap. "You surprise me," Carlisle said. "I thought you had skipped town."

Marigold's breast heaved. Or it would have heaved, were it not bound up so tight. "Pray do not make this more difficult than it is already!" she snapped, because she had worked herself into a fidget while waiting for Mr. Sutton to return, and now was trying not to notice that he was taking off his coat. "I have decided that I must not be always looking to other people to get me out of scrapes," Marigold continued. "So I have come to take my medicine."

Carlisle tossed aside his coat and loosened his cravat. "You look as though you expect to swallow something very sour. I promise it will not be so bad."

Marigold did not think it would be bad at all. That

was not the point. "I am perfectly aware that I must re-deem your uncle's necklace," she said stiffly. "It is the only *honourable* thing for me to do. I am also aware that I shall never be able to lay my hands on twenty-five thousand pounds."

It was not money that Carlisle wished to lay his hands on at that moment. "You look hot in that jacket," he suggested. "Why don't you take it off."

Mr. Sutton appeared a trifle warm himself. He was unbuttoning his shirt. "*And,*" Marigold continued with determination, "I am also aware of your terms."

She looked very stubborn. Carlisle folded his arms across his chest. "Are you come here to quibble, Miss Macclesfield? I had thought more of you than that."

The man thought nothing of her, and well she knew it. Marigold wished he would fasten up his shirt. "My name is Marigold, not Miss Macclesfield! I did not come here to quibble, but to do what I must. Still, I wish you to know that I am *not* a Paphian girl!"

How absurd she was, and how absurdly charming. Carlisle replied, "Who said you were? On the other hand, nor can you claim to be an untried maiden—Marigold."

Marigold was offended by this assessment. "That was different. I *married* them first!"

Carlisle frowned, and drew his shirt closer around him. "You can't wish me to marry you!" he said.

Marigold stared at him in horror. "Good God, no! I meant only that this is all very strange!"

Matters were to become even stranger. There came a knock at the door. "Sutton, I know you are there. We must talk!" Marigold grabbed her cap and jacket, and scuttled under the bed.

Carlisle opened the door. Magnus Eliot stood in the

hallway. "Do I interrupt?" he asked. "The innkeeper said you had a guest."

Mr. Eliot's voice was heavy with innuendo. The innkeeper had not been deceived by Marigold's costume. "What brings you here, Eliot?" Carlisle inquired.

"A conversation with Warwick." Magnus stepped into the room. "Apparently I have something that rightfully should be yours, and his lordship would be most grateful if we dealt with the matter between ourselves." Which removed Lady Georgiana from the equation, to Magnus's regret. Had the lady been a little more wicked, or he a little less—but one might as well wish for the moon, as Lord Warwick had succinctly pointed out.

Carlisle Sutton would have liked to be privy to that conversation. "You want me to give you the sum of twenty-five thousand pounds. I believe that was the figure. Have you brought the gem with you?"

Magnus reached into his pocket and removed a jewel case. "You are welcome to the bauble! It has recently come to my notice that having the thing in one's possession is an invitation to thieves."

Beneath the bed, Marigold squirmed and tried not to sneeze. If only she could see! She scooted forward on the dusty floor just a little, and then a little more. Perhaps the gentlemen were so rapt in their conversation that they would not notice her. Slowly, carefully, she lifted up the bedspread and peered out. And then she scrambled out from beneath the bed, and leapt to her feet. "Leo! What the devil are you doing *here?* And where the devil have you *been?*"

Mr. Eliot, for his own part, regarded Marigold with appreciation. "The beautiful ninnyhammer. I should have guessed. Don't eat me, Marigold! I didn't plan that matters should turn out as they did." He glanced at Carlisle Sutton. "Did I do you so great a disservice, after all, by shabbing off?"

So great was Marigold's agitation, so deep did her breast heave, that the buttons on her shirtfront popped. Marigold clutched at the edges of her garment. "You played fast and loose with me," she said, with immense dignity. "You broke my heart!"

Magnus eyed Marigold, and then Carlisle Sutton. "Hearts heal," he observed. "I suppose I should inquire, Sutton, if you are harboring intentions of a dishonorable nature toward my wife."

"Your *wife*?" Few things had the power to startle Carlisle, but he stared now at Marigold. "You are married to Magnus Eliot?"

Marigold looked from one man to another in bewilderment. "I was married to *Leo*. And then to Mr. Frobisher and Sir—Oh!" She paused, appalled. "If Leo is still alive—"

"Then you weren't married to those other gentlemen," Magnus said cheerfully. "Damned if you haven't become shockingly loose in the haft, Marigold."

"Of all the unjust things to say!" Marigold rested her hands on her slender hips, leaving her shirt to gape open as it would. "Who is this Magnus Eliot? You told me your name was Leo!"

Magnus shrugged. "I lied. It is a habit of mine. Precisely *why* I lied in this instance, I cannot remember. Now that you remind me, my middle name *is* Leo, although I have not used it in some years. As for the last name I used—what was it, do you recall?"

Certainly, Marigold recalled. "Flitwick!" she said.

Magnus's dimple flashed. "Ah, yes. Now I remember. What a delightful honeymoon we had, before I was forced to disappear."

"Before you took a powder!" Marigold grabbed her jacket and yanked her little pistol out of a pocket. "And left *me* with the reckoning! What a hateful wretch you are, Leo. Or Magnus! Pray tell me why I shouldn't shoot you dead."

With one swift movement, Magnus divested Marigold of the pistol and drew her into his arms. "Because you are my wife. Remember?" Wickedly, he smiled. "Marital difficulties can be much more easily resolved. I'll make you a different bargain, Sutton. I'll give you the emerald. You give me back Marigold."

Marigold struggled. "Damn you, Leo! You can't mean to take up where we left off!"

Of course Magnus did not. A wife would be most inconvenient in his line of work, unless she was sharp enough to help him in the gulling of lordlings, which Marigold demonstrably was not. For that matter, Magnus doubted that Marigold was in truth his wife, since the marriage had taken place under an entirely spurious name. But females were contrary creatures, bless them, and as soon as he told Marigold that he did not want her, she would wish he did. "Why not?" he said, therefore. "You *are* my wife."

Her poor Leo, so cherished in memory, revealed as this odious loose-fish? Marigold kicked and flailed. "I don't *wish* to be your wife!" she cried. "You *abandoned* me, you cad! Indeed, I do not think I ever wish to set eyes on you again in all my life. Now unhand me, at once!"

Magnus did so, abruptly, not because of Marigold's words but because she had kicked him in a tender spot. Marigold swore again as she landed on the floor.

"Do you know, I don't think I wish to be married to you, either," remarked Magnus, as he rubbed his injured shin. "You have turned into a termagant. Now, Sutton, about that emerald."

Carlisle had been following these proceedings with no little fascination, and more interest than he would have imagined. "I have a suggestion. For a consideration, I will take her off *your* hands."

Did Mr. Sutton *not* take Marigold off his hands, she would cost him a great deal more than twenty-five thousand pounds. Magnus held out the emerald. "I wish you joy of her," he murmured, and made Marigold a mocking little bow.

The door closed behind him. Carlisle looked at Marigold, who still sprawled where she had fallen. "Lady Georgiana has been hiding you all along," he said, as he pulled her to her feet.

Marigold brushed dust off her clothing. "Are you angry with Georgie? You should not be. I gave her no choice." Though Mr. Sutton had not removed his shirt, he had not fastened it, either. Marigold stared at his chest. "Am I mistaken, or did you just *buy* me from Leo?" she asked.

The notion was not particularly shocking to a gentleman who had spent a great deal of time in India. "Not precisely," Carlisle murmured. Marigold's shirt had lost all its buttons in the scuffle, and consequently afforded a most tantalizing view. "Or maybe just a little bit. Unless you should dislike the idea."

He pushed the shirt down off her shoulder. His touch sent shivers up and down her skin. "You are very wealthy, are you not?" Marigold inquired. "Because a fallen woman—which apparently I am, although I did not know it, so I am not entirely certain that it counts—should think about such things."

"Very, *very* wealthy." Carlisle picked her up into his arms.

Heavens, but it felt good to be carried in such a manner. Neither Sir Hubert nor Mr. Frobisher—And Leo—

The devil with Leo. That was then and this was now. Still, Marigold wished a certain reassurance. "I shan't go to gaol?"

How blue were the eyes that regarded him so warily. How golden was her hair. How pretty the plump breasts that he was releasing from their binding. Carlisle had captured his tiger. He didn't think he would be able to behead her for some time. "I was thinking more along the lines of India," he said.

Marigold's eyes widened. *"India?"*

"India is a country of many contrasts." Carlisle ran his fingers through her golden hair. "Calcutta. The jungle. Camels and monsoons and peacocks. Would you like to ride an elephant, do you think?"

Marigold thought that what lay on the road ahead might be very interesting indeed. "What an excellent idea! I believe I should like that above all things!" And then she gasped, because Carlisle had clasped the emerald around her neck.

"I've long had a desire to see you wearing this," said Mr. Sutton, "and nothing else." Marigold giggled, and pulled off her boots.

Thirty-two

The hour had grown somewhat advanced by the time Lord Warwick presented himself at Miss Halliday's front door. Tibble opened that portal. Garth prepared yet again to explain who he was. Before he could do so, Tibble spoke. "Warwick!" The butler beamed. "I got it right, didn't I?"

The old man's air of triumph was disarming. "Indeed you did," his lordship replied gravely. "Now may I come in?"

Tibble's smile faded. "You aren't really a groom, are you?" he asked.

Once again, Garth reflected upon the strangeness of Georgie's household. One would grow used to it, he supposed. "As a matter of fact, I am a marquess. Now will you please stand aside?"

"A marquess!" The smile returned to Tibble's face. "Then that's all right! You'll find Mistress Georgie in the drawing room." Tibble did not lead the way, as his lordship already knew it, but instead hastened to the kitchen to impart these tidings before he forgot what Warwick had said he was.

Georgie was in the drawing room, exactly as predicted, although Lord Warwick had not expected to find her sitting beside Lump on the faded rug. She was frowning over a letter. The hound's great head was in her lap. Lord Warwick cleared his throat.

"Garth!" Georgie scrambled to her feet. Lump opened one eye, recognized Lord Warwick, wagged his tail, and went back to sleep. All this jauntering about— and eating things one shouldn't—took the juice out of a fellow. Lump needed to rest and regain his strength.

Georgie stepped over her recumbent pet and held out the letter. "You have been very busy. It would appear that now I am in *your* debt."

Lord Warwick did not take the proffered letter, but instead closed the door behind him. To insure that it stayed closed, he wedged a chair beneath the knob. Then he turned back to Georgie, who was watching him with considerable interest. "Magnus Eliot asked me to bid you his *adieux.*"

"Oh? Mr. Eliot is leaving Brighton?" Georgie inquired cautiously, as she eyed the barricaded door.

"No." Lord Warwick looked forbidding. "But I do not think that your paths will cross again."

"Ah." Georgie gestured with her letter. "I have received a note from Marigold. She and Mr. Sutton have struck a bargain. Marigold is going to India with him and, she says, ride an elephant." At that very moment, a bemused Janie was gathering up the belongings still strewn about Marigold's bedchamber, Mr. Brown having finally been persuaded to go home. "Marigold also writes that she is married to Mr. Eliot—or *was* married to him, when he called himself Leo—and Mr. Eliot has very generously given Mr. Sutton the emerald."

There was no end to Mr. Eliot's chicanery. Lord Warwick had already paid him twenty-five thousand pounds. One had to admire the scoundrel's daring. Garth sat down on the couch.

"Mr. Inchquist has given his blessing to Andrew and Sarah-Louise," Georgie continued. She glanced again at the barred door. "Mr. Inchquist also said that you had applied for a divorce. Are you certain? I mean— The scandal, Garth!"

Now it was Georgie who talked to him of scandal? Odd, to see their roles so reversed. Scandal there would be in plenty, no doubt of that, for divorce could be obtained only by wealthy men whose wives had committed adultery, and involved details and proofs and the testimony of witnesses, and consequently afforded the gossips an entire barnyard-full of dirty laundry to rifle through and marvel at. "Yes, Georgie, I have begun the process of obtaining a divorce. I wish you would come here and sit down. Unless now you wish to run away from me?"

Georgie didn't wish to run away. More than anything, she wanted to fling herself upon Lord Warwick's chest, so that he might hold her, and she might forget the various events of this tiresome week. So odd was his mood that instead she perched on the edge of the couch.

Garth regarded her somberly. "The marriage was a disaster from the beginning. The man doesn't exist who can satisfy all of Catherine's whims."

One thing in particular struck Georgie about Garth's comments, and it wasn't his assessment of her cousin's character. "*Can*?" she echoed. "Garth, what have you found out? Do you know where Catherine is?"

"I know where she *was*. Her present whereabouts, I am in the process of discovering." Not that Garth particularly cared where his wife was in that moment or any other, and never wished to set eyes on her again. There was, however, the matter of the divorce, and that Garth wished for very much. "Magnus Eliot crossed paths with Catherine. She was in the company of a wealthy cit. I gather he was not her, ah, first travelling companion. I am sorry, Georgie. Your family will dislike me all the more by the time this business is finished."

Georgie couldn't have cared less about the feelings of her family. "They should be grateful to you for not announcing that she had run off in the first place. You saved Catherine's reputation—which she hardly deserved!—at the expense of your own."

Georgie looked so very lovely, with her absurdly belligerent expression. Garth wished she were not perched on the far end of the couch. "It seemed to me that if I could not love Catherine, I at least owed her that. Or so I thought then."

Georgie was distracted from informing Lord Warwick that Catherine would not have been—indeed, had not been—half so kind. "You did not love Catherine?" she echoed.

"I never loved Catherine," Garth said roughly. "It was infatuation, I suppose. Or—I don't know what the deuce it was, but it didn't last."

Georgie knew precisely what had caused Lord Warwick to do such a foolish thing as marry her cousin. "There is something I must tell you, Garth."

How serious she looked. Garth was intrigued. "Is it so very bad?" he asked.

Georgie contemplated Marigold's note, crumpled in her hands. "You may think so. I sat on Magnus Eliot's lap. I did not mean to—Lump knocked me over—but I did so all the same." At mention of his name, Lump sat up and wagged his tail.

Fortunate for Mr. Eliot that Garth had not known of this earlier. "Where did this lap-sitting take place?"

Georgie smoothed out Marigold's note, then crumpled it again. "Outside the library on the Marine Parade. When I went to try and persuade him to give the emerald back. I am surprised you did not hear about it, because the whole world saw."

Well could Garth imagine the scene. He tried to ignore Lump, who had come to lean against his knee. "And then what happened?" he inquired.

"Mr. Eliot helped me to my feet, and apologized." Georgie stole a peek at Garth. "He was very much the gentleman."

Magnus Eliot was no more a gentleman than Lord Warwick was a rakehell. Garth caught Georgie's hand and drew her closer to him on the couch. "Did you like it?" he asked.

Georgie was unsure what Lord Warwick had in mind. She was curious to find out. "Like what?"

She was so close now that Garth had a most enchanting view of her bosom in the low-cut blue gown she wore—donned, though he could not know it, in lieu of the tea-stained dress. "Do pay attention!" he said, as much to himself as Georgie. "We were talking about you sitting in Magnus Eliot's lap."

"We were?" Georgie blinked. Lord Warwick's proximity was having a most disruptive effect on her thoughts. "It was well enough. But I believe that I like sitting on your lap a great deal more."

So pleased was Garth by this admission that he drew Georgie again onto his lap. She curled up there and sighed. "Truly, there is no comparison. Your lap is *much* better than Mr. Eliot's."

Lord Warwick was happy to hear it. "You didn't kiss him, did you?"

That she had wondered what it would be like to kiss

Magnus Eliot would remain Georgie's secret. "I didn't kiss Magnus Eliot. Nor did I kiss Mr. Sutton." Abruptly, she sat up to look at Garth. "Did you kiss Marigold?"

Lord Warwick was appalled by the suggestion. "Devil a bit!" he said.

Satisfied by this response, Georgie settled back against his chest. "Did you learn any more about Mr. Sutton's association with Catherine, Garth?"

Lord Warwick didn't care who Catherine had associated with, or when, or even how. He did wish Georgie would hold still. "Who *did* you kiss?" he inquired. "Other than myself?"

What an odd question. Georgie sat up again. "You mean *ever?*" she asked.

'Twas not what he had meant, but now Garth wished to hear the answer. Not that he expected to like it. Georgie was a beautiful woman, six-and-twenty years of age. Naturally, she would have had *beaux*. Unthinkable that none of those *beaux* had kissed her. "Ever," he said, and waited. "The devil, Georgie, can it take so long to add them up?"

Lord Warwick looked so chagrined that Georgie had to laugh. "I am sorry to disappoint you, Garth. The sad truth is that I have never kissed anyone but you."

Naturally, Lord Warwick could only respond to this pretty confession by kissing Georgie again, not once but several times. When he finally paused in this most pleasant of pursuits, both of them were breathless and rumpled, and Georgie's hair looked as if several birds had decided to set up housekeeping there. Lump disliked to be left out of all this attention. He laid his head on Georgie's lap, and whined.

Absently, Georgie petted the dog. Garth smoothed her tousled curls. "I know you value your freedom, and I would not wish to change you in any way. And it will be some time before I myself am free. But when I am—It is clear to me that you are determined to make a scandal. Therefore, I think you should make it with me. Will you marry me, Georgie? My darling, I have never loved anyone but you."

Magnus Eliot had called her darling, also. Georgie had demurred. From Lord Warwick's lips she could hear no sweeter words. Too long overlooked, Lump tried to crawl onto the couch. "No!" she said, and pushed him away.

Lord Warwick looked at Georgie, uncertain whether she had been talking to him or to the dog. "No?" he echoed.

How absurd he was, for Garth must know she loved him, had always loved him, even when he married Catherine. "Clunch!" said Georgie. "You know I meant yes. But, Garth, I would like to know—how is it that you wish to treat me that you have not?"

Lord Warwick's smile was so wicked that he might well have been a rakehell. Or perhaps there is a little of the rakehell in even the most proper gentleman. He set about confirming Lady Georgiana's suspicion that the most shocking things were indeed the most pleasurable.

There! That was fixed up all right and tight. Lump yawned. Damned if he wasn't getting good at doing the work of Master Cupid. The great hound rolled over on his back, and began to gently snore.

ABOUT THE AUTHOR

Maggie MacKeever lives in Los Angeles. She's currently working on her next Zebra Regency romance, LOVE MATCH. Maggie loves to hear from readers and you may write to her c/o Zebra Books. Please include a self-addressed stamped envelope if you wish a response.

Put a Little Romance in Your Life With
Melanie George

__**Devil May Care**
0-8217-7008-X   **$5.99**US/**$7.99**CAN

__**Handsome Devil**
0-8217-7009-8   **$5.99**US/**$7.99**CAN

__**Devil's Due**
0-8217-7010-1   **$5.99**US/**$7.99**CAN

__**The Mating Game**
0-8217-7120-5   **$5.99**US/**$7.99**CAN

Put a Little Romance in Your Life with
Georgina Gentry